City Girl

Lori Wick

HARVEST HOUSE PUBLISHERS
Eugene, Oregon 97402

Unless otherwise indicated, all Scripture quotations are taken from the King James Version of the Bible.

Cover by Terry Dugan Design, Minneapolis, Minnesota

Cover photo by the Robert Runyon Photograph Collection, 00106, courtesy of The Center for American History, the University of Texas at Austin

CITY GIRL
Yellow Rose Trilogy
Copyright © 2001 by Lori Wick
Published by Harvest House Publishers
Eugene, Oregon 97402

Library of Congress Cataloging-in-Publication Data
Wick, Lori.
    City girl / Lori Wick
        p. cm. — (Yellow rose trilogy; 3)
    ISBN 0-7369-0255-4
        1. Ranch life—fiction. 2. Ranchers—fiction. 3. Texas—fiction. I. Title.
PS3573.I237 C58 2001
813'.54—dc21   00-064675

Printed in the United States of America.

      01   02   03   04   05   06   / BC-CF /   10   9   8   7   6   5   4   3   2   1

Love-at-first-sight had no meaning before I saw you.
I've never been crazy about surprises, but then I met you.
Always the same. Always different.
Thank you for being my Webster.
I love you more than words can say.
If the best is yet to come, I can hardly wait.

Acknowledgments

Bob Hawkins Jr. It's a delight to work with you and be a recipient of your warm, wonderful humor. My Bob and I love laughing with you. We treasure both you and Beth more than we can say.

Kathi MacKenzie-Foster, Nina Stianson, O.J. Acton, Walt Seward, Mike Bailey, Vince Attardi, John Hurley, Phil Fleming, Marion Smith, and Bob Boyne. I always enjoy any time we can spend visiting at CBA. Your hard work does not go unnoticed.

Vivian Danz. So many people fill my life with joy, and you are one of them. Thank you for your precious friendship, joyful spirit, and also your words of wisdom.

Jayne Wiese. Your quiet, gentle spirit is beyond precious to me. I learn something from you every time we visit. Thank you for keeping on and for helping me do the same.

Todd Barsness. We are often blessed by your words, hard work, and laughter. The coaching is just an added bonus. Thank you for hours of compassion and creativity, and for putting God first.

My Bob. Well, we made it! The Texas trilogy is complete. Thanks for cheering me on along the way. I tried recently to imagine doing a book without you and decided it can't be done. Fun as it is to write a romance about another couple, you're still the only romance I want. It's funny, but even when I'm furious with you, I'm still head-over-heels in love. Thank you for 20 years of patience, love, laughter, and especially your guidance.

Prologue

New York, New York
December 1882

REAGAN SULLIVAN PEDALED HER BICYCLE down the busy neighborhood street, calling greetings to everyone who spoke to her and trying successfully not to run over anyone's dog or child. She was tired after her day in the factory but jubilant over the news she'd received at the beginning of the week.

"You'd better watch yourself," a familiar voice called as she passed old man Cannon's house.

"I will, Mr. Cannon. How's your wife?"

"Pretty as the day I married her."

It was their standard exchange, and with a wave and a smile, Reagan moved on. She was almost home and sighed when she saw the sign for Mrs. Banner's Boardinghouse for Girls come into view. She hoped Mrs. Banner had a good meal for the night, one that included chocolate cake.

Pulling along the curb and swinging her leg over the bar to hop down, Reagan had the bike stopped and parked in the blink of an eye. She laid it against the stone steps that led up to the boardinghouse, and with the usual jog in her step, started to ascend.

A hand grabbed her arm suddenly as a voice called her name, but she wasn't too surprised.

"Just hold on now, Reagan," Tommy said, the usual smile in his voice. "You can just talk to me before the lady of the house catches you and says dinner is hot."

Reagan turned with a smile and looked up at Tommy Amhurst. He lived two doors down the block, and they had been friends for years.

"But dinner might be hot," Reagan returned in her normally straightforward way, "and I'm hungry."

"Never mind your stomach," he chided. "Tell me it isn't true. Tell me right now."

Reagan's smile grew by inches.

"But it is true," she replied, not feigning ignorance or able to conceal her excitement. "I'm leaving New York after the first of the year."

"For where?"

"Texas!"

"Texas? What in the world will you do there?"

Reagan nearly danced in her excitement.

"You happen to be looking at the newest nanny in town."

Tommy couldn't stop his mouth from dropping open.

"Nanny? Did you say nanny? As in a person who takes care of children?"

"That's right."

"But Reagan, you don't know anything about children."

The dark-haired, dark-eyed, petite woman only smiled.

"I'll just have to learn then, won't I?"

Tommy's finger came up to wag in her face. It almost touched her nose.

"You have had some mad schemes in your day, but this tops them all. What has come over you?"

"Nothing," she told him sincerely. "I just saw a way to get out and experience life a little, and I'm going to take it. I answered an ad, and the man even sent half my fare. I may never get an opportunity like this again." She suddenly smiled. "Not to mention, he's a widower. Maybe I'll find love."

Knowing Reagan as he did, Tommy's head fell back with his laughter.

"Reagan, are you out there?" a motherly voice called from the window. "Dinner's hot."

"Thank you, Mrs. Banner," Reagan called in return. She turned back to Tommy. "I've got to go in."

The man on the step below her only shook his head.

"You're really going to go?"

"Yes, I am, Tommy. I've run out of room for adventures in New York. I need the wide open spaces. On top of that, I'm not getting any younger."

Tommy knew he would miss her terribly, but in a way he envied her. He didn't know anyone half as gutsy or hardworking.

"I've got to go in," Reagan repeated as she started to turn away.

"You'll tell me the exact date?"

"As soon as I know for sure." Reagan turned with one more saucy smile. "And besides, if I don't tell you a date, you won't be able to put together a big send-off party in my honor."

Reagan slipped inside just as her stomach started to growl, still managing a smile at the sound of Tommy's laughter.

One Month Later

"You'll send my bike? I'm too rattled to bring it right now."

"I said I would," Tommy assured her again.

"But you didn't promise."

"I promise."

"You have the address?"

"In my pocket."

"All right. Do it right away."

"I will. Have you got everything?"

"Yes. I'm fine."

The two stared at each other before both smiled.

"I envy you a little," Tommy admitted and then added, "but not enough to join you."

Reagan laughed and hugged him.

"You've been a good friend, Tommy. Write me if you get married or something big happens."

"You do the same," he said, knowing she never would. She hated letters and anything else that made her feel sentimental.

The two hugged once more, this time to the accompaniment of the train whistle. Reagan boarded, and Tommy turned away. He didn't want to watch her go. He almost stayed on the busy platform, thinking she might want to wave to him one more time but then remembered that it was Reagan. She would want no such thing.

And he was right. That westbound, determined woman had already found her seat and sat with eyes straight ahead, only occasionally glancing out the window. She was off to new sights and adventures. And tempted though she was, she reminded herself that there was no room in her heart for looking back.

One

St. Louis, Missouri
January 1883

SLATER RAWLINGS CAME QUIETLY INTO the room where he hoped his wife, Liberty, would still be sleeping, but as soon as he neared the bed, he could see that her eyes were open. She lay flat on her back, staring at the ceiling.

"How are you?" he asked quietly.

"The nausea was supposed to go away after three months."

Slater sat on the edge of the mattress, bent over, and kissed her cheek. He knew she wouldn't actually be sick—it might be better if she could be—but at this particular time in her life, mornings were not very fun.

"How about some juice? My mother always has some."

"Fruit juice?"

"Yes."

"That sounds good."

"Coming right up."

Liberty lay still and listened to the sound of her husband's footsteps. They were muffled on the thick carpets that lined all the hallways of Slater's parents' home. Charles Sr. and Virginia Rawlings had a wonderful two-story home in a fine neighborhood of town. Liberty had only visited one other time since marrying Slater nine months before. The first time she hadn't been expecting.

9

She had hoped this visit would be as enjoyable as the last, especially since they had come for such a special occasion, but right now she was having her doubts.

Working at not being discouraged, she thought of the family that was gathered. The oldest brother, Charles Rawlings Jr., better known as Cash, had come from Kinkade, Texas. The middle brother, Dakota, was present; he had just resigned from his position as a Texas Ranger to take a sheriff's job in the small town of Jessup, Texas. And their grandmother, Gretchen Rawlings, from Hilldale, Texas, had also made the trip. Liberty reminisced over the time they had all gathered in Shotgun, Texas, for her wedding to the youngest brother, Slater.

"Here you go," Slater said, coming into the room with a large glass of juice in his hand. "How does orange juice sound?"

"Wonderful," Liberty said sincerely, scooting up against the headboard to drink. The first sip was just what she needed, and already feeling better, she drank more than half the contents.

"Thank you," she finally said, setting the glass aside and looking into her husband's eyes.

"I'm still asking myself if we should have come," Slater admitted.

Liberty opened her mouth, but Slater cut her off.

"And before you say anything about what Duffy had to say, you can let me have a second thought or two."

Liberty shut her mouth but still smiled a little.

Duffy was her stepfather. He was also her doctor. When word had come that there was to be a wedding after the first of the year, Liberty's heart had sunk, thinking it would be too close to her due date to travel, but then a second letter had come, saying the wedding would be in January. Liberty assumed they would go. Slater had other ideas. Liberty smiled as she remembered the conversation.

"Oh, Duffy and Slate, I was hoping I'd find you together," *Liberty said as she entered Duffy's office with a letter in her hand.*

"What's up?" her husband asked.

She waved a letter. "It's about the wedding; he's getting married in January. Isn't that good news?"

"We knew he was getting married, Lib, so why is this good news?" Slater asked.

"Now I can go with you," Liberty stated what she thought was the obvious.

"Let's get one thing straight," Slater said firmly. "I'm not going to the wedding without you, and since you can't travel, I'm staying home."

"But with the wedding in January, we don't need to stay home."

"It's still too close."

Liberty looked at her stepfather. "Will you please tell him?"

"It's fine, Slater," Duffy said, his bedside-manner voice becoming rather matter-of-fact. "With her due date, it shouldn't be a problem."

Slater's eyes grew suspicious. "Did she put you up to this?"

Liberty laughed out loud over this, Duffy joining her.

"Slater, Slater," Liberty said, her voice loving. "I'm fine, and the baby's going to be fine."

"You feel sick every morning," he argued.

"That's normal."

"It is, Slater," Duffy put in. "The stage ride to Keyes would be the most stressful part, and that's only 17 miles. Taking the train makes it a very easy journey."

"You did remember that we're talking about St. Louis, didn't you, Duffy? It's a long way."

The older man only smiled. Slater's eyes swung to his wife to find her smiling too. At that moment his face told them he was giving in.

"What's that smile for?" Slater now asked, breaking into Liberty's thoughts.

"I'm just remembering how panicked you were about my coming here."

"I have good reason. It's a long way in your condition."

Liberty could only grin.

"You are impertinent," Slater told her, but it was no use. As poorly as she had felt a few minutes earlier, she was glad she'd come, her smile attesting to that fact. Slater could frown all he wanted, but Liberty was delighted to be here for Dakota Rawlings' wedding.

❧ ❧ ❧

"You have that tense look again," Dakota said to Darvi Wingate, the woman who was scheduled to be his bride in less than a week. He had just arrived at her house, and they were sitting alone in the parlor.

Darvi was from St. Louis, and if the guest list was any indication, a boatload of family had come to wish her well. That, along with the wedding paraphernalia that could be seen everywhere, indicated it was going to be quite the occasion.

"I am tense," Darvi admitted. "The caterer informed us this morning that he didn't know we wanted candelabra."

"Do we want candelabra?"

"My mother does," came Darvi's standard reply.

Dakota couldn't stop his smile as he teased her.

"I'm not going to let you forget that it was my idea to elope."

"And have my mother hunting us down for the rest of our lives?" Darvi reminded him with a theatrical shudder. "I know you'll forgive me. I'm not too sure about her."

Dakota suddenly leaned forward and kissed her.

"What was that for?"

"Do I need a reason?"

"This time, yes."

He studied her. "You're fun, and I'm in love with you."

Darvi gazed at him, her own heart in her eyes.

"That was a nice reason. I'm glad I asked."

"Oh, Dakota," Mrs. Wingate said from the doorway of the room; the couple had not even heard her approach.

"I'm so glad you're here. Did you take care of the carriages?"

"Yes, ma'am." Having come to his feet, Dakota answered politely, not bothering to remind her that she had already checked with him on this subject. "They're all set."

"Good. There's no problem with your suit or those of your brothers, is there?"

"No, ma'am. Everything is in order."

Clarisse Wingate stared blankly at Darvi and Dakota for a moment before giving a small gasp and hurrying on her way.

"Is your mother going to make it?" Dakota asked compassionately when she had left.

"I hope so. When you consider that she wasn't even speaking to me in the fall of last year, we've come a long way. Having me marry in style has always been important to her. I took the chance away from her once; she's not going to be denied again."

"Well, if I have anything to say about it," Dakota said, sitting back with a smile, his eyes still on his fiancée, "she'll see you married."

"Is that right?" Darvi's smile held a teasing glint. "And what makes you so eager, Mr. Rawlings?"

Dakota tried to look nonchalant. He studied the ceiling with interest. "I'm just thinking that our trip to the gulf sounds nice. I've never been to the gulf."

Darvi laughed. She wasn't fooled in the least. He was looking forward to being alone and on their honeymoon as much as she was.

Dakota was reaching for her hand when Darvi had a sudden thought.

"Oh, Dakota, I just remembered something. Uncle Marty sent us a gift."

"That was nice. What is it?"

"I didn't open it. I wanted to wait for you."

Dakota watched her move from the room, loving how graceful and feminine she was. The uncle she spoke of had been Dakota's superior in the Rangers. He hadn't been happy when Dakota had wanted to leave but in the end had admitted that he understood.

"Let me get that," Dakota said as Darvi came back into the room, a large box in her arms.

Dakota waited for her to take a seat on the sofa and then set the box down so it would be positioned between them. Darvi had opened a few gifts already, presents from people Dakota did not know, so it was special for her to watch him open this box and remove the gift. It was a beautiful wall-mount coffee grinder.

"Oh, my," Darvi said as she took in the size and heavy cast-iron make. "This is wonderful. I think Uncle Marty knows how much you like your coffee."

"I think you might be right." Dakota suddenly stopped and stared at Darvi. "Are we thanking all these people at the wedding for this stuff or what?"

Darvi laughed until she was red in the face.

"Leave it to a man," she finally gasped, "not to know what's going on. If a gift arrives early, it's usually because the giver can't attend the wedding. I've been sending out thank-you cards as things come in."

Dakota looked rather sheepish but still laughed a little.

"Thanks for taking care of all this, Darv."

"You're welcome."

The couple's eyes met and held for long moments. Dakota was glad the box separated them. Darvi wished she could move it. Both were thinking: *Just a few more days.*

❧ ❧ ❧

Cash Rawlings sidestepped a running child and the woman darting after him and made his way into the downtown shop. Each and every time he was in St. Louis to see his parents, he took a gift to his housekeeper, Katy.

Knowing her personality, it had always been something practical. This time he was going to surprise her.

"May I help you, sir?" asked a friendly woman who met him in the middle of the store.

"Yes, please. I'm looking for something for someone who is a little older. I'm not even sure she'll welcome the idea," Cash added with a smile, "but I'm going to give it a try."

The perfume shop owner's smile was genuine, her eyes twinkling as she said, "I believe I have just the thing." She turned and led him to one of the three perfume counters, slipped behind it to face him, and from under that glass countertop withdrew a tray full of tiny bottles .

"Try this," she said, uncorking a small vial and waving the lid in his direction.

"That's nice," Cash said, but it had a scent he would term romantic. He almost shuddered as he pictured Katy's reaction.

"Too romantic?" the woman shocked him by saying.

Cash looked down at her and blinked. "As a matter of fact, I was thinking that very thing."

"I was hoping you were, in case you realize you have a second lady at home who would enjoy some perfume."

She was openly flirting, and Cash's smile was kind, but he stuck to the business at hand.

"I'll just shop for my housekeeper this time," he said, not unkindly. "Have you something else in mind?"

"I do," she stated, all at once becoming very professional. She put the first tray back under the counter and had Cash follow her to the next counter.

"This is what I should have shown you in the first place. I believe you will like it."

The woman was right. Cash inhaled the gentle scent and thought that not even Katy would be able to hide her pleasure.

"This is perfect," he stated quietly. "I need it gift-wrapped and able to travel."

"Right away," the woman agreed with a smile, wondering why some woman had not snatched up this charming, redheaded cowboy. His manners were faultless, and if the cut of his clothing was any indication, he was not living on the streets. But the thing she was most drawn to was his eyes. A deep shade of brown, they were so warm that even a stranger was made to feel as though he cared.

The package wrapped and secured for travel, the proprietress walked Cash to the door as if it were an everyday occurrence. It wasn't, but she couldn't deny herself the sight of watching him put his hat back in place and then seeing his long legs take him down the street. She knew her business would never survive out of the city, but for a moment she wondered just how far west she would need to go in order to find a town where the men were all like that.

❧ ❧ ❧

"How are you, Libby?" Virginia asked as soon as she returned from meeting with the dressmaker. Virginia's dress was done, but she had caught some of the excitement that surrounded this wedding and had gone in person to make sure it was being delivered that very day as promised.

Having removed her hat and gloves, she now came over to hug the younger woman and kiss her cheek. "I'm sorry I wasn't here when you came down."

"That's fine. I'm feeling much better, thank you. I had a good breakfast, and I just came back from a walk."

"Did Slater go with you?"

"No, a message came for Dak, so he went to Darvi's to deliver it."

Virginia took a seat but didn't bother to get comfortable.

"At moments like this, I wonder if any of us are going to survive this."

Liberty smiled with compassion. "When we went to dinner the other night, Darvi told us her mother wanted her to have a wedding she would never forget."

Virginia's eyes rolled. "She's sure to have that, and if it will keep peace in the family, then it's worth it."

Liberty didn't comment but was well aware of the story. Liberty also knew that at times Dakota found *his* mother rather stubborn on issues she felt were important. Virginia Rawlings was not as worried about St. Louis' opinion as Darvi's mother seemed to be, but when it came to spiritual truths, she was almost stiff with fear and pride. Mr. Rawlings had been more open, and the discussions with his sons had given them great hope, but Virginia still seemed to be digging her heels in on the subject. So much so, in fact, that Dakota had told Cash and Slater, *If it wasn't for Mother's hesitance, I think Father would have come to Christ by now. He won't have anyone to blame if he waits too long, but I do think Mother is holding him back.*

"Is there anything I can do to help?" Liberty asked, even as she prayed for Slater's parents.

"I can't think of anything just now. Be sure you get your dress to Winnie so she can press it for you."

"She came for it yesterday."

"Oh, that's right. I saw it in the back hallway. It's beautiful, by the way."

"Thank you."

Virginia sighed. "I've got so many lists in my head, I can't keep track."

One of the staff came to the door just then with a question for the lady of the house. Virginia stood as she answered, moving toward the doorway, but then remembered her daughter-in-law.

"Oh, Libby, how rude of me to leave like this, but the truth is, I'm going to be so busy today. Are you going to feel terribly neglected, dear?"

"Not at all, Mrs. Rawlings. Slater and his grandmother have plans this afternoon to show me where she used to live. Darvi and I will see you at dinner tonight," Liberty reminded her. "Your sons are going out on their own."

"I'd forgotten about that," she said with a laugh. "Look out, St. Louis!"

❧ ❧ ❧

"Do you remember the time you tried to hide from Father in a stall full of hay?" Dakota asked Slater that evening.

The three Rawlings brothers were in a small St. Louis dining establishment. Their table was quiet, as was the rest of the place, and the smells coming from the kitchen told them their father's recommendation had been a good one.

"How could I forget?" said the youngest brother, shaking his head at the memory. "I still have the scars from that pitchfork I never saw coming."

"I came into the house and thought you were dead," Cash added. "All because Dak stood in the hallway and howled all the way through the doctor's examination of you."

Dakota shook his head and smiled. "I hated the pain of one of Father's spankings, and I thought a pitchfork in the seat must have been a hundred times worse."

"At least I didn't get both," Slater added.

"He wouldn't have done that," Cash added with confidence. "I heard him and Mother in the kitchen later. He was too shaken up about the blood all over your pants."

Cash suddenly looked at Slater. "What had you done?"

"Ridden Father's horse after I'd been told not to. I thought Father had gone to town, but when I came past the pond, I saw him headed into the barn. He came out a second later shouting my name, and I knew I'd been caught. He wasn't even looking for me in that stall, he said later, but he decided to fork some hay into one of the stalls before he turned the ranch upside down to find me."

"Father's probably hoping you have a son that gives you twice the trouble."

"Me?" Slater looked to Dakota in amazement. "I was easy compared to you, especially after you'd decided to join the Rangers. Why, you arrested the dog every day over something. You practiced holding your toy gun on Mother and Katy so much, the two of them still don't flinch at the sight of a weapon."

Both Slater and Cash had a good laugh at Dakota's expense, and he couldn't help smiling as well. The threesome fell quiet for a moment, and after several seconds, Cash realized his brothers were exchanging a glance. Cash was about to ask what was going on when Dakota gave some instructions to Slater.

"All right, Slate, you go first."

Slater nodded and looked to his oldest brother.

"You have to get married, Cash."

"Is that right?" Cash asked calmly. He didn't know whether he should be laughing or his mouth should be hanging open at this unannounced change in topics.

"Yes. Marriage is wonderful, and now that Dak is taking the plunge, it's your turn."

"To any lady in particular?" Cash asked congenially.

Slater turned back to Dakota.

"Go ahead, Dak, you've been in his church. Who could he marry?"

With this, Cash started to laugh.

"Be serious now, Cash," Slater scolded him. "You have to let Dak think."

"You two are crazy. Do you know that?"

"Never mind now," Slater directed, starting to smile too. "Let Dakota think."

"There was that one woman," the black-haired brother said thoughtfully. "She was sort of tall with blonde hair, I think. Is she available?"

Cash shook his head in amazement.

"Maybe Libby and I need to go home by way of Kinkade, so we can find someone for you," Slater said so matter-of-factly that Cash began to laugh again.

"Let me ask you one thing, Cash." Dakota's serious face was almost comical. "Have you been looking?"

"Not specifically, no."

"She's not suddenly going to drop into your lap," the middle brother chided.

"She did for both of you," Cash stated mildly.

This silenced the younger Rawlingses. They looked at Cash and then at each other in surprise. The waiter came to their table before anyone else could comment further, and all three men realized they hadn't even glanced at the menus. The waiter stood by while they looked over the choices. It didn't take long, and after they'd given their orders and the man had gone on his way, Cash spoke in a voice tinged with laughter.

"Shall we start this evening over again, gentlemen, or does someone want to tell me what that was all about?"

"We honestly want you to get married, Cash," Slater admitted, his smile lopsided. "It's nothing more than that."

Cash gave a moment's thought to this and then asked, "Is there something in my life that makes you think I'm not trying?"

Both men shook their heads no.

"Then I don't know what else I can do. I certainly talk to the Lord about it, but in truth, there is no one at my home church, and I don't want a mail-order bride. You both found love, and I have to be honest and tell you I'm looking for the same thing."

Forgetting where he was for a moment, Dakota sat back in his chair, the front legs lifting from the floor. His dark gaze was intent on his brother.

"Darvi did drop into my lap, didn't she? I hadn't really thought about it like that."

"Yes," Cash agreed, "and Slater dropped into Libby's. It doesn't always happen that way, but since there aren't any single women my age at church right now..." Cash shrugged as he let the sentence hang.

"Well, I still think you should," Dakota said, his brow drawn down in a stubborn way.

"If you find someone for me, I'll listen to you."

"Darvi's cousin is a believer, and she's pretty too," Slater said.

"Who's that?" Dakota was all ears.

"I can't recall her name. She's the one we met the other night."

"If you're talking about Wendy, Mother told me she's 17." Cash put his oar in, wondering if he should stop them or just listen.

Thankfully, their food came in record time, and from there the conversation turned to business, Dakota's new job and the town it was in, where he and Darvi would live, Slater and Liberty's life in Shotgun, and finally the ranch.

Either by design or by oversight, the topic of a bride for Cash was put on the back burner, and Cash was rather thankful that it was. His brothers wanted answers. He had none. In his mind there was nothing to talk about.

Two

"THANK YOU FOR DINNER," Charles said, following Virginia to the kitchen and kissing her cheek after she set a large bowl down on the counter.

"You're welcome," she replied, smiling as she looked up at him. "Do you think the girls liked it?"

"Very much," he returned, his voice warming perceptibly. "I would say our boys have done very well."

"And a grandchild, Charles!" She grabbed his arm. "I'm so excited. I don't suppose we could talk Slater into moving back to St. Louis."

Charles laughed. "He loves Texas, Ginny, not to mention that you told me you were in as much a mood to travel as I was. We already put off our trip to Europe for the wedding. I was hoping we could leave after Dakota and Darvi are off on their wedding trip."

Virginia looked at him in horror. "I can't leave now."

"Why not?"

"The baby!"

"The baby's not due until June."

Virginia opened her mouth but quickly closed it again. She had just seen a side of herself that she did not like. For years women in her association had been making fools of themselves over grandchildren; something she had vowed never to do. She and Charles had only recently learned that Liberty was going to have a baby, and here she was trying

22

to fit her life around this grandchild instead of the man she'd been married to for more than 30 years.

"You're right," she said quietly. "The baby's not due until summer, and I did want to see Europe in early spring."

Charles put his arms around her and held her close. He didn't say all that was in his heart, but he was very proud of her. Unbeknownst to either of them, they were thinking of the same sets of friends who were grandparents. On Charles' part, he was picturing men whose wives would not stray from their grandchildren. The men were forced to sit and listen to tales of travel from other husbands whose wives accompanied them or who simply chose to travel without them.

Suddenly weary, Virginia thought she could rest in her husband's arms all night. But her daughters-in-law were waiting for coffee and dessert in the next room. After a warm kiss for the man she loved, she moved to get the good china teacups.

❧ ❧ ❧

"How are you feeling?" Darvi asked Liberty.

"Most of the time, I'm fine. Mornings are still rough."

"Was the trip a bit long for you?"

"At times, but I worked to hide it."

Darvi smiled. "Why was that?"

"Slater wasn't really sure that he wanted me to do this, so I was trying not to worry him."

"Tell me something, Liberty," Darvi suddenly sat forward and asked. "Were you surprised when you first met the brothers, how little they look alike?"

Liberty had a good laugh over this.

"It lasts until you get to know them and watch them interact. They become so similar then that you forget about their looks."

"I haven't had much time with all three," Darvi noted, wondering if there would be such a time. She had enjoyed some great visits with Cash in Texas but had only just met Slater and Liberty.

"Are you all set for the wedding?" Liberty asked.

"I think I am. I've told myself I can't go crazy over every detail, and that seems to help. I don't know if my mother is sleeping at all, but most of the time I'm peaceful."

"Are there days you wish you'd just up and married?"

"Every day," Darvi said dryly, as both women heard their hosts returning. And the timing couldn't have been better. Charles and Virginia had no more arrived with the tray full of coffee and cake than Cash, Dakota, and Slater showed up.

"How was dinner?" Charles asked first.

"Excellent," he was told, his sons thanking him for the recommendation.

"How are you?" Dakota asked, having sat close to Darvi and taken her hand.

"Fine. We had a wonderful meal."

The two smiled into each other's eyes for a moment.

Slater had slipped into the seat next to his wife, his eyes studying her as they often did, first her face and then her waistline. Following his eyes and train of thought, Liberty smiled, and he caught her. He was giving her a stern look for laughing at his concern when his mother offered him coffee.

"Yes, please."

"So did you boys do anything else?" Virginia asked when she had served everyone and taken her seat.

Slater gave the details of the evening, which did consist only of eating a leisurely meal and coming home. He ended by teasing his mother. "We looked over the desserts at the restaurant, but we knew we'd get a better offer here."

This said, he took a bite of cake, his eyes sparkling over his mother's laugh.

"Is that so?" She tried to sound outraged, but she was still chuckling.

"It worked, Mother," Dakota reminded her, and everyone laughed at her look of surprise.

"This sounds fun," said a voice from the edge of the room, and everyone turned to see Gretchen Rawlings in the doorway.

"Come in, Mama," Charles invited, standing to give her his seat. "Have some cake."

"I couldn't eat another bite," she told him, having just returned from dinner with friends and taking the chair he offered.

"What restaurant did you visit?" This came from Cash, and in the time that followed, the eight of them fell into good conversation. The topics ranged from old family stories to the latest political subject. Some resorted to filibuster tactics to keep the floor, and with plenty of cake and coffee, it seemed they would go all night.

Darvi didn't want it to end, but she knew that her coming in would disturb her parents and thought that an early getaway from the Rawlingses might be better. All were sorry to see her go, but everyone was gracious as she and Dakota walked to the door and made their way outside.

"Have I mentioned that I'm sick of walking you home?" Dakota offered, his hand holding Darvi's as they covered the distance between his parents' house and hers.

Darvi tried not to be hurt by his words but found herself glad that it was dark out.

"No," she said quietly, working to keep her voice normal. "I don't think you've said that."

They had arrived on Darvi's front porch, a dark place at this time of the night. Dakota waited only until they had stopped moving to bring her gently against his chest and whisper in her ear, "I want to keep you with me. I'm sick of leaving you at your door and having to walk away."

Darvi relaxed in his arms, so enjoying his tender hold.

"It's not long now," she said as she felt him kiss her brow.

"Forty-eight hours."

Darvi tipped her head back and tried to see him in the dark.

"Mrs. Dakota Rawlings. I like the sound of that."

Dakota bent and kissed her, not a long kiss—that had to wait—but one filled with the tenderness he felt for her.

"I'd better let you go in."

"All right. I'll see you tomorrow evening at the family dinner, and then on Saturday..."

Dakota laughed. "I'll be there."

With one more hug, he stepped off the porch and walked into the night. Behind him, he heard Darvi's door open and close. Just a few more days and she could be with him, but in the meantime, his family was gathered as they hadn't been for a long time. He was eager to get home and share in that celebration too.

❧ ❧ ❧

"Cash," his mother said to him much later that night. The family had laughed and talked until some were drooping in their seats. When people started to head off to bed, Cash grabbed the serving tray for his mother and walked it into the kitchen. He hadn't planned to linger, but she caught him before he could leave.

"Yes?"

"It's time you got married," she said without warning.

If Cash hadn't contained himself, he would have laughed.

"Why is that?" he managed, a small smile coming to his mouth.

"Well," she tried, her brow furrowed a little as if she expected him to already know. "I was just watching your brothers with Libby and Darvi tonight, and I thought, 'I want that for Cash too.'"

"I appreciate that, Mother, but sometimes it's easier said than done."

Virginia looked thoughtful. "I suppose it is." Her eyes shifted around the room, gazing lovingly at the contents before looking back to her son. "Between this house and the ranch house, I prefer the ranch house. Did you know that, Cash?"

"No."

Virginia smiled. "You father built that ranch house for us. This house was already built. I love the kitchen at the ranch house and all the rooms. I love the way it's laid out. We've had some great times in this house, and I wouldn't want to move back to Texas, but I do miss that house." She looked Cash in the eye. "But even with all of that, I have no problem with another woman living there. I want you to marry someone who will enjoy the ranch with you. I want your children to grow up there, as you boys did."

Cash so appreciated his mother's words, but he couldn't exactly promise to give her what she wished. He wondered what she would say if he told her what her other sons had said to him that very evening. He ended up smiling at her and saying nothing at all.

"Well, dear," she said quietly, in what Cash knew to be her *mother's voice*, "when the time comes, remember that your mother will be delighted."

"Thank you, Mother," he said sincerely, knowing no end of relief that she didn't expect to hear a plan to make this happen. And her eyes, just before she hugged him, told him how deeply he was loved. He took himself off to bed, his heart wondering if God was trying to tell him something or if Dakota's wedding had just put everyone into a matrimonial mood.

🌿 🌿 🌿

"You look a little pale," Cash said to Dakota just an hour before the big event.

"Do I?" Dakota asked, looking vague and not quite focusing on his brother's face.

"Sit down, Dak." Slater took his arm and led him to a chair.

"All right," Dakota agreed, but he sat for only a matter of seconds.

"Is it hot in here to you?"

Thinking that letting him pace might be the best thing, Slater and Cash stood back while Dakota moved to open the window.

At the same time, all three men heard laughter from the next room.

"It sounds like the ladies are having a party," Slater said casually, but Dakota did not appear to have heard.

"How are you?" Virginia asked as she sailed through the door, Charles at her heels.

"We're fine," Slater replied, his eyes sparkling. "Aren't we, Dak?"

But Dakota wasn't listening. He had finally sat down and was staring blankly out the window.

His father found this highly amusing and started to laugh. His whole family was nearly hysterical before the groom noticed.

"What did I miss?"

No one could answer him. It had been a busy time for everyone, which left a certain level of fatigue on each person's part, making the incident seem funnier than it might have been. Nevertheless Dakota began to smile. His father's face was getting red, and he laughed a little in return.

"I think they're ready for you," one of the wedding coordinators said to Charles and Virginia as she stuck her head in the door.

"Thank you. We'll be right there," Virginia responded agreeably, moving swiftly to hug Dakota and say something quietly in his ear. Charles didn't hug him, but he smiled as he moved out the door, an older version of the groom himself. Dakota had been watching him and smiled in return.

The room was still quiet after the older Rawlingses went on their way, but the tension was gone. Cash, Dakota, and Slater sat quietly and talked—something they never seemed to tire of doing—until it was their turn to join the wedding party.

⚜ ⚜ ⚜

Dakota's quiet and distracted state before the ceremony had not been the result of second thoughts. Not for a moment did he doubt whether or not he and Darvi should be married. But his heart had been prayerful, asking God to bless this union and help him to be the husband he needed to be. For this reason and many more, he was now able to stand in great joy and excitement and watch Darvi come up the aisle toward him.

Darvi's dress was a stylish creation of satin and lace, the very latest in fashion with a bustle that was just coming back into style. But the groom, had he been willing to admit it, didn't take much notice. His eyes intent on hers, he offered his arm when she neared, barely aware of the way Mr. Wingate let her go and took a seat with his wife.

Hundreds of people from St. Louis and family from far and wide had turned out to see these nuptials, but the bride and groom were hardly aware of them. Darvi heard someone sniff and thought her mother might be tearful, but she herself didn't want to cry at all. She worked to keep her eyes on Pastor Daniel Cooper, a man she had come to love and deeply respect since her conversion, but her gaze strayed repeatedly to Dakota, who was just as distracted by her presence.

They both grew solemn when it was time to repeat their vows, promises they were taking very seriously, and in rather short order, they were pronounced husband and wife. Mr. and Mrs. Dakota Rawlings turned to face the church and found smiles at every glance. The couple led the way out of the sanctuary to the large hall where a banquet had been prepared. Taking their seats at the head table, they were joined by the family, and the merrymaking began.

"She looks beautiful," Liberty said to Slater, her head bent forward slightly to see down the table.

"Um hmm," he agreed, looking at his wife's face. "Like another bride I remember."

Liberty smiled as they leaned to kiss each other.

Down the table, Darvi was saying to Dakota, "It went so fast. Beforehand it felt like forever, and now here it's all behind us."

Dakota smiled at her enthusiasm just as his stomach growled.

"Didn't you eat breakfast?" she asked him.

"I can't remember."

Darvi looked very pleased with herself. "Well, you have a wife now. She'll see that you don't go hungry."

And down the table some more, Cash was sitting with Darvi's youngest bridesmaid, a sweet girl of 11 who wanted to know all about ranching.

"How do the cattle get to market?"

"We round them up and load them onto the train."

Not wishing to be impolite, she tried not to show her dismay.

"Doesn't it smell rather bad?"

Cash smiled. "In summer it does."

"What do the people do, just ride with a hankie over their noses?"

"Well, the cattle are not with the people. They have special train cars."

Cash watched as she bit her lip and giggled.

"I thought they were right in with the people."

"That *would* smell rather bad," he said and made her laugh again.

❧ ❧ ❧

Hours later, after good food and lots of hugs and good wishes, the bride and groom climbed into a covered carriage and settled against the plush seat.

"You know," Dakota said for his wife's ears alone, his arm holding her close, "I couldn't help but notice that this dress has a lot of buttons down the back."

Darvi turned to look at him.

"It does, doesn't it? Do you think that will be a problem?"

"Not for me." He sounded very satisfied. "I'm a very patient man."

Darvi started to laugh, but Dakota caught it with a kiss before they both settled back to finish the ride to the hotel.

❧ ❧ ❧

"I've been reading the Bible," Charles told Cash at breakfast the next morning.

"What have you been reading?"

"Genesis," the older man answered and then seemed to be searching for words. "I'm a businessman, Cash. I try never to lead with my heart."

Cash waited, sure his father was going somewhere with this.

"I guess I'm just trying to say that I never saw God as logical before, but I'm very impressed with how He laid out the world and commanded Adam to care for it. And even after Adam and Eve had to leave the garden, God had plans for them. He never set them adrift, as it were."

"No, He sure didn't. Genesis is a great place to start, Father. That was wise of you to start at the beginning."

"There are some things that confuse me, though. I mean, why would Noah, after being so disciplined to do this huge job God gave him, get drunk?"

Cash smiled a little. "And why do I, knowing I was bought with a price, Christ's precious blood, commit sins and want my own way?"

"Why do you?" Charles persisted, truly needing an answer.

"Because I'm still a sinner. Scripture says the spirit is willing, but the flesh is weak. I've been saved from eternal death, but as long as I'm on this earth, the battle with my flesh will continue. I can choose not to sin at any time—God's Spirit inside of me gives me the strength to do that—but I don't always choose it. I sometimes want to sin and don't care that I've put myself out of fellowship with God."

"What does that mean, 'put yourself out of fellowship'?"

"My faith in Christ's life, death, and resurrection made me clean before God, but sin separates us from God, so when I sin, I lose communion with Him. I'm still His child—it's impossible to lose that—but until I confess my sin and repent of it, there's a barrier between God and me. He's a huge, forgiving God, so I have no excuse. I just need to agree with Him about my sin, and all lines of communication become open again."

Charles nodded, his face intent. He was opening his mouth to speak again but suddenly stopped. Cash saw his father's eyes dart across the room before the older man shifted his gaze to his coffee cup and took a drink.

Cash turned to see his mother had come in and let the door swing shut behind her. Cash watched her as she came to the table.

"You're talking about God, aren't you?"

Charles looked a bit sheepish, but Virginia sat down, her face open.

"It's all right, Charles," she shocked him by saying. "I've been doing some thinking of my own."

"On what exactly?"

Virginia turned and looked at Cash. "I've been patting myself on the back about this wedding." She smiled a little wryly. "I'm not sure why—Clarisse Wingate did all the work—but for some reason it's given me great pride that two of my boys have found wives. But in the midst of those thoughts, you came to mind. It's not that you're not married, Cash; it's what you believe. I was just short of taking bows over Dakota and Darvi's marriage, and then I thought you wouldn't feel that way. You would thank God for putting them together."

Cash only looked at her, still too surprised to speak.

"You would, wouldn't you, Cash?"

"Yes, Mother," he said gently. "I would."

Virginia sighed a little, her gaze going upward. "I just don't know if He wants me. I know Charles is interested, and I want to be, but I feel as though God is hiding."

"The God I believe in, the God of the Bible, doesn't play hide-and-seek with anyone. He's not capricious. Deuteronomy 4:29 tells us God can be found if we search for Him with all our heart and soul."

"Where does it say that?" Charles asked, standing as he spoke and moving to the small desk in the kitchen where he'd been keeping the Bible. When he came back, Cash opened the book and showed him the verse. Virginia pressed in to see as well.

For the next few minutes Cash took them to passages that spoke of God and His expectations of the people He created. Both Virginia and Charles were very attentive. Cash didn't press his parents, and after just a short time, he sat back and was quiet.

Virginia was the first to speak. "Charles, would you mind terribly if we didn't leave for Europe this month?"

"No, I wouldn't, but why wait?"

"I just want to hear more of what Pastor Cooper has to say. I want to go this morning and next week too. If we're leaving soon, I might be distracted."

Charles took her hand, and for a long time they looked at each other.

"I'm a stubborn old man," he said, having forgotten Cash's presence.

"You're in good company then," Virginia said, her eyes still on his. "You're married to a stubborn old woman."

Charles raised Virginia's hand and kissed it, but they weren't distracted with each other for very long. This subject was too urgent in their minds. Only seconds passed before they had more questions for their oldest son.

❧ ❧ ❧

"What are you doing?" Liberty asked her husband when she found him poised outside the closed kitchen door. She was ready for the service long before she needed to be, and because she'd already had some juice, she was hungry.

"Cash is talking to the folks about spiritual issues," Slater responded, his voice low. "I don't want to interrupt."

Liberty nodded. She couldn't really hear what was being said, but she was quiet with her husband. They stood for a moment longer until Slater glanced at his wife's face. As usual she looked a little pale in the morning. He knew it would help if she could eat.

"How about," he started, "I take you out to breakfast?"

"All right. Do I need a sweater?"

"I'll keep you warm."

Liberty smiled in delight as he took her hand and led her to the front door. An impulsive outing was always fun in her mind, and she loved having time with her spouse, but even as they left, both husband and wife remembered to pray for the people in the kitchen.

Three

"YOUR FATHER GAVE ME THE LONGEST hug he's given me in years," Gretchen Rawlings told Cash, Slater, and Liberty after the train pulled out of the St. Louis station. "I don't know when I've seen him so tender."

The older woman's eyes misted over, and her three grandchildren let silence fall, but they understood just what she meant. The questions and discussions they'd had in the last few days and the interest they saw in Charles and Virginia had given them all renewed hope that someday they might set their faith, their future, in Christ.

It was five days after the wedding and time for all of them to head home. Before catching their own train back to spend a week on the gulf, Darvi and Dakota had spent a few days on their own and then come back to the Rawlingses' house to open gifts. Now these other four would ride together as far as Dallas before Slater and Liberty would connect to one train and Cash and his grandmother to another.

Everyone was on the quiet side. It had been a tiring time—fun, but draining both physically and emotionally. The family was weary. And Liberty was not just tired—she was hungry. She had not felt up to eating before they left, so it wasn't surprising that she was ready for food not too many miles down the tracks. The young couple asked the others to join them in the dining car, but both Cash and Grandma Rawlings declined.

"I'm rather glad we're on our own for a moment, Cash," Gretchen turned from the window to say.

"Why is that?"

"I've been meaning to tell you that you need to get married."

Cash looked at her, hardly able to believe his ears.

"You're the fourth person to tell me that in a week," he admitted quietly and found his grandmother's eyes widening in surprise.

His face was so serious that she put a hand on his arm.

"I'm sorry, Cash. Truly I am. That was very insensitive of me."

And that was all. No "buts," no explanation of good intentions or having only his happiness and well-being in mind—just an apology.

Cash smiled at her and she smiled in return, and although they shared no other words, Cash's heart was very thoughtful.

It was never my intention to be the last one, but it's not as if I'd planned it. I couldn't be happier for my brothers, but seeing them get married doesn't change anything in my life. Cash let his heart be quiet for a moment, and then he spoke to the Lord. *You don't have this for me yet. I don't need to even ask about it. I can see it with my own eyes. I feel I'm ready to be married, but You know me best.*

Cash could see that this was all he could say to God. He could thank God and trust Him for the future, but he couldn't expect God to act on something just because he felt the time was right in his human mind.

Cash's own sense of weariness suddenly intensified. He was so glad for the time he'd had with the family, but right now he was tired. A glance at his grandmother, whose stamina always amazed him, told him she was settling in for sleep too. Cash had no problem joining her. Even knowing he would have to move when Slater and Liberty came back, he stretched his long legs toward the seat across from him and let his body slouch down into comfort so he could sleep.

❧ ❧ ❧

Kinkade, Texas

There weren't too many trains into Kinkade each day, but Reagan had taken an early one. She had a name, William Harmond, and an address, and in her mind that was enough. She wasn't as fresh as she would like to have been for a first meeting with her new employer but felt sure he would understand.

The platform cleared swiftly, and Reagan was glad to have a moment to look around. She liked what she could see of Kinkade. It looked to be on the quiet side and nowhere near as large as her neighborhood in New York; she could tell that it was a town just her size.

"Excuse me," Reagan said when a man in uniform passed by. "May I ask you a question?"

"Certainly, miss. What can I do for you?"

"I'm looking for a Mr. William Harmond. Could you possibly tell me where he lives?"

"Yes, ma'am, it just so happens he lives next to my aunt. You go to the middle of town, and then a block to the north, turn left, and he's the third house on the right."

Reagan beamed at him. She never dreamed she would hear such clear directions.

"Thank you, sir."

The man watched her walk away, a small smile on his face as he shook his head a little. She had smiled at him as though he'd given her a sack of gold.

Reagan did not look back. She moved toward downtown, a woman with a mission, her eyes swiftly scanning the storefronts. She watched the door of the general store just being opened, reminded again of the early hour. It was

a brisk day, but not at all cold like New York. Reagan had
everything she could do not to smile and greet everyone
she saw.

A bit of preoccupation over one advertisement in the
barber shop window almost made her miss her turn, but
with just a few maneuvers, she was on her way again. It
didn't take long to find that the instructions had been perfect. Doing exactly as she'd been told, she stood in front of
a large, well-kept home and saw the name Harmond on the
porch. Thinking there was no time like the present, Reagan
started up the walk.

A brisk knock on the wide wood door produced a
woman. She didn't look like a servant, and Reagan could
only hope he hadn't hired someone else.

"May I help you?" the woman asked.

"Yes, please. I'm Reagan Sullivan. I'm looking for Mr.
William Harmond."

The woman nodded, and Reagan thought she looked at
her oddly.

"I'll get him for you" was all she said before leaving
Reagan on the front porch.

"Well, at least she didn't shut the door completely," the
nanny muttered, wondering what to think of what had just
happened. She wasn't given much time. Within seconds
the door opened wide and a man stood there.

"Miss Sullivan?"

"Yes. Are you Mr. Harmond?"

"I am. Won't you please come in?"

"Thank you."

Her heart surging with excitement, seeing now that it
was all going to work out fine, Reagan stepped across the
threshold.

"You didn't get my letter," Mr. Harmond began before
Reagan could even set down her bag.

"Yes, I did," she said plainly. "I wouldn't be here otherwise."

William Harmond hesitated, his mind scrambling for words.

In that instant, Reagan knew something was wrong, and it wasn't hard to figure that the woman at the door had something to do with it. Nevertheless she was going to wait for this man to admit it.

"How is it you got my letter if you're just now arriving? I mailed it two weeks ago."

Reagan smiled. "I left early and took a little time to see the country."

Mr. Harmond nodded. He had hoped to avoid this, but now he had no choice.

"I must tell you, Miss Sullivan, that since I contacted you the first time, I've taken a wife."

"Have you now?" she asked calmly.

"Yes."

"And that would have been mentioned in this letter that I missed?"

"Yes. I'm sorry you've had to come all this way."

Reagan eyed him for a moment and then let her gaze take in the foyer. It would have been a nice place to work.

"Well, I guess that's the end of it," she said, not with a stinging tone but one that spoke of regret.

"I'm sorry."

Reagan smiled at him and started toward the door. Mr. Harmond was there ahead of her, his gaze anxious as he watched her. For this reason he saw the exact moment she stopped. He froze when she turned to him, not at all sure what she might do or say.

"Who did you marry?"

Nearly flabbergasted at the question, the man still managed, "Beth Barton."

"Where did she work?"

"She was a cook at the hotel."

Mr. Harmond was awarded one of the smiles that drew people to Reagan.

"I'll have to head there then, won't I? They'll be needing a cook."

William Harmond couldn't stop his shoulders from shaking. He'd never encountered anyone with such charm and pluck.

"Good day," Reagan said as she moved out the door, across the porch, and down the steps. She was halfway down the walk when he called her name. Reagan turned to see him approaching.

"This is for you," he said, his hand outstretched to offer money to her. "I only sent half your train fare because I didn't know if you'd really come, but this should be enough to get you home if the hotel has already hired someone."

Reagan took the money without hesitation.

"I thank you, Mr. Harmond. As I don't even know where I'm sleeping tonight, I thank you indeed."

They parted company then, Reagan back to the main street of town and Mr. Harmond back to his wife. Mr. Harmond was not sorry he'd married; indeed, he was quite content, and Reagan, although sorry the job didn't pan out, felt it was early enough in the day to still land on her feet.

❧ ❧ ❧

Russell Bennett, a mountain of a man, wiped the sweat from his brow, put down his hammer and tongs, and stepped away from the forge in his blacksmith's shop. He needed a drink and a rest from the fire. Business was brisk, and this was his day to work in the shop. He wouldn't make calls to the ranches until Monday. Not only taking a drink but pouring some on his neck as well, Russell had only just set the water jug aside when he spotted her.

Standing in the middle of the double doorway, right where the horses came and went, was a small, dark-haired woman. She stood erect, a single bag grasped by both hands and held in front of her.

"Can I help you?"

"I don't know, but I was wondering what I need to rent one of your stalls for a time."

"You need a horse."

Reagan nodded.

"Would you say a horse is a pretty expensive item, something a person would want watched with care?"

Trying not to smile, Russell said, "I would agree with that, yes."

"Well, that being the case, would it be possible to leave my bag in a stall for a time? I've got business here in Kinkade, and the bag's heavy enough to add inches to my arms."

Russell did smile then. He also pointed toward a stall.

"No one will disturb your bag if you leave it right there."

"Right here?" Reagan asked, setting the bag down so that it couldn't be seen from the door.

"That's the place."

Regan brought up the small purse that hung from her wrist to look for a coin.

"You don't need to pay me."

Reagan eyed him.

"Are you going to rent that stall and let some animal step on my things?"

Russell laughed at this, a booming sound that made Reagan smile.

"No," he told her, still chuckling. "I close down at five. Just be back before then so you can get your things."

"I thank you, sir."

"What's your business?" he asked her as she began to walk away.

Reagan answered with only a glance over her shoulder. "I'm job hunting."

That said, she continued on her way.

Russell stood still for a moment, a smile on his face. His own dear Holly would have to meet this one. Unless he missed his guess, she was too independent by half and just might need a friend in Kinkade.

❧ ❧ ❧

"I need to see the manager," Reagan said for the second time.

"What about?" the little man at the rear of the dining area asked again. She hadn't been willing to give her name, and he thought this might work.

"I'll tell the manager when I see him."

It went a long way toward strengthening Reagan's resolve to hear pots crashing behind the closed door to the right of her and a woman's voice above it all. It didn't take any great skill to hear that she was unhappy.

"Do you have an appointment?"

"Do I need an appointment?"

The little man gave up, saying with long-suffering, "Wait here."

Going through the very door Reagan knew led to the kitchen, the man disappeared. As Reagan watched, her eyes caught a glimpse of a kitchen she felt sure had seen better days. For a moment she doubted her idea, and at that moment a woman appeared.

"Meddlesome busybody," she muttered. "As if I can't use a few minutes out of that steaming kitchen." The flushed woman didn't see Reagan until she was almost on top of her, but she didn't look sorry, only hot and cross.

"Are you the manager?" Reagan asked.

"I am. What can I do for you?"

"I hear you need a cook. I'd like to apply for the job."

Much as the woman looked as though she needed relief, she still asked, "Do you have any experience?"

"Not much, but I'm a fast learner."

The woman's eyes rolled heavenward. "As if I have any time to teach you."

Reagan eyed her, taking in the stains on her apron and the beads of sweat over her upper lip.

"Maybe you're right. It doesn't look like much fun."

Reagan was turning away when the manager said, "It pays well if you're experienced."

Reagan turned back in surprise. Had she not heard her say she wasn't?

"What does it pay if you're not experienced?"

The manager smiled. "I like your honesty."

"I won't promise something I can't give you."

The two eyed each other.

"So how much experience have you had?"

"I can cook anything. I've just never done it for a large group."

"Well, that's a start."

"You didn't answer me about the pay."

The woman quoted a wage that was so low Reagan was outraged.

"*A week*?"

"That's right."

"I'm used to twice that."

"Where are you from?"

"New York."

"This is not New York."

"I know that, but I don't even have a place to stay. It could cost a fortune to live in this town!"

"It's not that bad, especially since you can eat here anytime you cook. That would leave most of your pay for rent."

"And clothing. Kitchen work is murder on fabric."

The manager smiled; this one was as dumb as a fox.

"I'm Sally March, by the way." The woman offered her hand.

"Reagan Sullivan."

"Megan?"

"No, Reagan with an *R.*"

"That's different."

"*I'm* different."

"I can see that. I'm willing to give you a try, but it's only fair to warn you that my cousin from Cincinnati is supposed to be coming to take this job. If he ever shows up, I might not need you."

"Well, at least for the moment I'll have work, but I'd better warn you, I plan to eat plenty."

Sally's eyes twinkled. She didn't know what the food would taste like, but the new cook was sure to lighten the load and the atmosphere. There wasn't much to her, but over the years Sally had found that the plucky applicants worked the hardest. Indeed Sally was getting ready to put her to work when Reagan moved as if she was leaving.

"I thank you for trying me, Mrs. March. I'll see you tomorrow."

"It's Miss, and you can call me Sally. I was thinking you'd be starting right now."

Reagan faced her squarely.

"I just got off the train. I don't have a place to live, and I haven't eaten yet today. If I find a place to stay, I'll come back as soon as I can, but for right now, I've got to make plans for tonight."

"Fair enough. Plan to eat when you get back here, even if you don't have a chance to work. The least I can do is feed you."

Reagan smiled and left without another word. She wasn't at all sure where to start, but start she would.

"A place to stay on only my new salary," she said quietly to no one but herself. "This could take awhile."

❧ ❧ ❧

"Whose bag is this?" Holly Bennett asked of Russell when she brought him his lunch.

"Some little gal's. I didn't get her name."

"Did she take a horse?"

"No. She said she was job hunting and the bag was heavy."

Russell smiled at his wife's wide eyes.

"She knew what she wanted, Holly. You would have liked her."

Holly looked at him teasingly. "I don't know what you're talking about, Mr. Bennett. You speak as though I've been strong-willed in the recent past."

She chose to turn her back on him and jumped a little when he landed a swat on her seat.

"Russell Bennett! Someone could have seen that."

But the blacksmith had just put half his sandwich in his mouth and managed to look innocent as he chewed.

Holly only shook her head. He was always so much fun.

"Where's Alisa?" Russell asked.

"Mrs. Ellis stopped in and offered to stay with her, but I should probably get home."

"Thanks for lunch."

"You're welcome. I'll see you tonight."

A quick kiss later, Holly went on her way. Russell watched as she turned back at the door and waved at him the way she always did. He waved in return, but as soon as she was gone, his eyes landed on the bag that had been left. He wanted to laugh all over again. He also wondered how the mystery woman was doing.

※ ※ ※

"This door has no lock on it."

"You want how much a week?"

"I have to share a bed?"

Those were Reagan's three responses to the three places she checked. Kinkade was not lacking for rooms to rent, but it was also clear why some of them were empty.

Nevertheless she was undaunted. At the moment, Reagan was following directions she'd been given at the general store and found herself wishing she'd started there. The lady had been kind, almost motherly, and not asked a dozen questions that Reagan did not have time to answer.

"This must be it," she said, still talking to herself.

Knock on the door of the big house, not the little one.

"I don't even see a small house," Reagan mumbled as she remembered the woman's words and climbed resolutely onto the porch. She was about three blocks from Mr. Harmond's place and thought that if this didn't pan out, she might have to ask him for help, at least for the night.

"Of course Sally might have an idea. That would probably be..."

"Hello."

Reagan had not heard the door open, so she was startled to hear someone speak to her.

"Hello. My name is Reagan Sullivan, and the woman at the general store said you might have a room to rent."

"Oh, I do, yes. Did you say your name was Megan?"

"No, it's Reagan with an *R.*"

"It's nice to meet you, Reagan. My name is Holly. Would you like to see the house?"

"It's a house?"

Holly Bennett smiled. "A small one."

"How much is the rent?"

She named a price that made Reagan's heart sink.

"Would you still like to see it?"

"Well," she said honestly, her truthful nature rising to the surface, "it's a little steep for my pay right now."

To her surprise the woman smiled.

"Why don't you see it anyhow?"

Not sure if this was wise or not, she agreed.

Holly Bennett led the way around her own house and down a short lane. About 20 yards behind the main house was a small structure. A shed might have been the best description, but it was in good shape and had windows and a front door that made it look like a small house.

Following the woman, Reagan walked over the threshold behind her host, and in the space of one heart-beat fell in love. All in one room, this tiny house had every amenity. In one corner was a brass bed, and next to it was a low table. Opposite the door was an overstuffed chair with an ottoman, and behind the chair was an oak dresser. A tiny stove sat next to a table for two and there were even shelves for a pantry. Holly opened a closet that had been built in behind the front door, and Reagan could only stare.

Reagan had never imagined such a place. Visions of living alone, something she had never done—quiet mornings and no one snoring in the night—floated through her mind.

"How much did you say it was again?"

Seeing her face, Holly made herself quote the price she and Russell had decided on. It was hard to do because she wanted this woman to move in, but she remained true to her agreement.

Reagan licked her lips. She would probably be in rags because she wouldn't be able to afford new clothes, but she couldn't let this get away.

"Is there a lock on the door?" she remembered to ask at the last minute.

"Of course," Holly answered in surprise.

Reagan felt a smile building up inside of her. She wouldn't even have a blanket for the bed that night, but the thought of being chilly didn't stop her. Before she headed back to the livery for her bag, she gave Holly Bennett the money for one month's rent.

Four

RUSSELL REALIZED SHE COULD HAVE taken her bag and left, but she didn't do that. He had been busy shoeing a horse when she returned, and when he looked up she was standing there, the bag at her feet.

"Thank you for watching my bag."

"You're welcome," the big man said as he used his handkerchief on his face. "How did the job search go?"

"I found one, and a place to live as well."

"Well, now, you've been busy."

Reagan couldn't hide her pleasure and didn't try.

"So where do you work?"

"At the hotel, in the kitchen."

Fearing that her skills would be inadequate, she hesitated to call herself a cook and then find herself out of work in a week.

"So you cook?"

Reagan smiled. "I hope so."

The big man laughed again.

"And where did you find a place to live?"

Reagan's guard went up in a hurry. She had learned many survival skills living in New York City, and one clear law was not volunteering information to strangers. Her hand came out as if he hadn't spoken. Russell shook it automatically.

"Thank you again for watching my bag."

"You're welcome."

With that she moved on her way.

The blacksmith was not exactly sure what had happened, but a customer came in the door looking for his horse, and he ran out of time to speculate.

☙ ☙ ☙

"Well, you certainly can eat a lot, can't you?" Sally said about an hour later, having watched Reagan methodically polish off a large plate of food.

"It's good food."

"We certainly want the customer to feel that way," she said pointedly, but Reagan only smiled.

"Actually," Sally started again, "I need to tell you that I want you to come in the mornings and bake. If the truth be told, I don't mind the cooking. It's the baking I hate."

"All right. I can do that. What time?"

"You'd best be here by four, since the first breakfast customers come between five and half past. You'll bake all the bread, rolls, pies, and cakes for each day."

"All right, and when do I get my first raise?"

"Raise? You haven't even started."

"I know that, but you said my pay was because of inexperience. I just figured when I had some experience, it would be worth it to you."

Sally's look was shrewd, but Reagan met it unflinchingly.

"I'll let you know" was all she would say.

"Oh, don't worry about it," Reagan replied lightly, "I don't mind asking again."

Sally was taken off guard and found herself laughing. She'd have kept on laughing if she hadn't heard an impatient sniff. She turned to see her front-desk man standing nearby, his face disapproving when he saw that Reagan was eating. It told him she'd been hired.

"What is it, Pierce?"

"I was wondering if you'd had a chance to look at those ledgers yet."

"Yes, they're done and on my desk."

"Thank you."

After he walked away, Sally shook her head.

"He drives me crazy."

"Why do you keep him on?"

Her brows rose as if Reagan should know.

"His manners at the front desk are excellent. The customers love him."

She sounded so aggrieved that Reagan smiled.

"Well, if you're finished eating, you can clear out."

"You don't want help tonight?"

"Tonight's all done—that's what you're eating. I'm always done cooking by three, and the waitresses, who will be here any minute, do the coffee and small stuff."

Reagan stood. "So I'll see you in the morning."

"Four o'clock."

Reagan stared at her for a moment.

"Thank you, Sally, for everything."

"You'll earn it, Reagan," the older woman said confidently, albeit kindly.

Reagan retrieved her bag from near the door and stepped outside. It was time to head home.

❧ ❧ ❧

"Here you go," Holly said to her daughter that evening as she handed her a piece of bread.

"Thank you, Mama."

"How about you, Russ?"

"Yes, please. Elly, would you please pass me the butter?"

The ten-year-old handed it to him and then realized she needed it back for her own bread. They spent a little time working together and then laughed when seven-year-old

Jonah realized he needed bread with butter too and the passing began all over again. Nine-month-old Alisa sat in the high chair, smiling at anyone who would look her way and cheerfully eating whatever was offered.

"Someone is in the little house, Papa," Jonah announced to his father.

"Mama told me," Russell said. "Did you meet her?"

"No, she's not home now, so we can't meet her."

"I think I might have met her earlier today," Russell told his children. "A woman asked me to watch her traveling case, and I think it might be the same one."

Having said this, Russell found his wife's eyes on him.

"What's the matter?"

"Is that the only bag she has—the one you watched for her?"

"I don't know."

Holly worried her lower lip for a time.

"Russell, she probably doesn't have sheets or blankets or anything. I left a lantern, but would she find it and the matches if she didn't return until dark?"

Husband and wife finished eating as soon as they could, and leaving Elly in charge of her siblings, took their own lantern to the rear of the lot toward the little house. Even from a distance they could see a light burning. Holly knocked on the door but still called out so as not to frighten their new tenant.

"Reagan, it's Holly."

The door opened.

"We're sorry to disturb you, but we thought you might need some things."

Reagan didn't answer. She was too busy staring at the large man behind Holly. When he smiled, she recalled her manners.

"Come in," Reagan invited and stepped back. Even so, Reagan took a moment to recover, especially since the room shrank visibly with the blacksmith inside.

"We wanted to make sure you had everything you need, Reagan," Holly said again, having already taken in the things laid on the dresser, but also seeing absolutely nothing on the bed. The room was warm from the fire Reagan had lit in the stove, but Holly was not comforted.

"I'm doing fine," Reagan assured her landlady. "But if I could impose upon you for one thing, I would be very grateful."

"Just name it."

"A pillow. I don't think I'll sleep well without it."

"But you do think you'll sleep well without blankets and sheets?" This came from Russell before he realized they'd never been introduced. "I'm Russell, Holly's husband."

"I'm Reagan," that lady told him. "Did you put this little house together?"

"Yes, ma'am."

Reagan took in the way his head almost touched the ceiling.

"How did you manage that?"

"It wasn't easy," he replied, smiling in a way that belied the words.

Reagan and Holly laughed a little just before both of them heard a small voice.

"Papa?"

It was Elly. Russell opened the door for them, and Reagan smiled as Elly entered with Alisa in her arms and Jonah coming just behind.

"It looks like the whole family is going to welcome you, Reagan. I hope you don't mind."

"Not at all."

"This is Elly, and next to her is Jonah, and the baby is Alisa. Children, this is Miss Sullivan."

Holly plucked Alisa from Elly's arms as the two older children came over to shake Reagan's hand.

"You're the first one to live here," Jonah informed her. "I wanted to live here, but my room is in the house."

"Well, you'll just have to come and visit me. Will you do that?"

Jonah was only too happy to nod in agreement, and he might have had more to say, but Russell was ready to bring the party to an end.

"All right, children, let's give Miss Sullivan a little privacy now. We'll head back to the house and leave the ladies alone."

"Thank you," Reagan said when they all turned to tell her goodnight. In just a moment she was alone with Holly.

"Reagan, do you have pots or pans or even anything to eat?"

"I don't, Holly, but I'll be doing most of my eating at the hotel, so that's not really much of a concern. I guess it would be nice to have a blanket, but I've got plenty of clothes and the stove is going to keep me nice and warm."

Holly didn't comment on that particular remark but did say, "I'll head back to the house and gather some things for you. We have plenty to spare, so there's no need for you to be going without."

"Are you certain, Holly? I mean, you have three children."

The other woman was already shaking her head.

"It's not a problem."

Reagan stood in a mix of emotions when her landlady left, so pleased to have a place to live and a job, but also feeling the effects of a long day. She was tempted to sit down but knew it would be too hard to get back up. It was with relief that she heard Holly returning.

"Okay," Holly said when she was back inside, a basket overflowing with a pillow, a quilt, one blanket, a set of sheets, and several sizes of towels. "I took you at your word about the food, but you can't sleep on a bare bed."

Reagan smiled at her adamancy.

"Oh!" Holly suddenly remembered, her hand going to the pocket of her apron. "Russell sent this out to you."

Reagan looked at the money in Holly's hand but didn't take it.

"What is it?"

"Russ has lowered the rent, and this is the difference."

"Why is he doing that?"

"I told him it was a bit steep for you, and he doesn't want you to struggle."

Reagan didn't speak, but she was thinking, *Could these people be real?*

"Take it, Reagan." Holly pushed the money toward her. "He won't want it back."

Reagan took the offered money, not sure what she thought.

"Can I help you with anything, Reagan? We could have this bed done in no time."

Reagan looked into her kind face and thought she really had landed on her feet in this town. Almost all the people in Kinkade had been kind, and her landlady was especially so.

"Thank you, Holly, but it's no trouble. You've been very kind, and before it's over I'll probably need something else, but for right now, I'm doing fine."

"I'm glad, Reagan. Just come right to the back door if you find you do need something, even if it's in the middle of the night."

Holly took her leave, and Reagan found herself alone once again. Not until that moment did she remember the money in her hand. She looked down at it, her brow furrowed in thought. Had the blacksmith asked where she'd found a place to live only out of curiosity and kindness, or was there something more?

"His wife is beautiful," Reagan said quietly, "but more than one man has wandered in spite of that."

She hoped she had read the situation all wrong, but why would he return about a quarter of her money in exchange for nothing?

Reagan had a sudden need to check the already locked door. She went to each window and found them secured as well. Not liking the thought in her mind, Reagan nevertheless faced the fact that Russell Bennett might not be as respectable as she first thought.

❧ ❧ ❧

"Is she settled, Holly?" Russell asked once the children were in bed. He'd taken his bath and gone to the bedroom to find Holly changing into a nightie and starting on her hair.

"I think so. She looked tired to me, but she didn't want help with the bed." A huge yawn escaped her. "If she's like me tonight, she'll sleep hard."

"What did she say about the returned rent?"

"Not much, but I'm not sure she liked it."

Russell was quiet over this. He had debated what to do about the rent, and in the end was glad he'd given some back, but there was a chance he could have given the wrong impression, or even that they would find themselves taken advantage of. He wasn't all that keen about being a landlord in the first place, and he and Holly had both decided that if it didn't work out, they would not rent "the shack," as they called it, to strangers again.

"Of all the people I tried to imagine would be our first tenant, Holly, I don't think Reagan fit the bill."

"What type of person did you expect?"

Russell's smile was lopsided. "Some homeless man with a drinking problem, maybe. I don't know."

Holly only watched him climb into bed.

"Did you get to know anything about her?" he asked as he lay down on his back.

"Not before I let her rent the place. I mean, she mentioned that she couldn't afford it, and just now she told me she's working at the hotel, but you had already mentioned that." Holly chewed on her lip, a sure sign she was worrying. "Did I mess things up, Russell?"

"No," he said quietly. "But when I'm feeling tired, like I am tonight, having someone else in my life to take care of makes me weary."

Holly was now ready for bed and joined her husband.

"Well, you might have emotions involved simply because she's the type of person who causes that, but something tells me that Reagan is used to taking care of herself."

"You're probably right."

Both husband and wife had run out of steam. Neither one moved to kiss the other goodnight. Russell simply reached for Holly's hand to squeeze it, and Holly mumbled a goodnight. Russell was thinking that he loved her and should say so, but sleep was rushing in fast.

🌺 🌺 🌺

"Have you got those biscuits in?" Sally asked a little before five the next morning.

"In and almost done," Reagan informed her, her arm still mixing the batter for two cakes.

"How much longer?"

"Only about five minutes. The bread is rising nicely."

Sally stood back in approval, thinking Reagan was going to work out fine. Sally had all but taken the morning off, since the baking had to be done first, and for the first time in a month, she wasn't tense before she started to cook.

Even if Cousin Leslie shows up, I might just keep Reagan too.

"We have customers," Pierce put his head in the door to announce.

"Well, where is Missy?" Sally demanded.

"I haven't seen her."

Sally's face went red very quickly as she whipped her apron off and went out to the dining area to do someone else's job. Her peaceful thoughts about Reagan's hard work evaporated.

Reagan noticed the exchange but kept her thoughts to herself. She wondered at people these days who didn't have enough pride in their work to show up on time and do a good job but then remembered that it was none of her business. The event lingered on her mind, however, so when she finished her work in the kitchen, she removed her own apron and went out front to see if she could help. Sally was still taking orders, so Reagan started around with the coffeepot and a tray of mugs.

"Well, now," one cowboy spoke amid a table full of cowboys, straightening when she got to his table. "You must be new."

"I might be." Reagan was noncommittal. "Do you want coffee?"

"I do, ma'am, yes, but only after you tell me if you're on today's menu."

"Do you want the coffee on your head or in your cup?" was Reagan's only reply as she counted heads, set mugs on the table, and began to pour. The men at the table had a good laugh over her words, but to a man they tried to catch her eye.

"You have flour on your cheek," the man alone at the next table told her.

Again Reagan was nonchalant.

"Do I?"

"Yes."

"Would you like coffee?"

"Here, let me get the flour off for you."

Reagan was two arms' lengths away from the table before the man saw her move. He sat with his handkerchief in hand, just staring at her.

"All I'm offering is the coffee," she clarified. "Do you want some?"

Not able to get anything more than an impassive stare from her, the man gave in. He nodded and watched as she poured but wasn't able to miss that she left his table without a backward glance.

"They seem to like you," Sally commented when Reagan came back to the kitchen to help dish up eggs and bacon.

"I'm the new girl, that's all."

Sally took in that head of dark wavy hair, the dark sparkling eyes, and the small but shapely figure, and wasn't convinced. And she was right. Two weeks passed, and the men still watched for Reagan. She had a way of lighting up the dining room with her candor, her quick smile, and her no-nonsense service. Sally had been smart enough to offer her a little more money, so each morning when she was finished with the baking, she moved to the dining room to wait tables. She was already used to being proposed to and took it in stride, but she didn't tolerate unwelcome caresses. More than one mess had to be cleaned up because Reagan had been forced to discourage a suitor by dumping his food on top of him.

The Wednesday of her third week began just this way. Reagan had not slept well and was not in the mood for games. A man whom she had not met before wouldn't take no for an answer, and Reagan had thrown his water in his face. The man was outraged, but Reagan had had enough. Exiting to the kitchen, she spoke as she gathered her things.

"I'm leaving for the day, Sally. I'm tired of being treated like something on the auction block." She turned and gave her employer a hard look. "From the outside this place looks classy, but some of your breakfast customers act like animals."

Not sure she still had a job, Reagan moved to the door. She headed down the alley, not really keeping track of where she was headed. She wasn't upset so much as she was tired. The man really hadn't been that obnoxious, but she hadn't been in the mood to deal with him.

A good walk; that's all I need. Without my bicycle I just don't get out enough.

"Good morning, Reagan," a voice suddenly called to her, and she realized she'd walked all the way down to Russell's livery.

"Hello, Russell," Reagan said easily enough, approaching where he stood in the alley behind his shop. She still didn't know the man very well, but at the moment he was a kind face, and Reagan felt very alone.

"Did you work today?"

"I did, yes, but I left early."

"Are you not feeling well?" he asked with genuine concern. "Holly has everything you can think of if you're under the weather. Just stop and see her."

"No, I'm all right."

The big man studied her.

"Your face says you aren't."

Reagan smiled and laughed a little.

"Sometimes men are so rude!" she suddenly blurted, and Russell had all he could do not to laugh.

"I can't disagree with you there."

They were silent for a moment.

"What happened?" Russell finally asked.

Reagan shook her head in wonder. "One of the hotel patrons could not keep his hands to himself. I threw his water in his face."

Russell's booming laugh brought a smile to Reagan's face.

"Good job. You keep them in their place."

Reagan was fascinated. This was the last thing she'd expected from him.

"Do you really think it was all right that I did that?"

"Of course I do. A woman alone can't let her guard down for an instant."

Reagan couldn't have felt better if he'd offered her the moon. Smiling a little, she thanked him and turned to go on her way.

"Oh, Reagan," he said, stopping her. She looked back. "How are things in the little house? Everything working well?"

"It's wonderful," she told him honestly.

"Well, if you need something, you know where to come."

With a wave Russell went back inside, and Reagan moved toward home. She was inside the safe walls of her little house a short time later, feeling as tired as if she'd worked her regular day.

Sitting down in her chair and putting her feet up, she found herself thinking of New York and growing sad over what she'd left behind. It hadn't been much, but it had been familiar. Tommy hadn't even sent her bicycle yet, and for one ridiculous moment Reagan thought she might cry.

"This won't do," she said quietly. "I must be more tired than I first thought."

But not even hearing the sound of her own voice could convince Reagan. She dozed off for a nap before she could put her finger on what was truly wrong.

Five

"I'M SUPPOSED TO BE WATCHING CHILDREN," Reagan muttered in low fury just two weeks later, her arm scrubbing furiously at a pot. "Kind, gentle little children who adore me. I'm supposed to be sitting under shade trees and reading storybooks. I should be eating little cakes and fanning myself if I'm warm." Reagan shook her head in irritation, blew the air from her brow, and picked up the bucket of water that needed dumping.

It wasn't enough that waiting on tables had been added to her original job as baker. Now, added to those jobs was pot scrubbing. It didn't matter that she was being paid more. She didn't like it! Nearly stomping to the back door, Reagan took barely a step outside before she tossed the bucket of water into the alley. She would have turned right around and gone back in, but a deep gasp stopped her. Peeking around the doorjamb that hindered her view, Reagan caught sight of a tall cowboy. He was dripping wet from his mid-chest to his knees. Reagan's hand came to her mouth.

"I'm sorry!" she exclaimed. "I didn't see you."

"It's all right," he said, still looking surprised but not angry.

"What were you doing back here anyway?"

The apologetic, concerned face of the woman with the bucket was transfigured into a frown. The wet man looked a little taken aback but still answered, "Just taking a shortcut, ma'am."

Reagan did little more than nod, not aware that she was still frowning in ill humor. Not until the cowboy went on his way without another word did she think she could have at least apologized again. She had not only soaked him with dirty wash water but intruded into his business as well.

I've got to get out more, she decided as she went back into work. *I'm wilting here in Texas, and it's only been a month. If Tommy would just send my...*

"Reagan, what are you doing just standing there?"

Sally had not asked in outrage, but Reagan was not in a pleasant mood. She caught herself before she snapped at the woman.

"Just emptying the bucket. And yes," Reagan added before Sally could ask her usual question, "everything is either baking or cooling."

Sally smiled and teased her.

"What put a burr under your saddle?"

"I don't know," Reagan admitted as she put the bucket down. "I don't like scrubbing pots—that much I know— but other than that I'm not sure."

"If you don't like scrubbing pots, why did you agree to do it?"

"The money."

"Well, is it worth it?"

Reagan looked at her, thinking for the first time that she *had* been a fair employer, not overly harsh, but at times single-minded in purpose because she had a business to run and reliable people were not always available to help her. Reagan smiled for the first time all day.

"Actually, it is, but I just needed to complain for a time."

Sally shook her head in mock exasperation and went to peek into the ovens. Reagan got fresh water and went back to scrubbing pots.

❧ ❧ ❧

Holly was hanging out the wash when Reagan arrived home. They hadn't seen too much of each other outside of Reagan's paying the rent and returning the borrowed things as she'd purchased blankets, sheets, and towels of her own.

"How are you, Reagan?" Holly asked. Reagan smiled at the sight of Alisa asleep in a basket at the end of the clothesline.

"I'm doing fine. How are you?"

"Very well, thank you. Jonah found a handkerchief in the bushes," Holly said as she plucked a small white cloth from her pocket. "Is it yours?"

"It is," Reagan said after she studied it. "Thank you. It must have blown away when I pegged out my own wash."

"Are you free to come to dinner tonight?" Holly offered on the spur of the moment. "I've got a chicken stewing, and you're welcome to join us."

"Why, thank you, I am free tonight."

Holly smiled at her.

"Is there something I can bring?"

"Just yourself."

They didn't talk much longer, but after learning the time to arrive, Reagan went to her little house, her mood very light.

"That's it," she concluded as she prepared to bathe. "I don't have any friends here. That's why I'm so down. Tommy hasn't sent my bicycle, and I have no friends. Who wouldn't be down?"

Having concluded this, Reagan stopped worrying about her mood. She had a plan now, and that was all she ever needed.

❧ ❧ ❧

"I don't like school as much as Elly does," Jonah informed Reagan that evening. Holly would not accept her help with dinner, so she sat in the living room with Alisa in her lap and Jonah visiting at her side.

"Why is that?" Reagan asked the seven-year-old boy.

"Elly can read lots better than me."

"But you'll learn, won't you?"

"That's what mama says."

Reagan smiled down into his dejected little face and thought she might be seeing herself. Most things came easily to her. When they did not, she wasn't very patient.

"What *do* you like about school?"

His face lit up in an instant.

"I like taking lunch in the tin with Elly, and I like to hear the teacher read, and I like it when Timmy Bolthouse plays with me."

"Who is Timmy Bolthouse?"

"He's my friend from school. He can spit water out his teeth!"

"I can do that."

Jonah's eyes and little open mouth spoke of his awe.

"Can you teach me?"

Reagan saw her mistake.

"Well..." She tried to find words.

"Can you teach me?" he asked again, thinking she might not have understood.

"Jonah," Holly suddenly called from the kitchen, "please come help Elly with the table."

The little boy was clearly in agony. Reagan barely kept her mouth shut as she watched Jonah look between her and the door that would lead to the kitchen.

"Go on now, son." Russell suddenly appeared to give his boy the urging he needed.

"I'm sorry," Reagan began as soon as the child was gone. She had shifted Alisa in her lap, but that baby had yet to do anything but sit complacently and play with her toes.

"For what?" Russell asked when he took a seat across from their guest.

Reagan gave him a quick rundown and watched him laugh in delight.

"I'm glad you're laughing," she said when her host quieted.

"So what did you tell him?"

"I didn't."

"Well, I think you should," Russell surprised her by saying. He grinned boyishly. "Then he could teach me."

Reagan laughed so suddenly that the baby jumped.

"I'm sorry, Alisa," she said quietly, and for the first time Alisa caught sight of the silver necklace that hung down the front of Reagan's dress. The baby's hand was reaching for it when her father called her name.

"Alisa, don't touch that," he said, and she looked at him and looked back at the enticing locket.

"Alisa," he called her name again.

She looked at him.

"No," he said quite firmly when they had made eye contact.

For a moment she looked as though she would pout or cry, but another look from her father put an end to that.

Reagan didn't know if she was impressed or concerned at how stern he had been. She had to admit to herself, however, that it was nice not to have her necklace grabbed and possibly broken.

A glance at the baby gave her further pause. She was smiling across at her father as though he'd hung the moon. In fact, just a moment later her pudgy arms went out to him. When he took her, Alisa giggled and snuggled up against his chest as though she'd been waiting to do so all day.

"I think we're ready in here," Holly called from the kitchen before Reagan could comment. And just a few minutes later, Reagan found herself at the kitchen table set for five, with Alisa's high chair close by her mother's seat. The rolls were directly in front of her, and she was about to take one so she could pass the basket when Russell's voice stopped her.

"I think it's my turn to pray tonight," he said.

Reagan was glad she'd not made a move. She bowed her head along with everyone else and waited for one of the memorized prayers she'd heard off and on over the years.

"Father in heaven," Russell began, "thank You for this wonderful day and the way You blessed us each hour. Thank You for all Holly's hard work and this great food we can eat. Thank You that Reagan could join us. What a blessing to have her live in the little house and be such a good neighbor. Bless us as we eat and spend the evening together, and may we ever be mindful of Your presence and blessing in our lives. In Christ's name I pray. Amen."

Reagan managed to raise her head, but the rolls and other food were forgotten. No one had ever prayed for her before. She hadn't even known that a person could talk to God like that. If she hadn't known better, she'd have wondered if Russell might not be a man of the cloth.

"Would you like some potatoes, Miss Sullivan?" Elly was asking, and Reagan was jerked back to the present.

"Thank you," she said, her head bent low to cover her red face. What had she done in those seconds of distracted concentration, and had this family noticed?

"I think I'll hold this chicken platter for you, Reagan," Russell was saying. "It's rather hot."

"Thank you," she said again, and for more than one reason: It seemed they hadn't noticed anything odd in her behavior.

"How is work at the hotel, Reagan?" Holly asked when everyone had been served.

"Most days, it's fine."

"Is that what you did in New York?"

"No. I worked at a factory. It was monotonous, but at least we had one day off a week."

"That must have been nice," Russell put in. "I'm not sure all factories do that."

"No, they don't. Many of the girls in the boardinghouse worked seven days a week."

"Where is your family?"

"They're all gone. I've been on my own for some time."

"What do you do at the hotel?" Elly asked, and Reagan began to fill her in.

"And then today," she concluded, her eyes rolling at the memory, "I needed to change my wash water when I was scrubbing pots, and I threw a bucket of water on a man in the alley."

"Oh, no!" Elly gasped, her eyes large.

Reagan shook her head in self-deprecation.

"Was he angry?" This came from Jonah.

"No," Russell answered, and all eyes turned to him.

"Did you see it happen?" Reagan asked.

"No, but the man was a friend of mine, and he was on his way to see me."

"Who was it, Russ?" Holly wished to know.

The big man's eyes sparkled. "Cash."

Holly and the children all laughed over this, and Russell turned to Reagan to explain.

"Cash is a good friend. We've known each other for years."

"And he wasn't angry?" Reagan asked with a small amount of anxiety.

"Not at all. He was laughing by the time he got to me."

Reagan sat back with a sigh. "I'm glad to hear it, but he would have been more than justified."

"He doesn't anger easily."

"I've never seen him angry," added Holly.

These comments were of great interest to Reagan. She didn't have much of an impression of the man from the alley, having only seen him for a few moments, but these people she rented from were somehow different; she figured their friends must be too. Reagan couldn't put her finger on an exact incident, but something here was not what she was used to. For an instant she remembered the way Russell prayed.

"We have cake for dessert," Holly announced. "Anyone interested?"

Even Alisa seemed to light up over these words, and Holly gave out generous slices of cake just a few minutes later. As coffee cups were refilled, the conversation started up all over again.

"I had a big one come in today," Russell began. "One of the biggest horses in town."

"Was he nice or mean?" Jonah, who loved his father's work, wished to know.

"What was his name?" Elly stuck in.

"His name was Sam, and as for temperament, he was somewhere in the middle. I've had some big ones you could swing by the tail and they wouldn't blink, but this one liked me in his sight and was happy as long as I kept talking."

"Have you ever been seriously injured?" Reagan found herself asking, fascinated.

"Yes. I have a cavity on the outside of my leg from a severe kick more than ten years ago."

"And you still wanted to be a blacksmith after that?"

"Yes, ma'am," the big man replied contentedly. "I can count on one hand the number of days I've wanted to quit."

There was something in the way he said this that made Reagan smile. She couldn't think of anything more wonderful than having a job she loved. The question was, would *she* ever feel that way?

Hours later Reagan climbed into bed, tired but not exhausted, that question and the whole evening still on her mind. It had done her heart a world of good to have some fun. Typically her friends from New York were single men or women, but getting to know a family here was a wonderful new experience.

The thought of family suddenly made her lie very still.

Maybe I haven't gotten too close to a family in the past because I didn't want to know what I've missed.

Almost afraid to let her thoughts go on but not able to stop them, Reagan thought about how she'd grown up, and how cruel life could be. If she had learned anything, it was this: To love someone was to give them the power to hurt you. Not by plan or design did Reagan live this out, but by instinct.

Her thoughts unsettled, Reagan rolled into a ball to get comfortable, reminding herself that morning came whether she was ready or not, and she would be a bear if she didn't get her sleep.

🌹 🌹 🌹

"What was *that?*" old Hank Demby exclaimed. He stood at the checkout counter at the general store, his eyes on the large glass window that overlooked the street.

"That was Reagan on her bicycle," Lavinia Unger, the proprietress said. "Have you not see her before?"

The older gentleman didn't answer. He'd gone to the door to try to catch sight of it again. Lavinia joined him and, sure enough, they were swiftly rewarded with a view of Reagan as she left the bank, hopped on her bike in the most amazing way, and began to ride toward them.

"Good afternoon, Mrs. Unger," she called when she was abreast of them.

"Hello, Reagan."

Pedaling along as if she hadn't a care in the world, Reagan gave a wave and kept going.

"How long has that been here?" Hank asked, his mouth still slightly agape.

"I think only about a week. It came in on the train. Reagan had told the boys at the station to watch for it, and when they sent word that it had arrived, she was down there in a flash—didn't even remove her apron."

"Disgraceful!" a woman sniffed as she came up the boardwalk toward the door. "Completely improper! These easterners coming west with their strange and unprincipled ways."

"Now, now," Lavinia tried to soothe her. "Reagan's a good girl. She works hard."

"Where's she work?" Hank found himself curious about the rider as well.

While this exchange took place, Reagan, who was uncaring of any attention she might draw, finished her errands. She was down to her last stop, and that was the livery. She found Russell shoeing a horse, lifting the animal's leg as though it weighed like a coin.

"Hello," Reagan greeted him when he heard her and glanced up.

"Well, now," he said as he finished with the last nail, dropped the hoof, and straightened to look at her. "Been riding that bike?"

Reagan smiled.

"How can you tell?"

Russell didn't answer, but he always knew. Her eyes would be especially bright, and if the day was brisk, her cheeks would redden, but the real giveaway was what it did to her hair. Always a bit unruly, Reagan's coiffure had been blown around until black curls and wisps finally fell on her forehead and down her neck.

"I've just come to tell you that Holly wasn't home when I got there, so I left the rent on the table."

"She goes to Bible study on Wednesdays, and then sometimes the women visit," Russell said almost absently. "You did the right thing. She'll find it."

"All right."

It had been on Reagan's mind to ask why Holly was studying the Bible, but she decided against it.

"So, are you out on business or just getting some exercise?" Russell asked.

"I'm doing errands until I meet the children at school."

"Oh, that's right. Elly said you were coming to walk them home."

"She's getting quite good on my bicycle."

Russell grinned. "Only one scraped knee."

"It helps that she's tall."

"Has Jonah ridden yet?"

"Not on his own. The pedals are too far away."

"Well, be sure and tell me if they don't thank you for all this fun."

Reagan only laughed at what had been a serious comment from him and started on her way. Somewhere along the line she had decided that Russell and Holly took obedience a little too seriously. They had good kids. Reagan could see that. It seemed to her that they need not worry so much about all the little details.

Hopping on her bicycle yet again, Reagan rode toward the schoolhouse. She was running a little late, and the school was uphill, but she arrived just as the children were dismissed for the day. Several of them stopped to see her two-wheeled conveyance and were suitably impressed, but in short order she was walking along with the Bennett children.

"How was your day?" she asked them.

They both tried to answer at once, but then Jonah let his sister talk. Reagan listened with genuine interest until they were over halfway home, then agreed to take Elly's books so she could ride the rest of the way. Once Reagan and Jonah were alone, the little boy told her about his day.

"I had to spell words up front."

"How did you do?"

"I got them all right. Jimmy got one wrong, but teacher let him do it over."

"That was nice of her. What word was it?"

"What."

"What word was it?"

"What," he said again, turning his head to look at her, and Reagan began to laugh. Hearing her laugh, Jonah caught on and laughed too.

"We could have gone on with that for a long time," Reagan commented as both her little house and Jonah's came into view. Out front, Elly was still atop the bike, going in big circles. Reagan heard Jonah sigh.

"I wish I had long legs."

"You will before you know it."

"That's what my mother says too."

Reagan smiled at his sweet little face. She had never yearned for a family, but this little boy touched something inside of her that she had never felt before.

"Watch me, Miss Sullivan," Elly called just as Holly came to the porch with Alisa.

The adults clapped and cheered while Elly leapt off and stopped the bicycle. Reagan then gave Jonah a ride, basically pushing him while he steered. Elly cheered her brother on from the porch, and Reagan was again struck by the closeness of these two children.

A moment later Holly told the children she had a snack for them on the kitchen table. She invited Reagan, who declined. Much as she enjoyed being with this family, at times she was oddly uncomfortable.

Not willing to think on it, Reagan took herself home. She had no specific plan, but she needed to do something to elude the feelings that seemed to pester her.

Six

A Sunday morning off! Reagan could hardly believe her luck. Not that she would ever want anyone to be harmed, but having a small fire in the hotel kitchen on Saturday night had meant the dining room would be closed all day Sunday. It hadn't allowed her to sleep in because she didn't know about it until she arrived for work, but that didn't diminish her joy. She hadn't had a morning off since arriving in Kinkade, so she wouldn't have wanted to lie in bed anyway. There was too much to see and do!

For the first time since her bicycle had arrived, Reagan left it at home. She had ridden to work but now returned home, spent time mending a torn seam, puttered around her small house, and eventually put on her better dress and set off on foot. It occurred to her somewhere along the line that she had not had breakfast, but she dismissed the thought for the moment. If she got desperate, she could throw herself on Sally's mercy to let her use the kitchen long enough to prepare a meal.

Thoughts of all she might do with a full day ahead raced through her mind. Because her business rarely took her to the east end of town, she decided to head that way. She was enjoying a few new sights when she heard singing.

Reagan stopped and listened to what sounded like a choir in full voice. It was in front of her somewhere, and after a few seconds, she moved toward the sound. A small white church came into view. Reagan didn't know why the idea of a church hadn't immediately occurred to her, but now that she saw where the sound was coming from, she smiled at her own surprise, shook her head, and started to turn away. At almost the same moment, she remembered that she had nowhere else in particular to go.

Walking slowly and enjoying the voices, Reagan went ahead to the church and stopped a few feet from the closed door. The closer she neared, the more beautiful it sounded. Church was not a place she'd visited much, hardly at all if the truth be told, but she felt mesmerized by the music she was hearing. Even when the singing stopped and didn't start up for a few seconds, Reagan remained still. The singing resumed, and the congregation must have been on their fifth number when Reagan's feet moved again, this time all the way to the door. Working not to be noticed, she opened the portal and slipped inside. To her surprise, no one turned. They were all standing, facing front, hymn books in hand, singing their hearts out.

Reagan couldn't say exactly what compelled her, but she slipped into the last pew and sat down just as they finished. There was no one directly in front of her for two pews as she moved as far to the wall as she could get, and the people in the next two pews were closer to the aisle.

Reagan gazed at the man up front and listened to the sound of his deep voice. He was reading from the book in front of him, and although the words were not familiar to Reagan, she knew it must be the Bible. With almost no idea how she'd come to be there, Reagan found herself quite rapt.

"'The angel said unto him, Fear not, Zacharias; for thy prayer is heard; and thy wife Elisabeth shall bear thee a son, and thou shalt call his name John. And thou shalt have joy and gladness; and many shall rejoice at his birth. For he shall be great in the sight of the Lord, and shall drink neither wine nor strong drink; and he shall be filled with the Holy Ghost, even from his mother's womb. And many of the children of Israel shall he turn to the Lord, their God. And he shall go before him in the spirit and power of Elijah, to turn the hearts of the fathers to the children, and the disobedient to the wisdom of the just, to make ready a people prepared for the Lord. And Zacharias said unto the angel, Whereby shall I know this? For I am an old man, and my wife well stricken in years. And the angel answering said unto him, I am Gabriel, who stands in the presence of God; and am sent to speak unto thee, and to show thee these glad tidings.'

"This news from Gabriel was huge," the pastor intoned, looking up from the pulpit and smiling kindly at the people in the pews. "A special child is about to be born to Zacharias and Elisabeth because Zacharias and Elisabeth are special. Verse six describes them as blameless. They had clearly shown God that they were up to the task of raising this child.

"John is going to be a man with a very special job. The angel compares him to Elijah, one of the most powerful prophets of the Old Testament. We've taken a few weeks to come to these verses because I didn't want to rush. I wanted you to be prepared for the special words here."

Reagan watched as the man paused, his eyes scanning the pews.

"Look at verse 17. It says John is going to go before Him. Do you understand who the verse is talking about here? Who that *Him* is?"

Reagan could see some heads nodding, but she didn't have a clue.

"It's Jesus Christ," the pastor continued. "John is coming to prepare hearts for Christ when He starts His earthly ministry. God's Son, who has come to bring salvation to mankind, is going to be announced by John."

For a time, the man's words were lost on Reagan. She had never heard of this, but she found it riveting. It was almost as if her questions were being answered, but she hadn't asked any questions.

"The events that follow in the book of Luke have paved the way for what we believe today, and we will get to many of those in the weeks and months to come, but don't rush past verse 17. Let me read it to you again. 'And he,' that's John, 'shall go before Him,' Jesus Christ, 'in the spirit and power of Elijah, to turn the hearts of the fathers to the children, and the disobedient to the wisdom of the just, to make ready a people prepared for the Lord.'

"What is the first thing Jesus is going to address? The fathers! Of all the things that could be at the top of the list during this time, we find that God wants fathers to father their children. I don't know about the rest of you men in the room, but this gives me a wake-up call. Are my children hearing from me the way of salvation? Do my children know that my main priority is to teach them of their Creator, their Savior, their God?"

The pastor shook his head in wonder, smiling a little as he leaned forward on the pulpit. "I'm excited about this verse. God never demands something of me that is impossible for me to do. He came to turn my heart to Him, and to help me, as a father, put my children in the right direction as well. With God's help I can do this."

Again Reagan was swept out of the room as her own father's face sprang to mind. The pastor concluded with a final prayer and an announcement, but Reagan did not hear much of it.

"Father in heaven, thank You for bringing each one here today. We praise You for Your Word and Your love for us. May we go from this place better prepared to serve You and return next week if You do not come for us before that time. In Christ's name I pray. Amen.

"Don't forget now, come out the side door today and see all the remodeling in our home. We'll meet in the side yard for prayer in a few minutes, and then we'll eat. It looks as though we have enough for an army, so don't hesitate to join us."

The pastor, his family, and almost the entire congregation moved forward to a side door to exit, but Reagan was still in New York as a child. She was aware of things around her but felt apart and separate, her heart a little bruised. It took a few moments for the room to quiet down, and when it did, Reagan finally realized someone was standing in the aisle staring at her. Her head whipped over, and her eyes met those of the cowboy from the alley.

"Do you have your bucket with you today, or am I safe?"

Reagan relaxed in the light of his humor and laughed. When she did, Cash came forward.

"I'm Cash Rawlings," he said, putting his hand out.

Reagan shook it.

"I'm Reagan Sullivan, and I've wanted to tell you again how sorry I am about the water."

Cash shrugged. "Accidents happen."

Reagan shook her head. "You might be more understanding than you should be."

"I don't think so."

"Actually," Reagan admitted, "Russell Bennett told me you weren't angry."

"Do you know Russ?"

"Yes."

"They're here," Cash told her. "Come on. I know they'll want to see you."

"They go to this church?" Reagan asked as she moved out into the aisle between the two pews and toward the door where the others had gone.

"Yes, they do. Did they know you were coming?"

"No, it was a last-minute decision," Reagan said, her voice having dropped some. She also had come to a halt.

Cash watched her stare at the pulpit as though Pastor Ellis were still standing there. She then looked to him.

"I think there might be something to this salvation thing."

"I certainly think so."

Reagan's eyes widened. "Then you've done it? You know about salvation?"

"Yes, I do."

"Salvation from God, from His Son?"

"That's right."

Reagan could only stare at him. Her mind moving faster than she could keep up, Reagan was unaware of the way she gawked at the man, making him feel that he shouldn't question her.

"Cash!" a voice called from without before Russell Bennett came through the door. "Reagan?" he said in obvious surprise.

Reagan seemed to snap out of her trance.

"Are you a Christian?" she blurted, nearly accusing Russell.

"Yes."

"But you didn't get your Bible out and try to convert me as soon as we met."

"No." Russell was as calm as ever. "I wouldn't have done that for a number of reasons."

"Like what?"

"Well, for one you're a woman, and I wouldn't want to give the wrong impression. Also, you didn't show any interest, so why would I shove it down your throat?"

"That didn't stop certain people in my old neighborhood," Reagan grumbled.

"Listen, Reagan," Russell said, having come to a swift decision as the entire church was waiting, "we need to talk about this, but right now Cash has to come and pray for our meal."

"Oh, right," Reagan began as she started to back away.

"Come and eat with us," Russell invited as his huge hand took Reagan's wrist. "Holly is right out here."

Cash smiled at the stunned look on her face as she was hauled out the door. Russell landed her next to Holly and then walked with Cash to the front.

"That was subtle," Cash teased him.

Russell smiled. "I had her this far. I didn't want to let her get away."

"Oh, here's Cash now," Pastor Ellis said as the men neared.

"Let's pray," Cash said when he stepped up front next to the pastor and his family. After a few moments of silence, he began. "Father in heaven, thank You for the work that was done here. Thank You for the willing hands and hearts that made all of this possible. We are so blessed, Father, to have Pastor and Noelle with us, and their children, and by giving to them we have an even greater blessing. We pray, Lord, that they would enjoy this wonderful home for years to come.

"Thank You for this food, Father. Thank You for all who worked to make it. May we remember Your goodness to us as we enjoy it. In Your name I pray. Amen."

In the back, Holly opened her eyes and looked over at Reagan. Their renter was a bit shorter than she was, so it was easy to watch her expression. Holly had not really had time to find out how Reagan had come to be there, and she desperately wanted her to stay but knew that forcing her would never work.

"Reagan," she finally called her name.

Reagan looked at her.

"I hope you'll want to stay, but please don't feel you must."

"I didn't bring anything to share."

"If you mean the food, I brought two dishes, a pie and a beef and bean casserole. We always have plenty at these gatherings."

"So you've done this before?"

"Eaten together, you mean?"

"Yes—I mean, you don't just come and sit in the pews and then go home?"

"Sometimes we head right out, especially if the children have had trouble sitting still and we need to get home and talk about it, but the majority of the time we visit, and often we eat with another family or have a family to our house."

Reagan was on the verge of saying she'd never seen anyone there and then remembered she was always working. As though she'd said this out loud, Holly asked her about it.

"Did you get the morning off?"

"Yes. There was a fire in the hotel kitchen last night, and Sally shut the dining room for the day."

"Was anyone harmed?"

"No, nothing like that."

"I'm glad. Will it be open tomorrow?"

"I think Sally was planning that. I'll check with her later."

"Hi, Miss Sullivan," Jonah, who had suddenly run up, greeted her. "Are you going to eat with us?"

"I think I am, yes," Reagan said, and it was the last thing she said for a while. What followed was a celebration unlike anything she'd ever known. With everyone laughing and talking, the group lining up to eat couldn't have been more friendly or generous. Men allowed their wives to go first and then stayed to help with the children, much the way Reagan had seen Russell and Holly interact. It was interesting to watch one family in action; it was nothing short of amazing to watch a hundred people acting the same way.

Reagan caught male eyes on her from time to time, but none of the men had inappropriate looks on their faces, and none of them stood with a woman at his side.

"Have you seen the house?" Russell asked Reagan as the event was starting to wind down.

"No. Why did the pastor want everyone to do that?"

"Because we've been doing some remodeling for the past nine months, and it's finally done. The house is not that old, but the original owner had skimped in some areas, so there was rain damage in a number of places. Once we started working, we found even more places that needed repair, and so we did the whole job. You should go in. It won't be as good as seeing it before, but you'll still enjoy it."

Once Reagan left the table with Holly and Alisa, Cash joined Russell.

"I've set up an elders' meeting for the twenty-fifth. Is that going to work for you?" Cash asked.

"That should be fine. I'll tell Holly, and she can remind me."

"Okay. I've got to let Jarvis know before I leave."

"Are we going to be discussing the widow and orphans' fund at this meeting?"

"Yes. I've got that on my list. Have you had more feedback?"

"Yes, some good comments. I've made some notes, and I'll bring them with me."

"All right."

Jonah, who had played with his friends but was now tired, had made his way into Cash's lap, and for a time the tall cowboy let everything else slide.

"How are you, Jonah?" he asked, his arms holding the boy close.

"I rode a bike."

"A bike?" Cash frowned as though he'd not heard right.

"It's Miss Sullivan's."

"Oh."

Cash was so stopped by this that Russell began to laugh. Cash looked up at him.

"She has a bicycle?"

"Yes. Elly can ride it alone, but Jonah needs a push."

"Well, now." Cash looked down into the little face again. "That sounds very fun. Have you done it very often?"

"Every week."

"Wow. And you don't fall?"

"No. Elly has, but Miss Sullivan hangs onto me."

"She sounds very nice."

"She's here today! She ate with us."

"I saw her."

Jonah suddenly laughed. "She threw water on you."

"Did she?" Cash asked angelically while his fingers found Jonah's ticklish sides. The little boy squirmed with laughter as Cash took his revenge.

"I didn't have any cake!" Jonah announced. Cash had stopped tickling him, and he had remembered his stomach.

"Well, go have some."

The little boy was off in a flash, and the men went back to talking. Cash had horses that needed shoeing and some work on a few broken wagons.

"I can come out Tuesday," Russell told him. "Will that work?"

"Yeah. Come at noon. I'll tell Katy to plan on you."

"How are you for hands these days?"

"I have plenty of men. Brad is the best foreman I've ever had. As you well know, I didn't even have to help with roundup this year. He can charm the hat off the most cantankerous cowboy and still get two more hours of work out of him at the end of a long day."

Russell was chuckling at this description when Holly and Alisa joined them. Reagan was not with them.

"Did you lose Reagan?" Russell asked as soon as Holly sat down.

"In a way, yes. I think she was a little overwhelmed by all of this. It seemed to come on her rather suddenly. I could tell she wanted to think and take it all in. When we finished in the house, she said she was headed home. I don't think she ate much, but I didn't want to say anything."

"It's hard, isn't it?" Cash interjected. "We don't want to come across as crazed, but we believe we have the best news in the world to share."

The Bennetts were in full agreement with that sentiment.

Jonah chose that moment to return with his cake. His baby sister saw it and all but crawled from her mother's arms to get at the plate. Cash volunteered to go for the dessert and rescue all of them. They stayed to visit until

Alisa's cake was gone and she was drooping in her father's arms.

If someone had reported the event in the local paper that week, it would have said, "A good time was had by all."

౩ ౩ ౩

"What do you mean you need Sundays off?" Sally asked in surprise. "What for?"

"Not the whole morning, just long enough to go to church."

Sally looked clearly skeptical. "And who takes the cakes from the oven when you're gone?"

"That's what I've been trying to tell you. I'll come early enough to have the baking done. When I come back, I'll clean up and help with tables."

"Reagan, you don't strike me as the type who needs religion. What's gotten into you?"

"I don't know," the younger woman said honestly, her dinner plate forgotten in front of her. She had been too nervous to eat much at the church gathering and had found herself hungry that evening. She'd gone to Sally's without a backward glance and found her in the kitchen fixing her own meal. The way she'd welcomed Reagan had done the younger woman's heart a world of good.

"I just found myself at that church this morning. I'm not even sure how. And once I got inside, I was just so drawn to what the pastor was saying."

"Pastor Ellis?"

"Yes. Do you know him?"

"No, but his wife is a real person—I know that."

"Noelle. I met her too. Even their children are nice. Just like Russell and Holly's family."

"They go to that church too, don't they?"

Reagan nodded.

"And you want to find out why they live the way they do."

Reagan stared at her.

"You've wanted to as well, haven't you, Sally?"

The hotel owner shrugged. "Maybe."

"Why haven't you looked into this?" Reagan demanded. "You've lived here for years!"

"Reagan," she said with a shake of her head. "I don't have time for church. This place takes every minute of every day. Can't you see that?"

Reagan's eyes narrowed. "Of course I can see that, Sally, but you're not going to be here forever! You can say something to shut me up for the moment, but when you're on your own, are you happy with who you are, fine hotel or not?"

Sally's eyes narrowed right back, but she didn't say anything right away.

"You can take off on Sundays to go to church unless it doesn't work."

"Why wouldn't it?"

Sally shook her head in amazement. "You have more guts than anyone I know, Reagan. I hand you a favor, and you're ready to argue."

Reagan didn't reply. In her haste to have her own way, she often forgot that Sally was her boss.

"Thank you for giving me time to go to church."

"If you get all religious, are you going to start carrying your Bible and drive us all crazy?"

In a heartbeat, Reagan thought of the difference between the two Christians she'd known in New York and Russell Bennett. It was not hard to answer Sally.

"I won't say anything unless you ask me."

"Fair enough. Had enough to eat?"

"No," she said, tucking back into her plate. "Let me finish, and I'll clean up for you."

Sally, who'd had a long, arduous day, was not going to argue with that idea.

❧ ❧ ❧

"Was she here this morning?" Russell asked Cash before their meeting started at the church just two weeks later.

"Yes. Just like last week. I think she must slip in just before we start and back out again on the last song. Have you had a chance to ask her about it?"

"Not really. Holly and I are both afraid of pressuring her. We're both praying that she'll know where to come if she has questions."

Both men would have been delighted to know that Reagan was on her way to Holly's door right then. She was not aware that Russell was not at home, but she had some questions and could only hope that someone in the big house had the answers.

Seven

"HOLLY, ARE YOU BUSY?"

"Not at all, Reagan. Come right in."

Reagan entered the familiar home, but unlike the first time, she didn't enjoy her surroundings. She was too distracted for that.

"Have a seat," Holly invited. She had a word with one of her children in the kitchen and then joined her guest.

"What can I do for you?"

"I have a few questions."

"All right."

"I went to church this morning—last week too."

Holly nodded. She hadn't been certain of this, but she was glad nevertheless.

"If I believe as your church does, do I have to get married?"

Holly had all she could do not to look surprised. This was the last thing she expected.

"May I ask you a question?" Holly said after a moment's recovery.

"Yes."

"What do you mean, 'believe as my church does'?"

"Become a Christian—be saved—like Pastor Ellis talked about."

"Like the Bible explains?" Holly questioned again, hoping they were talking about the same thing.

86

"Yes. Believing on the Lord Jesus Christ and living for Him."

Holly nodded, now feeling satisfied that she and Reagan were on the same track.

"No one in our church is going to force you to get married, no matter what you believe."

Reagan looked so relieved that Holly smiled.

"Why did you ask, Reagan? Can you tell me?"

"It's not something I want, Holly. Marriage, that is. I don't want a husband. I don't want a man to rule over me and control my life."

"What about a man to love and cherish you?"

Reagan smiled a little. "I don't think I'm the love and cherish type."

Holly could not have disagreed more, but she didn't argue with her.

"Is that all that's on your mind, Reagan? Are you understanding what you're hearing in church?"

"Yes," she said with excitement, leaning forward a little. "I've never heard any of this, and I think it's wonderful. What Christ did was wonderful. I don't think I could have done it."

"I know I couldn't have," Holly agreed. "Only God could do that for us."

"How do we really know that Jesus is God?"

"The Bible."

"But what if the Bible's not right?"

"That's a good question, Reagan—one that many people have asked. I think the first thing we have to establish is whether or not we take the Bible as God's Word or something less than that. The answer to that question determines our response to the answers for all the other questions we ask."

Holly had believed this for so long that she'd started to take it for granted, but Reagan looked amazed.

"That's it, isn't it? It's all about how I view the Bible!"

To Holly's surprise, Reagan got up and began to head to the door. The hostess watched as she had her hand on the knob and then caught herself.

"Oh, Holly, I'm sorry. I just have so much to think about. I didn't mean to be so rude."

"It's all right. Can I help with anything else?"

Reagan looked at her. "Do you have an extra Bible I could read?"

"Yes, I do. Let me just get it."

It sounded as though someone dropped a plate in the kitchen just then, but Holly didn't go there. She disappeared into another room and returned to give Reagan a dusty Bible.

"This was my father's. You read it for as long as you like."

"Thank you, Holly. I'll take good care of it."

"I'm not worried about that. May I tell you something, Reagan?"

"Sure."

"I'm praying for you."

Reagan didn't know what to say. She wasn't overly surprised, but she still didn't know how to answer.

"I've been meaning to ask you, Reagan," Holly continued, "do you have Sundays off?"

"Not the whole day, but Sally has given me enough time to go to church."

"That was kind of her."

"It was, wasn't it?"

Reagan left then. She had not known exactly how to thank Holly or say goodbye, but it seemed to Reagan that she understood.

❦ ❦ ❦

"What is it that makes her tick?" Russell asked that night.

"I don't know. She hasn't really said anything about herself, and she certainly shows no sign of hating men, but she's not going to trust one to be in charge of her."

"I can honestly say that I've never known anyone like her."

"I wish you could have seen her face when I made that statement."

"About the Bible?"

"Yes. She was flabbergasted. And then after she left I realized there was so much more I could have said."

"Maybe it was best that you didn't."

"Maybe."

A very sleepy Alisa sighed softly from her quilt on the floor just then, and Holly remembered that she wanted her in bed early. Russell volunteered to do the honors, and Holly sat down in the living room to read a book to Jonah and Elly.

"Did Miss Sullivan come today to talk about God?" Elly asked before the book was opened.

"In a way she did. She's been coming to church and had a few questions."

"Does she love God like we do?"

"I'm not sure what she believes, Jonah. I think she's searching for answers to things in her heart."

"Do I have questions in my heart?"

"I think you must."

"What are they?"

Holly smiled. "Well, the first would be if you have questions in your heart."

The little boy smiled then, and Holly bent to kiss his adorable face.

"We didn't pray for her at dinner tonight," Elly said, her little brow furrowed in thought.

"Didn't we?" Holly honestly couldn't remember.

"I don't think so."

"Well, we can pray right now. All right? Jonah, would you like to pray?"

The little boy nodded and began.

Returning to the living room while Jonah prayed, Russell listened quietly.

"And please God, help Reagan to be saved. Help her to want Jesus in her heart. Help her not to be afraid anymore. Amen."

Russell looked at his son.

"Do you think Reagan is afraid of something, Jonah?"

"Well, maybe she's not, but she might be afraid that God wouldn't want her."

Russell smiled at him very tenderly. The little boy had summed up so neatly what many people believed. His own sister felt that she had to clean herself up before she could approach God. Nothing Russell and Holly had ever said could sway her. His sister was still trying to work on her life so she would be "saveable" in God's eyes.

In truth Russell and Holly didn't know if this was Reagan's problem or not, but when the quiet time was over and their two older children were in bed, they prayed for Reagan about that very thing.

❧ ❧ ❧

Reagan had all she could do not to growl with frustration. She had thought the Bible would be so easy to read and understand, but the different passages she turned to were about as clear as mud. She read that evening until she had to turn in and even tried again before work the next morning, but it was no use.

She wasn't in the best of moods to be heading to work, but she was liking her job more and more, having found the best method to do things and settling into her routine with Sally very nicely. And of course the dining room always made for a change. One could never anticipate exactly what would happen.

For all Reagan's sarcasm and sometimes-sharp tongue, she knew she was genuinely liked by the men who ate breakfast at the hotel each morning. Some were rather persistent about her joining them for a cup of coffee. She always said no but never grew angry or irate as long as they kept their hands to themselves. Indeed, she took it all in so calmly that they found her all the more intriguing.

Reagan had learned early on never to tell a man that she had no plans to ever be married. Men could be counted on to respond in one of two ways. Some said they were fine with that plan since they were only looking for a little fun and not a ball and chain—something Reagan found highly insulting. She thought the term "ball and chain" fit a man much better. Others attempted to talk Reagan into agreeing with them on the spot that every woman needed a husband. The term "ball and chain" was the last thing on their minds. Reagan had learned that both conversations were futile.

Nevertheless, some days she was flattered. A few men were so charming and persistent that Reagan had to stop herself from smiling for fear of encouraging them. One such man was Tyrone Arnold. He went by the name of Ty, and there was no getting around his good looks and fine manners. He looked at Reagan as though she were the last woman on earth, and never once had he intimated that he was just out for a few laughs. At the same time, he never once proposed or asked to take her out for the evening. He always made Reagan feel as though she'd made his day simply by waiting on his table.

Today was about to be different.

Reagan worked on pies until it was time to go out front. As always, the door opening from the back brought the delicious smell of food along with Reagan's presence, and the men loved it.

"We thought you'd never come," one young cowboy complained. He would take Reagan out every night if she would only agree.

"I can see you've suffered greatly," she said dryly, filling his cup without giving him any encouragement.

"When do I get a ride on that bicycle?" he asked, but Reagan didn't answer. She was getting coffee, talking to a little girl who was out for breakfast with her father, and taking an order from Ty, who had just sat down.

"Whatever Sally has hot and ready," he said congenially.

"Hungry this morning?" Reagan knew she could ask this man and not get a lewd comment.

"Starving."

"I'll get her right at it."

"Hey, Reagan," someone else called in full voice as she moved back to the kitchen. "You still haven't answered the question I asked you yesterday."

Reagan glanced over her shoulder to answer but kept moving.

"I can't remember what you asked, but whatever it is, the answer's no."

Reagan exited on a wave of laughter.

"They sure like you," Sally said as she entered the kitchen.

"That's because they don't know me."

With no time for chitchat, the women sped headlong into the morning. Reagan waited tables, finished the baking, and was scrubbing pots when the back door to the kitchen opened. Ty was standing there.

"Hello, Ty," Reagan greeted him. "Are you looking for Sally? She's in her office."

"Actually, I came to see you."

Reagan's guard went up, but she tried to brush it off.

"Did I leave a strip of bacon off your plate?"

"No," he said with a smile. "You never make mistakes with my breakfast."

There was a warm tone in his voice that Reagan didn't like, but she only looked at him.

Ty was swift to see that she wasn't smiling at him in return and knew it was time to get to the point. He did so, keeping his voice even and businesslike.

"I didn't want to ask you in front of the others, Reagan, because I wanted you to take me seriously, but I was wondering if you'd have dinner with me some evening this week?" Reagan was already shaking her head when he added, "I want to talk to you about a job."

Reagan was suddenly all ears.

"A job?"

"Yes."

"What kind of job?"

"I want to tell you about it over dinner."

Reagan shook her head. "You've got the wrong girl, Ty. Any job that has to be discussed over dinner..." She let the sentence hang.

"It's not like that, I assure you, Reagan. I have tremendous respect for you and a job that would be perfect for you if you're interested. It's not a job I'm offering to anyone else, so you let me know if and when you want to hear about it."

To Reagan's amazement, he turned for the door and exited. He was only a dozen feet down the alley when Reagan, whose curiosity had gotten the best of her, made it outside and stopped him with one question.

"Can I meet you somewhere for dinner?"

Ty turned.

"What do you mean?"

"I don't want to be picked up at my house. I'll come to dinner and hear about the job if I can meet you."

"That's fine," Ty agreed, coming toward her a ways and gaining tremendous ground by agreeing to this term.

"How about this Saturday night?"

"How about Tuesday next week?"

Ty grinned, knowing he was doing the right thing.

"Tuesday, it is. Where do you want to meet?"

"Right here in front of the hotel."

Ty tipped his hat. "Tuesday, seven o'clock. I'll be here."

Reagan watched him walk away without a single romantic thought in her head, but she didn't think his handsome face would be hard to look at if she actually went to work for him.

☙ ☙ ☙

"Okay, Reagan," Russell said the next evening as he did odd jobs in the little rental house. "Try that."

Reagan opened the cupboard door and found it working fine.

"It's perfect, Russell. Thank you."

"With all your independence," he teased her, "I'm surprised you didn't fix it yourself."

Reagan grinned.

"I left my tools in New York."

Russell smiled in return.

"Okay. What was next?"

"This window. The lock is a little loose. I've been thinking about buying a gun, but I haven't done it yet."

On his way toward the window, Russell stopped and turned to look at her.

"Are you saying that if you had a gun, you wouldn't need window locks?"

Reagan looked thoughtful.

"No, but I wouldn't be as concerned about them."

"Have you ever handled a gun?"

Reagan met the eyes that were trained on her and answered slowly.

"No, but I didn't think it could be too hard."

Russell's finger came up. "You do not make one move toward a gun without talking to me first. Do you hear me, Reagan?"

"Yes, Father."

"You can *Yes, Father* me all you please, but you do as I say."

Reagan's head tipped as she looked at him.

"What do you fear would happen?"

Russell looked shocked enough to cause Reagan to laugh.

"This is not funny, Reagan," he responded, trying to be stern. "You could shoot yourself or someone else."

"I think that would be the point."

Russell leveled her with a look.

"I'm not fixing another thing in this house until you agree to consult with me about any and all weapons."

Hands to his hips, the hammer held easily under one huge thumb, Russell waited.

"All right," Reagan said with a tolerant shake of her head. "I'll be sure to tell you, but you don't need to be such a tyrant about it. I don't know how Holly stands it."

"Holly isn't wandering around with a naive view of guns," he muttered as he went to work on the window. "Sometimes you scare me."

"I can take care of myself."

"That's what scares me."

Any stinging retort Reagan might have had was interrupted by Jonah's arrival. He'd been helping his father by finding a needed tool.

"Have you got it?"

"I think so. Is this it?"

"That's the one," Russell congratulated the little guy as he took the tool from his open palm.

"How are you, Reagan?"

"Miss Sullivan," his father corrected, his back to them as he worked on the latch.

Reagan only winked at Jonah and brought out a jar of candy she had bought at the general store.

"Would you like a peppermint drop?"

"Yes, please."

"How was school today?"

"It was fun," he answered around the ball of candy swelling his cheek. "I like school, but sometimes I miss Alisa."

"She probably misses you too."

Jonah gave her his shy smile, and, as always, Reagan's heart melted a little.

"Jonah," Russell called to him then, "climb up here and hold this for me, will you?"

The little boy was swift to help, his eyes catching Reagan's one more time and with one glance telling her how proud he was to be asked to help his dad.

The Bennett "men" finished up at Reagan's a short time later, and as nice as it was to have everything repaired, Reagan hated to see Jonah go. Quite suddenly she wanted to be with that little boy whenever she could.

❧ ❧ ❧

"You're coming on Saturday, aren't you, Reagan?" Jonah asked as Reagan walked him home from school, forgetting again to call her Miss Sullivan.

"What's on Saturday?"

"The party at Cash's ranch!" Jonah looked up at her with huge eyes, as if her not knowing was some type of crime. Elly had ridden ahead on the bike, and Jonah and Reagan walked slowly along behind her.

"I don't think I'm invited, Jonah," she said, feeling a need to be honest.

"Everyone is! Pastor Ellis said so."

"Is it a church party?"

Jonah nodded with great enthusiasm. "We have lots of fun. We get to swim in the pond, play games, and even ride horses all by ourselves! And then we eat dinner under the big shade trees by the house."

"That does sound fun. Are you sure everyone is invited?"

She was treated to another nod. Huge eyes punctuated his words. "Pastor said. He was about to tell everyone they could stand, and then he reminded us."

"So this has been planned for a while?"

"We always go. Every year. Mama says it's tramition or something like that."

"Tradition?"

"Yeah. Tradition."

The house was in sight now, as were Elly and the bike. The little girl was jumping off, however, and running to hug her mother, who stood on the front porch.

"I think Miss Sullivan spoils you," Holly said as she wrapped her arms around her oldest child.

"She's so nice, Mama. Jonah and me like her so much."

"Jonah and I. And your father and I like her too."

"Mama," Holly heard Jonah calling as he ran, "Reagan can come to the party, can't she? I asked her and told her about the pond."

"Reagan," Holly asked as soon as she was within earshot, "did you not hear the announcements these past weeks?"

"I guess not. The whole church is invited?"

"Yes. It's a wonderful time. We go every year. It starts at about two o'clock, and we often stay until dark."

"This Saturday?"

Holly nodded, trying to gauge by Reagan's face whether she would attend. Holly would have been doing well to figure it out as Reagan was not certain herself. She had a meal with the Bennetts almost every week and saw the children daily, but other than a brief exchange about how the Bible reading was going, neither Holly nor Russell could gain an idea of what Reagan thought of the church family.

They shared little more conversation just then. Reagan gave Jonah a quick ride on the bike and then went home.

Once in her house, Reagan sat at her little table trying to figure out the yearning inside of her. She desperately wanted to attend the party and be with these people as she had the first morning when she hadn't needed to rush off for work. At the same time the idea terrified her, and she had no idea why.

Before walking back to the hotel, she sat for just a few minutes more, all the while telling herself she just wouldn't go. No one was forcing her, and she didn't have to!

"But I'm sure not going to show up without a cake or something," she muttered as she hit the back door of the kitchen, knowing she would have to borrow a pan from Sally or go empty-handed. She was also sure that if anyone could have read her befuddled thoughts just then, they'd have committed her to an asylum.

Eight

IT HADN'T BEEN EASY, BUT SHE HAD done it. Still vacillating right up to the end, Reagan ended up having to ride her bike to the Rawlings Cattle Company—not a long journey, but made a good deal more challenging by the need to carry a frosted layer cake in one hand.

Reagan rode under the arch of the gateway at the head of the driveway, not letting herself do more than glance at the sign, and in no time at all the house and many wagons came into view. To Reagan's surprise, Cash Rawlings himself came down the driveway to meet her.

"Well, hello," he said, managing to take the cake and catch and steady the bike all in one smooth movement. "Welcome to the ranch," he continued, as if people always arrived in just that manner.

"Thank you," she said as she jumped down, still breathing hard. "I'm a little late."

"Not at all. The games are just getting started. Thank you for bringing the cake, by the way."

"Oh, you're welcome. I wasn't sure what to bring."

"The cake is fine," he said, not willing to tell her that this was not a potluck.

"Something sure smells good."

"That's the beef we've got turning over the fire. It does smell good, doesn't it?"

"Spoken like a man who eats beef every day."

Cash laughed. "It kind of goes with the job."

"Where should I put my bike?" Reagan suddenly wanted to have her hands free.

"Why don't you put it there by the Bennetts' wagon? Then you can hop a ride home."

Cash waited for Reagan to come back from propping it against the wheel. He kept the cake and escorted her up the drive.

"How did you know which wagon belonged to the Bennetts?" she asked.

Cash smiled. "I don't know."

"How about the others?"

Having never given a moment's thought to this, Cash was nevertheless able to stop, look down the line, and name the owners of every wagon or buggy.

"Is it that you're a rancher or that I'm a city girl?"

"I don't know." Cash was again at a loss. "Can you pick a woman out by just the color of her dress?"

"Of course. What does that prove?"

"Maybe nothing, but maybe it's about interests and not just about living out of the city. I can't say that I would know a woman if I caught sight only of her dress."

Reagan looked up at her tall, redheaded host. She saw a kindness and a humility in him that she hadn't encountered very often. She was still thinking on it when the house, with many empty tables in front of it, came fully into view.

"Where is all the food?"

"Still in the kitchen."

"How did you make it fit?"

"Well, most of it's still in pots or in the oven. And don't forget, the beef is on the spit out back."

Reagan was not long in putting two and two together.

"This wasn't a potluck, was it?"

"No."

"Were you going to tell me?"

"Certainly not! You might have taken your cake back."

Reagan found herself laughing. She hadn't expected to. She was ready to be embarrassed about bringing food to a gathering when it was not needed, but suddenly that didn't matter.

"Hello," a woman called from up near the house. "Did you make that cake? She didn't have to make a cake, Cash," the woman said to him as though it was all his fault. "Land sakes alive! Give it to me now and go join the games. This one's going to make my cakes look terrible. Look at all that frosting."

Reagan stood with her mouth open as the scrappy little woman had her say, took the cake, muttering the entire time, and disappeared inside the huge ranch house. She finally looked up to see her host smiling at her and remembered to shut her mouth.

"That was Katy," Cash supplied. "She takes care of me."

"Do you need someone to take care of you?"

"Constantly," he said dryly. "Come on, Reagan. Let's join the party out back."

❧ ❧ ❧

"Is it me?" Reagan asked of Holly a few hours later, "or is everyone here extremely nice?"

Holly smiled. The two women were walking alone near the pond. People were milling everywhere, but no one else was a part of their conversation.

"That's a hard one to answer, Reagan," Holly said, opting for complete honesty.

"Why is that?"

"Because I don't want to lead you to believe that we're perfect. We all have feet of clay."

"Feet of clay?"

Holly was swiftly reminded of how Christians can fall into using clichés that aren't helpful to others.

"That saying comes from the book of Daniel in the Old Testament. The passage is talking about a statue that's made of fine gold and silver, but its feet are made partly of clay and partly of iron, so it's vulnerable in that area.

"I just now used the phrase since I'm afraid that your brief time with us has given you the wrong impression. Yes, people are nice—very nice—but that's only because of the work God has done in our hearts. We still sin, and sometimes we're not kind to each other, but most of the people here have made a personal commitment to God through His Son, and because of that, we're changed."

Reagan nodded but didn't comment. The women continued to circle the pond, sometimes walking among the pecan trees that bordered two sides. Holly kept glancing at Reagan's face, and when she could read her expression, she had to ask the question in her heart.

"Have I said too much, Reagan?"

"No, but it takes a little getting used to."

"What does?"

"People who call themselves Christians but are humble about it."

"Reagan," Holly said firmly, "I think it's time you tell me what kind of Christian you've known in the past."

"I thought the usual kind," Reagan admitted, "but you're smashing all those notions."

"How am I doing that?"

"By admitting that you still sin. The Christians I've known made me feel as though I was the only sinner in the world. They never once talked about not being perfect."

"And you knew better."

Reagan stopped and stared at her. Holly stopped with her.

"They would carry their Bibles everywhere but not stop to give a coin to someone starving in the street! They went to church and talked with each other, but they only came near the rest of us when they were ready to preach a street sermon. I told myself that if that's what becoming perfect means, they could have it!"

"And well you should," Holly shocked her by saying.

"You agree with me?"

"Of course I do. Clearly these people hadn't spent much time looking at the life of Jesus Christ. He went wherever He was needed. He was thronged by the sick and helpless. His own comfort was never foremost in His mind. He always looked for a way to teach. At times He preached, but often He healed the sick with just a word or two about who He was. He saw to the physical needs as well as confronting the spiritually sick time and again, but anyone who did call on Him, anyone who wanted to know the way of salvation, was never turned away. It's the same today. We can call on Jesus Christ, and He will save."

"When did you call on Him, Holly? When did you believe all of this?"

"When I was a child. My parents believed in Christ, and one night when I was frightened by the dark, my father talked with me about God's being everywhere, whether it was dark or light. Then he said God wasn't in one place that he knew of, and I naturally wanted to know what he meant. My father was talking about my own heart. So that night he explained to me the way Christ died for me, and I believed."

"The next race is starting!" The loud call came to everyone within earshot of the pond. "Line up behind the house, and we'll group off by ages."

Holly glanced up and then back to Reagan.

"Do you want to keep talking about this, Reagan, or join the race?"

"Let's go watch the race," Reagan said without hesitation, but then asked, "Is that okay?"

"It sure is, as long as you know where you can come with your questions."

"I know, Holly." Reagan put a hand on her arm. "Thank you."

The women moved with the group toward the rear of the house, and for the moment, the subject was dropped.

❧ ❧ ❧

"She rents from you?" Jerome Hill, one of the single men from church, clarified as he sat at a table with Russell and Cash.

Russell nodded. "Since the middle of January."

"And how did she end up at our church? Has she said?"

"It wasn't by her design, I know that. She was walking through town on a Sunday morning and heard us singing."

"And what does she think?"

Russell smiled. "Last I knew she was still trying to figure us out."

"So you don't think she's a believer?"

"No, I don't. She's searching—Holly and I can see that—but I can't tell where she'll end up."

Jerome nodded, his face not giving anything away, but Russell understood the questions. Theirs was a church unlike others in that they had a surplus of single, interested-in-marriage men. There was not one single young woman in the church, for the simple reason that nearly all who entered found themselves courted and married. This didn't happen all that often, but when it did, it gave the waiting men more hope that God might have a bride for them, one who shared their beliefs.

"I wish I could tell you she was a believer, Jerome; not just for her sake, but for yours as well."

"Well, I can still pray for her, can't I? Even if nothing ever comes of it for me, I can still ask God to save her."

"Indeed, Jerome. Someday she might even thank you for that."

Jerome didn't stay at the table too much longer, but the moment he left, Russell confronted Cash.

"Why haven't you asked me about Reagan?"

"I was the first one to meet her that Sunday, Russ. I know the situation."

"True, but you've never mentioned her need for salvation."

"But you know I'm aware. I pray for her every time God brings her to mind."

"And how often is that?" Russell asked, watching him closely.

Cash smiled. This was the crux of the matter, and they both knew it.

"There are two problems here, Russ, and you know the first one."

"Yes, I do," he admitted quietly, knowing this conversation was one between good friends. Russell Bennett would never wish for his friend to marry an unbeliever, no matter how endearing. He now stated it plainly.

"You can't go falling for a woman who isn't a believer."

"Exactly."

"But I don't know the second reason."

"That has to do with Reagan herself," Cash explained. "Even if she did come to Christ, I can see that she doesn't want a man of her own. She doesn't mind being friendly to all of us, women and children included, but she isn't looking for a husband."

Considering that neither Russell nor Holly had told Cash this, Russell thought him rather astute.

"You're right. She fears having a man control her."

"I thought as much. I would say she's wise about living life on her own, and because of that, I think she's a little short on trust."

"She's used to taking care of herself; I can tell you that."

Cash suddenly laughed. "She rode up the drive on that bicycle, the cake held in one hand...I was very impressed."

"Did she think it was potluck?"

Cash nodded.

Cries from Alisa stopped the conversation. They both looked up to see Holly coming with the baby in her arms, a red-stained handkerchief held against the child's head.

"She pulled herself up next to a tree," Holly explained, "and then proceeded to fall against it and cut her head on the bark."

"Go on into the house, Holly," Cash instructed as Russell rose to hold the door. "Katy's in the kitchen."

Cash smiled at the big, tragic eyes that looked at him from Alisa's tiny face just before she buried it against her mother again.

"How is she?" Reagan asked, coming up as they went into the house, a baby's blanket in her hands.

"I think she'll live."

"You're sure to be right. She's the third, and they're usually pretty tough."

"Do you speak from experience?"

"Not personally, no, but several large families lived on my street in New York. I was close to one of them, and we ended up with the saying, 'There's no one tougher than the youngest Caminiti.'"

"And who was the youngest Caminiti?" Cash asked, working to get his mouth around the different-sounding name.

"Tony," Reagan said with a smile. "An adorable, round-faced two-year-old who had a smile for everyone."

"You miss them, don't you?"

"The people, yes, but not New York." Reagan glanced around. "The sky here is so big, even at night. There's more dust than I thought existed anywhere on the earth, but I can live with that."

Cash looked down into her earnest face, the creamy complexion, the dark, curly hair and intense dark eyes, and found himself praying for Jerome. There was no doubt about the right thing to do, but if the men in the church weren't careful, they were going to succumb to this woman's charms.

⁂

"Thank you for everything," Reagan told Katy at the end of the evening. Her bike was already loaded in the rear of the Bennetts' wagon, but Reagan didn't want to leave without thanking the woman who had done so much work.

"Well, don't be a stranger," the ranch housekeeper said. "You come back anytime. That cake was a good one. Have you got your plate?" she asked for the third time.

"Yes, ma'am. Thanks again."

Katy waved her off, dismissing the words—something, Reagan noticed, she did with everyone. A few minutes later Reagan found herself in the back of the wagon with the Bennett children, darkness coming fast. They made the ride home in near silence, the children almost asleep at the end of the drive, and the adults alone in their thoughts.

Reagan enjoyed picturing the ranch in her mind. She thought it was a wonderful place, so wide open and grand. The trees that sat in front of the large two-story ranch house had provided abundant shade. Reagan had walked through the barn, which had dozens of horse stalls, and stood at the corral fence. This city girl wasn't any judge of horseflesh, but Cash's horses seemed very fine indeed. And the pond. Reagan smiled at the memory. Pecan trees, wooden benches, and a nice expanse of water all lingered in her mind as she watched the children swim, sat with the adults to visit, or walked with Holly around the perimeter.

Some of her conversation with that lady came back to mind, but her brain was too weary to take it in.

Had she but known that Russell and Holly were in the same position, she would have laughed. Both of them wondered if she'd had a good time and what she'd thought of the day and the people, but neither one had the energy to ask.

Home came into view when all were more than ready to arrive, and with only the briefest words of good night, they unloaded the wagon and went their separate ways.

❧ ❧ ❧

"You're meeting who for dinner tonight?"

"Ty. He says he has a job for me. And you know I'm always trying to better myself."

Sally's brows rose. "What's the job?"

"He wants to discuss it with me then."

Sally looked more than a little skeptical, and Reagan was not going to let that pass.

"Should I not trust him?"

"I didn't say that."

"But you're thinking it."

"No, I'm not. Ty is utterly respectable, but he doesn't have the type of job that would need a woman's help."

"What does he do?" Reagan asked, knowing full well she should have asked the man himself.

"He builds houses."

Reagan blinked.

"Like with a hammer and nails?"

Sally laughed. "Yes, just like that."

Reagan chewed her lip a moment. The breakfast crowd was long gone, and she was working on cleanup. A moment later, the same dry pot in her hand, she told herself to go through with the evening's plans.

"Well, I'm going to meet him and at least hear him out."

"Why isn't he picking you up? In my day, a lady didn't meet a man on the streets."

"You make it sound clandestine. I just feel safer not having men know where I live. 'In your day,'" she went on to mutter. "You sound 102."

"I feel 102, believe me."

That night, as Reagan stood and waited for Ty to arrive, she remembered the conversation from the morning. She wasn't really worried, but she was early for the meeting in hopes that her escort would come soon and she could ask him about his business and the job he had in mind.

"Well, Reagan," said a male voice to her right side.

Reagan turned to see Cash coming up the street.

"Hello," she greeted him.

The tall cowboy came up the boardwalk and stopped as Reagan turned to speak to him.

"You look as though you're meeting someone."

"I am."

"What's her name?"

"It's not a woman."

Cash frowned. "A gentleman asked you out for the evening but didn't offer to escort you from home?"

His tone put Reagan off a bit, but she still admitted, "I asked to meet him."

"Why would you do that?"

Reagan's gaze shifted away and back again before she answered.

"I didn't want him to know where I lived."

Cash's face told her she'd shocked him.

"Let me get this straight," Cash said, a little too calmly. "You're going to spend the evening with this man, but you don't trust him enough to tell him where you live?"

Reagan's gaze shifted again. She started a little when Cash suddenly moved and sat on one of the benches in front of the hotel.

"What are you doing?" Reagan asked as she turned to watch. He was only ten feet away.

"I'm sitting here to make sure you're going to be all right."

"You might be used to people taking care of you," Reagan informed him, her mood growing dark, "but I do just fine on my own."

"That's why you're sitting safely at home waiting for this man to escort you safely to dinner."

Reagan frowned at him.

"Who is it, by the way?"

"Tyrone Arnold."

Cash didn't comment, and Reagan got angry.

"You don't have to do this," she hissed at him.

Cash only stared back at her, crossed his booted ankles, and settled in, looking for all the world as though he was staying the night.

"You have a huge nerve, Cash Rawlings," Reagan told him, clearly not happy with his actions.

"And you have more guts than good sense."

Reagan's gaze narrowed. Russell Bennett had said something very similar to her, and she didn't like it. Who did these men think they were?

"I want you to leave."

Cash shrugged. "I'm just sitting on a public bench in front of the hotel."

"We both know that's not true."

"We also both know that you're more worried about this meeting than you're letting on."

Reagan's chin rose in the air, but she didn't deny it.

"If you're not," Cash pressed her, "move down the walk a ways. I'm sure Ty will still find you."

Reagan turned her back on him. She didn't know when she'd been so angry. She did not, however, move down the walk. She told herself she didn't have to. If anyone should move, it should be Cash! But even in her anger she wasn't quite convinced. It was on her mind to simply turn and walk home. She didn't have to meet Ty. No one was forcing her, and she certainly didn't have to answer to Cash Rawlings.

Reagan decided to make her move. She would give Cash a few more words to put him in his place and then walk home. In her mood, she'd be there in a matter of seconds.

But in truth, more time had passed than she figured. Before she could do anything, she looked up to see that Ty was nearly upon her.

Nine

"HELLO, REAGAN," TY SAID, A HUGE SMILE on his face. "You look nice."

"Thank you," Reagan said, relaxing a little. Why hadn't she just told Cash that she didn't fear Ty and let it go at that? Indeed, looking into his handsome, smiling face, she couldn't think why she hadn't told him to come for her at the house.

"Are you ready to go?" Ty asked; he hadn't even noticed Cash's presence on the bench against the building.

"I am, yes, but I do have one question. What kind of work do you want me to do?"

Ty licked his lips. "Can't we talk about it over dinner?"

"Well, in truth," Reagan improvised, trying to keep her voice normal, though she was suddenly nervous, "you shouldn't have to spend money on a meal for me if I wouldn't be suited for the job. Why waste your time and efforts?"

"It's no waste of time, Reagan." His voice grew perceptibly warmer. "I want to buy you dinner."

Reagan caught the tone and stiffened her resolve even as she sensed the whole evening was about to fall into a heap around her ankles.

"Please tell me."

Clearly he didn't want to, but there was no missing the set line of her jaw.

"Reagan, if only..." he began, but Reagan shook her head. "All right," he conceded, his voice sounding weary and cautious. "I want you to become my wife and take care of my children."

Reagan couldn't keep her mouth shut.

"You have children?"

"They're my sister's kids. She died a year ago, and I can't do it on my own anymore. That's the job I'm talking about—being my wife and mother to Sammy and Kara."

Reagan felt sick to her stomach thinking about all his smiles, warm looks, and kind manner. He wasn't being friendly. He wanted to marry her!

"I'm sorry, Ty. I have no interest in being married, not to you or anyone else. It's nothing personal, and I can certainly understand why you didn't want to discuss this while I was on the job, but I'm not the woman you need."

Tyrone Arnold was a desperate man. He needed a wife very badly. But he was also proud. With little more than a brief nod of his head, he turned and went on his way. He had thought the children would sway her. He'd worked for hours on the meal they would eat, not willing to tell her until the last moment that they wouldn't be going to a restaurant, so sure that meeting his niece and nephew would help her to see his position.

As he walked on, he determined that she'd never know how hurt he was. As tears of frustration and helplessness filled his eyes, he determined to walk away and never look back.

Still standing just where he'd left her, Reagan stood like a statue, her heart a lump of iron in her chest. It wasn't supposed to happen this way. He wasn't supposed to look so hurt and vulnerable. She didn't want to marry. Had he offered her a nanny's job, she would have heard him out, but not wife—not now, not ever.

"Are you all right?" Cash asked from her side. Reagan had all but forgotten him.

"I'm always all right," she answered without thought.

Cash made a small sound in his throat and took her arm. "Come on."

"I want to go home."

"You will, eventually."

"Where are we going?" she asked.

"We're going to see Holly and Russell."

"How do you know they're home?"

"Because I was already headed there."

Reagan didn't respond, but neither did she argue. At the moment there wasn't any fight in her at all.

❧ ❧ ❧

"Reagan, why did you agree to go out with this man?" Holly asked, trying to gain a clear picture with the little bit that Cash had shared. The four adults were sitting in the Bennetts' living room.

"He offered me a job."

"Ty Arnold?" Russell questioned. "He builds houses."

Reagan glanced at Cash.

"I found that out only this morning. The job he had for me was to be his wife and take care of his children."

"I didn't know he had children."

"He said they're his sister's kids. He said she died a year ago and he couldn't do it on his own anymore."

The Bennetts were quietly shocked. They had been expecting Cash, but not with Reagan in tow. And not just any Reagan, but a subdued Reagan who had frowned at Cash at least once and looked over at him often. That she found him highhanded was obvious, but they both understood why he'd brought her with him. Had he not been coming for the evening, he probably would have dropped Reagan off and left.

"Why were you looking for another job, Reagan?" Holly asked.

"I'm trying to better myself, Holly. I don't want to bake cakes and wash pots for the rest of my life—not unless I'm running my own place."

Holly nodded in understanding.

"I mean," Reagan went on, warming a little to her subject and hoping that Cash was listening, "the secret to this life is knowing what you want and going after it. No one is going to take better care of me than I am, so I've got to do it to the best of my ability."

No one in the room commented on this, and Reagan knew exactly what they were thinking. She stood, her movements agitated.

"Yes, you can all stay very quiet, you who have this knowledge about God, but not all of us share in that."

"But you can, Reagan," Russell said. "It's yours for the asking."

Reagan knew that now was the perfect time to admit to them that the Bible had been as clear as mud to her, but pride kept her mouth shut.

"May I ask you something, Reagan?" Holly put in when Reagan remained silent.

The other woman nodded and sat back down. She had other friends in this town, but it wasn't her choice to be at odds with anyone, and these people had been more than kind to her; not to mention they were her landlords.

"I don't know what you have come to understand and what you aren't getting," Holly began, "but I'll start by asking if you realize that *you* have to make a step here? God is waiting for you to humble yourself and believe. Does that make sense to you, Reagan?"

"I think so."

"Why aren't you sure?"

Reagan looked at her lap. "The Bible hasn't been very clear to me."

"That's no surprise," Holly said, and Reagan was amazed at how often Holly took her off guard.

"What do you mean?"

"I mean, the Bible is a love letter to believers. I can understand if it's not clear to you. Prior to someone coming to Christ, he doesn't have God's Spirit to help him. I'm not saying that a person can't understand, but when he doesn't, I'm reminded to whom the Bible is written. It's for Christians."

"So how do I stand a chance?"

"You stand a chance because God says that anyone who asks may receive, and God never lies. You've told me that you understand what's being taught on Sunday mornings, but what I think you're missing is that you have to own that belief yourself. You can't just spend time around Christians and hope that what they have will rub off on you.

"You can admire us and be fascinated all you want, but until you reach out in faith to God, you won't have the eternal life we possess. We aren't going to love you less, Reagan, if you don't believe, but I would be no friend to you if I didn't tell you plainly what you need to do."

"Like God being everywhere, but not in my heart."

"Exactly. God doesn't force Himself on us. He'll only be in your heart if you'll open it to Him."

Reagan was quiet for a moment, and the others let her be.

"May I think about it?"

Sitting across from Reagan, Russell and Holly both smiled. Naturally Reagan looked surprised.

"We're smiling," Holly explained, "because I used to feel that a person must believe on the spot. Russell was the one to point out to me what a huge step believing is. God takes it very seriously, and so should you. You should not jump into this blindly. God requires no less than full commitment from His children."

Reagan closed her eyes. She wasn't sure she wanted to hear this. Fear about what God would require of her filled her, and she wanted to escape.

"Would you care for anything to eat, Reagan?" Russell suddenly asked. "You didn't get dinner, did you?"

"I'm not very hungry, but thank you."

With that she stood, knowing she could do so without offense. "I thank you for your hospitality, but I think I want to go home."

"That's fine," Russell said, his deep voice calm.

"Reagan," Cash spoke. The small woman turned to him. "I'm very sorry if you're upset with the way I handled things. I just didn't want to see you hurt."

"It's all right, Cash. I was upset, but I do understand, and I thank you for caring."

Reagan moved to the door, thanking her hosts again, but Russell caught up with her on the front porch.

"Reagan, if you do decide to read the Bible again, work on the third chapter of John."

"The third chapter of John? Is that the same as St. John?"

"Yes. The New Testament starts with Matthew, then Mark, Luke, and John. John 3. It's all there."

Reagan sighed a little.

"Don't be discouraged, Reagan. Holly is a good friend to lay it on the line to you. Trust us when we tell you, God never hides from those who seek Him."

Reagan looked into his smiling face and smiled in return as her heart reminded her that this man had been different from others she'd known. His life did not contradict his words. She could say the same for his wife and his friends.

Not willing to tell him that at present, she went on her way, thinking she might actually do as he suggested.

❧ ❧ ❧

Katy Sims headed into the general store a day earlier than usual. Saturday was her usual day to stock the pantry and get supplies, but the big party always depleted her stores, and she thought Friday afternoon was as good as Saturday morning when she was low on sugar.

"Hey, Katy," Lavinia called when she entered.

"How are you for raisins right now, Lavinia?"

"Just in."

And with that they were off. Katy was one of the pro-prietress's favorites. She was picky to a fault and would brook no nonsense, but that she patronized her store spoke volumes to the other establishments in town.

More than an hour later, Katy finished and was ready to leave. She left instructions about the way she wanted things loaded into the wagon, telling Lavinia she had busi-ness down the street and she would return.

"You keep an eye on things, Luke," she said as she did most weeks, addressing the new ranch hand who had been chosen to drive her. "I won't be long, so you wait for me right here."

"Yes, ma'am," Luke responded with the utmost respect, having taken his cue from a certain ranch owner, who, although he teased his housekeeper, still treated her like a cherished family member.

As usual Katy was in a hurry. The day was warm but not hot, and she was due for an outing, but having come into town in the afternoon put a damper on any kind of window shopping. She needed some molasses candy, the kind Cash liked, and only Reynolds carried it.

Katy was almost to the other store when Reagan sailed by on her bicycle. The older woman stopped in surprise. Reagan caught the movement out of the corner of her eye, and when she glanced back, she saw it was Katy. Reagan quickly turned and rode up parallel to the boardwalk.

"It's you!"

Reagan smiled, glad to see Katy. She had liked the out-spoken older woman. Not sure why, she was nevertheless very drawn to her.

"How are you, Katy?"

"You're going to kill yourself!"

Reagan laughed. "No, it's fun. You should try it."

Katy's eyes grew huge, but in truth she was fascinated.

"No," she said, having regained her good sense. "I'd fall and break my neck."

"No, you wouldn't. I'd help you." Reagan glanced around. "No one's watching."

"Oh, go on with you! I can't do that in town."

Reagan smiled again.

"I'll have to come out to the ranch."

Katy only waved her off, but Reagan thought she had seen a sign of genuine interest. Not even bothering to return Reagan's goodbye, Katy went into the store, found the candy for Cash, and went on her way. It didn't take long before she was back at the wagon, and after Luke helped her aboard, they started home.

In less than a minute, town and all she had seen were forgotten. Dinner had to be made and supplies put away. Anyone listening to Katy's thoughts would have said that she took her job too seriously. Katy would have scoffed at such a notion. There was nothing serious about it. It was her job, and it had to get done!

"You can help me unload, Luke," Katy announced when they returned to the ranch house, the hand having taken the wagon around back so they were closer to the kitchen. His reply was a simple "Yes, ma'am." He'd been told by the ranch's foreman, Brad Johns, to expect anything and to stay until he was dismissed.

The ranch house at the Rawlings Cattle Company was as modern as any home in the area, and the kitchen was no exception. It was a cook's dream for meals and baking. Spacious, with work area and floor space and a pantry you could walk into, the kitchen area allowed Katy to put out a meal for 30 without even breaking a sweat.

"How about these sacks of sugar?" Luke asked, both shoulders laden.

"Bottom shelf on the right. You'll see the space."

"Do you need some help?" a male voice asked from the doorway. Katy turned to see Max, the ranch hands' cook.

"I think there's still some in the wagon," Katy told him. "Wipe your feet."

"Yes, ma'am," he drawled, having known just what she was going to say.

Katy had washed her hands and was getting ready to mix biscuit dough when Max returned.

"Why'd you go today?"

"I'm out of things," she said, as if it was the most logical reason in the world.

"I'm goin' tomorrow."

"Good. If I remember I've forgotten something, I'll put it on your list."

"My own list is plenty full."

"Well, one more item won't hurt. What are you making the men tonight?"

"Fish stew. Luke's brother caught a slew of bluegills and landed them all in my kitchen."

"I thought they hated fish stew."

"No, they don't!" His voice grew indignant. "It's that lamb stew I tried! I had a revolt on that one," he muttered, but there was a twinkle in his eye. Katy smiled a little herself.

Max Reed and Katy Sims had been friends for more than ten years. Max wasn't as old as Cash's housekeeper, but age had never been a factor. Their jobs—the very nature of being at the ranch nearly every day and not out on the range—simply drew them together.

"Is that wagon done?" Katy asked Luke when he came back with yet another load.

"Just about."

"Well, when you finish, you just get yourself over to that jar and get some cookies. Do you hear me?"

"Yes, ma'am," Luke replied, just barely holding his smile.

"And you get out from under foot, Max Reed. I've got Cash's dinner to put on."

"I'm goin'. I'm goin'. I got my own work to do."

Katy snorted as though he didn't know the meaning of the word and kept on with her dinner preparations. Cash came on the scene about an hour later when supper was just about ready.

"How were things in town?" he asked while having a quick wash at the basin. She'd told him that morning she was going a day early.

"Did you know that Reagan Sullivan rides a bicycle?" she demanded, turning toward him.

Cash laughed. "I take it you saw her?"

Katy shook her head in amazement. "She's going to break her neck!"

"I don't think so," Cash said confidently. "If anyone can take care of herself, it's Reagan."

Katy looked at Cash, her eyes narrowing.

"You sound interested."

"In what?"

"Reagan."

"You mean as a woman?" He looked confused.

"No, I mean as a horse. Of course, as a woman!"

Cash was already shaking his head.

"Now don't you say no to me, Charles Rawlings! She couldn't be sweeter, and something tells me she's a hard worker."

"I'm sure she's all of that, but she doesn't share my faith, Katy," Cash told her soberly.

The woman's eyes widened.

"But she came to the church party, and I've seen her at church too."

"Well," Cash kept his voice gentle and worked not to show his surprise, "we both know that attending church does not mean you believe."

This shut Katy's mouth. Cash had not intended to put her in her place, but she simply had no argument, and they both knew it. And the reason was a simple one: Katy had been attending church off and on with Cash for a couple of years, but never once had she been willing to talk about what she was hearing.

One Sunday morning Cash had asked her outright if she had ever gotten serious about her relationship to God. Katy had not pretended ignorance. She told him plainly that she didn't think she was a sinner and didn't believe God would condemn anyone He had created. And that wasn't the end of it! She had made it very clear to Cash on that day that she didn't wish to discuss it anymore.

But they had been sharing the same house for a long time, and he knew from other comments she made that a lot of her beliefs stemmed from her relationship to his parents. When he had first come to Christ, she had naturally wanted to know how his beliefs were different from his parents'. His explanation had not been well received. She thought the sun, moon, and stars rose and set on the senior Charles Rawlings and his wife and would hear no word to the contrary. Cash could still recall the scene.

How could you say such a thing, Cash Rawlings! Why, your mother took me in when I didn't have a thing. We've worked side by side in this house since the first year it was built, and now with them in St. Louis and not even here to defend themselves, you say they're not Christians!

"Dinner's ready," the housekeeper announced, her voice sounding completely normal.

"It smells good. What is it?"

"Veal medallions in peppercorn sauce. And if you'll check the little bowl in the living room, I've got your favorite molasses candy in there."

"What would I do without you, Kate?" Cash asked as he sat down to eat.

"Just curl up and die, I 'spect."

Katy didn't stick around to eat with him as she often did, and tonight Cash was thankful. He had little choice but to leave the subject of faith alone, but not having her in the kitchen allowed him to spend a little extra time in prayer. As he did often throughout the day, he asked God to soften Katy's heart so that she could see her need of Him.

Cash finally tucked into his meal but had only taken a few bites when his foreman knocked on the back door.

"Come in," he called.

Brad entered, taking his hat off before seeing that Katy was not in the room. Cash smiled when he replaced it and sat across from him.

"I'm headed out now."

"All right. Who're you taking with you?"

"Dusty and Zeke."

"Zeke?"

"I'll tell you, Cash, if you can get past that baby face, there's a lot of man there. He never complains, and because he was raised in the hills, he's a good man to track those coyotes."

Cash nodded. "I'll leave it up to you."

"One of the girls has a cold by the way," Brad added, talking about one of his two daughters. "I told Brenda to come up here to the big house if it gets worse."

"Good. I'll have Katy check on her tomorrow."

"All right, boss," the cowboy stood, his hat still in place. "I'll see you next week."

Cash waved him on and went back to his meal. Of all the changes he'd made since taking over the ranch from his father, the best was putting in a house for his foreman. Prior to that, his father had been through several foremen. They had been young and lacked experience. Men with better qualifications usually had wives and children. With no place for another family to live at the ranch, it was very difficult to offer the job to such a man.

"Where did she get that bicycle anyhow?" Katy demanded, suddenly coming on the scene. Cash nearly choked on his food for laughing.

"Are you still thinking on that?"

"Have you seen her?" the woman asked, as though that explained it all. This said, she went on her way, leaving Cash to wonder just what kind of impact Reagan Sullivan was going to have on them all.

Ten

REAGAN HAD MEANT WHAT SHE SAID. She had no doubt in her mind that anyone could ride a bicycle, and now she was headed to the ranch to let Katy try. This trip to the ranch, however, was a bit different. There was no cake in her hand, and she was not late and in a big hurry. Letting herself look all around, Reagan rode as though she didn't have a care in the world. And if she worked hard enough, she could even convince herself that she didn't.

It had been more than a week since she'd been scheduled to meet Ty and ended up in the Bennetts' living room. She hadn't touched her Bible or gone to church since she left them. She wasn't angry, but she just didn't think she could agree with their way of thinking. The whole idea of letting God rule over her ran her blood cold. What if He demanded more than she could ever give? What if she had to give up what she found most dear—her freedom?

Reagan's thoughts were interrupted when she realized the gateway to the ranch had come into view. She could hardly wait to see the surprise on Katy's face. Indeed, she was still laughing at the older woman's proclamation that she would break her neck.

She picked up the pace a little, excitement running in her veins, and before she knew it, she was hopping off the bike, bounding up the steps, and scooting across the wide porch to knock on the big wooden door. Feeling antsy, she wiggled around a bit when no one came. Making a harder ball with her fist, she came close to pounding this time, and sure enough, she heard someone speaking as she approached.

"You'd think it was locked," Katy muttered as she pulled the door open and found a smiling Reagan on the porch.

"I'm here with the bike!" she announced, her dark eyes sparkling.

Katy stared at her.

"You said you wanted to ride."

"Land sakes! Have you lost your mind?"

"Not at all. You can do it, Katy. A woman in my neighborhood in New York learned to ride, and she was much older than you."

"How old?" Katy shot at her.

"Very old," Reagan assured her.

"Oh, for pity's sake!" Katy exclaimed, but she also came onto the porch and walked to the top of the steps where she could look down to where the bike leaned against the railing.

"You do it," Katy suddenly turned and demanded.

Not saying a word but smiling hugely, Reagan descended the steps, put the bicycle into position, gave it a little push, hopped on with the ease of breathing, and rode in a little circle as though she'd been doing it all her life.

"Where did you get that?"

"I sent for it," she called from the leather seat. "It was in a catalog."

"How did you learn to ride?"

"I just did it. I held onto the side of a building when I first got going. It took only a few hours. It'll be easier for you, since I'll be here to help and steady you."

Katy licked her lips. Cash was always teasing her about being old and set in her ways, but what if he came off the range tonight and found her riding a bike? Reagan could stay for dinner, and Katy could greet Cash from the seat of that metal contraption.

Having convinced herself, Katy moved down the steps. Reagan all but shouted with enthusiasm and jumped off the bike to let her have a try.

"Okay," she urged the older woman, who was smaller in frame and height than she was. "Gather your skirt to one side with your left hand, and take this side of the steering bar with your right. Okay? Good. Now, let the bike roll a bit and then make a quick jump, releasing your left hand very fast, and grabbing the bar, just as you land on the seat."

"You must be out of your mind," Katy said with complete conviction.

"Here." Reagan took the bike from her. "Watch me. I don't have to hold my skirt over anymore, but I'll do it so you'll understand."

Katy stood back and watched as Reagan made it look very easy. She even hopped off and started again to show her.

"What if I tip over?"

"I'll run alongside and catch you."

Katy just about said no but then remembered how hard it was to surprise Cash.

"You'll stay right with me?"

"Yes. I won't let go unless you tell me."

Her mouth pursed with determination, Katy tried it and was surprised into a breathless gasp that it actually worked. Reagan kept her hand on the bar and seat, running alongside and encouraging her all the way. Katy made it several feet before she got wobbly and had to jump off.

"It just about jars your teeth out!"

Reagan smiled. "I know! Isn't it fun?"

Katy couldn't help but laugh as she said, "All right! Let's go again."

This time they got down to real business. The housekeeper even commanded Reagan to let go. She did very well for a good ten yards before taking a spill. Recovering very nicely, she even fussed over the dirt on her dress.

"Are you hurt?" Reagan asked as she rushed up.

"No. I want to ride some more."

Reagan laughed. It had been the same for her. Once she'd gotten the hang of it, she hadn't wanted to do anything else. In the next half hour the two had more fun than either could remember in a long time. Reagan even showed Katy a few tricks she had taught herself. Not warm by nature, Katy was thinking that she didn't ever want this girl to go home.

"I'll have a try at one of those tricks," Katy said.

"Maybe you'd better give it some more time, Katy," Reagan cautioned.

"I didn't mean it," she said as if Reagan should know. "I just want another ride."

Reagan stood back and watched her hop on. She headed down the driveway and then turned to come back. The turn was what ended the fun. She started to fall, and just as Reagan had taught her, put her foot out. This time, however, she was moving too fast. Her leg could not support her and down she went at an awkward angle. Reagan thought it looked painful and swiftly rushed to her side.

"Are you all right?"

Katy didn't answer.

Reagan moved so she could look right down into her face. The housekeeper's complexion had gone very pale.

"It hurts," she said.

"Where, Katy?"

"My leg. I can't move it."

Reagan could have died on the spot. That Katy might get hurt had honestly never occurred to her.

"I'll go for the doctor," she said, her voice rising in panic.

"No, send Max."

"Where is Max?"

"In the bunkhouse. You know the one?"

But Reagan didn't answer, she was already running, her skirts hitched up to give her freedom. She was fairly certain which building was the bunkhouse, but when she pounded and yelled, a woman answered.

"Where's Max?" Reagan demanded.

"In the bunkhouse. What is it?"

"Which one's the bunkhouse?"

"There," the woman pointed. "What's happened?" she called again, this time to Reagan's retreating back.

"Katy's hurt! We need the doctor," she yelled as she moved to the other building, not waiting to see if the woman heard her or not.

❧ ❧ ❧

Today they were branding calves. Normally Cash would not have been directly involved, but with Brad gone, he felt he needed to be on the job. That morning he had met with a man who hailed from the east and wished to go into ranching. Cash didn't think he would actually do it—he'd been too horrified by the smell of cattle—but Cash had been more than willing to answer his questions and offer help in any way he could.

The event caused Cash to think about the type of man his father was. Charles Rawlings Sr. had been born and raised in the city, but when an opportunity came to turn his hand to Texas ranching, he had jumped at it and been successful in the bargain. The ranch he handed down to his son was very prosperous.

Working without having to give the branding any thought, Cash let his mind wander to his family. He'd been with all of them just that January, but it seemed so long ago. He'd received a letter from Darvi the week before saying she and Dakota were doing well and settled in a small house in town. Cash was glad that the town was small. He liked thinking about his brothers ensconced in small, close communities like Kinkade.

"He's loose!" one of the men yelled when his rope slipped. Cash jumped to his feet—lariat in hand—to rope a runaway whose mother bellowed to him from outside the makeshift pen.

It was while Cash was finishing rounding up this stray that he looked up and saw Brenda riding toward him at a furious pace, her hair and clothing blowing out behind her. Cash's heart plummeted with fear, knowing she wouldn't be out here for anything short of an emergency.

"It's Katy," she called as she reined the horse to a hard stop. "She fell hard."

"Todd," Cash ordered, his voice belying the feelings inside, "go for Doc Bruce."

"Max went," Brenda told him, still breathless.

"Who's with Katy?" Cash asked, even as he moved toward his mount.

"Some woman. I didn't have time to get her name."

With this cryptic news, Cash's horse left Brenda's in the dust as he rode for all he was worth back to the main house. He went in the back way, and when he couldn't find her inside, he rushed for the front yard.

A mixture of surprise and concern filled him when he saw the bike, Reagan, and his housekeeper, who was still lying in the dirt.

"Katy!" he said, running fast and dropping to her side.

"I've done it this time, Cash," was all she said, her eyes clouded with pain.

Afraid to move her or even touch her, he naturally turned to Reagan for answers.

"She fell off the bike," Reagan told him, her face showing her own measure of misery. "She was doing so well..."

"It's all right, Reagan," he said, hoping it was true. "The doctor is on his way. He'll get her all fixed up."

Part of which proved to be true. The doctor was on his way, and when he arrived, they moved Katy, a terrible ordeal for the older woman, to a bed in the small downstairs bedroom. But fixing her up was not going to be so easy.

"Her hip is broken," Dr. Bruce told Cash, Brenda, and Max after they'd waited outside the closed bedroom door for about 20 minutes. Reagan had gone in to help. "She'll be laid up for a good long time."

"How much pain is she in?"

"Right now it's intense. She needs to lie still and not worry."

The doctor continued to speak with Brenda and Max, but Cash needed to see Katy. He slipped past the threesome and entered quietly.

The curtains were pulled back, allowing plenty of light to filter in. Cash found Reagan sitting next to the bed gently bathing Katy's face and hands. The fact that his housekeeper allowed this spoke volumes to him concerning her condition.

Cash took the other side of the bed. There was no chair, so with a hand to the oak headboard, he leaned down to speak into her face, asking himself as he did if she'd looked that old at breakfast that morning.

"How is it?"

"I've never broken anything, Cash."

He nodded. All three of the Rawlings boys had broken and cracked various bones, and although Katy had been as compassionate as they'd ever known her in her ministrations of them, she had not experienced this pain before.

"The doctor says you have to lie still and not worry."

"How am I supposed to do that? Who's going to take care of you?"

It was her standard line, and Cash smiled at her, glad to hear she had at least one small tease left.

"Maybe it's time I grow up."

Katy sighed. "I should have insisted that you take me to my house," she said, referring to the small bungalow that sat next to the foreman's house.

"Then I wouldn't be able to take care of you like I can now," Cash reasoned.

"You've got a ranch to run."

"Brad will be back in two days. When he's here, I'm not even needed."

Had Katy not been in so much pain, she would have given her customary snort. Instead she closed her eyes, thinking she might cry for the first time since Virginia Rawlings moved back to St. Louis.

Seeing her eyes closed, Cash motioned to Reagan. The two left the room together. The doctor slipped back in to check on his patient, and Cash was glad for a few minutes alone with his guest.

"You're not to blame yourself for this," he said to Reagan's set features.

"She didn't ask me to bring the bike. I just thought it would be fun."

"So you forced her?"

"No, but—"

"There are no 'buts.' It was an accident. She'll be fine."

"She's not a young woman, Cash. Why didn't I see that?"

"She'll be fine. It will take awhile, but she'll be back to her old self again."

Reagan only half heard him. She was already making plans to fix things, and her mind had shifted away from the man who faced her.

"All right, Cash," the doctor interrupted him, "come in here, and I'll tell you what she needs."

Without being asked, Reagan joined them. She listened in silence, but with every word the doctor spoke to the rancher, her resolve strengthened.

Cash did not comment as Dr. Bruce mapped out his expectations, but he could see that it was going to be a lot of work in the weeks and months ahead. The doctor had a powder for the pain, but not enough with him. The men eventually exited the room so Cash could send a man to town to get the medicine.

Reagan went back to the edge of the bed. Katy's eyes were still closed, but her mouth was open and her breathing told Reagan she was lying in very great pain. Without a word, the small, dark-haired woman exited— not just the room, but the ranch house itself, heading for her bike. She was back on the road just a minute later and headed for town. She had a lot of work to do before night-fall.

❧ ❧ ❧

"You're not riding back there in the dark!" Sally said for the second time. "And I mean it."

"But don't you see, if I go now it won't be dark."

"That's not true, Reagan. The day has gotten away from you. It'll be dark in an hour, and you said you haven't even gone home."

Reagan sighed.

"I know what this is about," Sally guessed. "You haven't told Cash Rawlings that you're going to do this, and if he hears a wagon, he'll send you packing before you can even climb out."

Reagan looked away from her and admitted, "I'm going to do this, Sally, with or without your help."

"That's just it, Reagan. I am willing to help you."

She turned back.

"So you understand?"

"Completely. Now, I think you should head home and get your stuff. Talk to Holly or Russell if you can so they won't worry, and then come back here. I can take you almost all the way there, and you can ride yourself the rest of the way."

"I don't know what I'd do without you, Sally."

"Well, I know what I'm going to do without you," she retorted. "I'm going to get up before dawn tomorrow and start baking."

Reagan gave her a hug. She couldn't help herself.

"Get out of here," she ordered, and Reagan hurried on her way.

Just 30 minutes later she was back, not having been able to speak with her landlords. Sally promised to tell them about the change. As soon as Reagan was ready, they settled into Sally's buggy and that woman, good friend that she was, took Reagan as far as the gate.

Reagan put her carpet bag handle over the bar on her bike and rode as steadily as she could manage. It was almost fully dark, but she could see what she needed. Heart pounding in her chest, she knocked hard on the door and waited.

"Reagan," Cash said with surprise. He answered the door, a lantern in his hand. "I wondered where you'd gone."

"I had to go home to get my things."

This said, she scooted past him and walked to the living room, looking for all the world as though she was there to stay. A moment later, Cash learned that she was.

"I'm here to take care of Katy and to do her jobs until she mends."

Cash stared at her, finally taking in the bag.

"You don't have to do that," he tried.

"But I'm going to. I've quit my job; I have money to live on for a time, and I'm here to do whatever needs to be done."

"You will not quit your job," he started to declare, but to his surprise, Reagan turned her back on him and started toward Katy's room. Cash was hard on her heels.

"Reagan," he began again, but she marched resolutely away.

"Reagan?" This time the name came from Katy as Reagan crossed the threshold of her room. "I was looking for you."

"Well, you don't have to look anymore. I'm here to take care of everything."

"You're not," Katy said, hoping above hope that it was true.

"Yes, I am. I'm going to take care of you and this house until you're up again and as bossy as ever."

Cash had entered the room right behind Reagan, so it would have been impossible for him to miss the sob that broke in the old woman's throat.

"I didn't know what I was going to do," she cried softly. "I've got to take care of Cash and this house. It's my job."

"It's all right," Reagan said gently, coming to take her hand. "I'm here now, and I'll see to it."

Cash had never seen this woman cry. He didn't know she was capable of such an act. He stood still while Reagan bent over her, talking in soothing tones and bathing her face again. Even in the lantern light he could see some of the worry lines easing around Katy's brow and temples.

He had no idea how it could possibly work to have Reagan living and working in his home, but sending her away from Katy right now was just not something he was willing to do.

Eleven

REAGAN SULLIVAN IS SLEEPING DOWNSTAIRS *with Katy,* Cash told God that night, speaking as though this would be news to Him. *I'm not sure I can do this. I'm not sure I can have her here. There's so much I don't know about her, and she doesn't know anything about us either. I understand that she's here because of what happened, and I can see why she'd blame herself, but in the space of a few hours, she quit her job and moved here!*

For a moment Cash only lay on his back and stared at the ceiling. The events of the day had put him in a near state of shock. It broke his heart to see Katy as he never had: broken and flat on her back. And then to have Reagan show up at the door! It was all too fantastic to be real.

Help me, Father. I need to take care of my Katy. Maybe this is what will draw her to You, but before I can help her spiritually, I have to figure out a way to help her physically. Brenda is willing to help, but she has the girls to care for, and if her changing shape is any indication, she has another one on the way. I'm willing to do anything Katy needs, Lord, but I'm not a woman and...

Cash's mind came to a complete stop. He had been staring up with his eyes open, but they now closed as he remembered Reagan.

I think You must have sent her, Lord. I would never have asked her to come, but Katy was so glad to see her. I have never seen Katy cry.

Cash's own throat closed at the memory. It had been awful to see her vulnerable and tearful, but the more he thought about Reagan's presence, the way she comforted Katy, and the fact that that woman even accepted it, the more a peace stole over his heart. He would not have planned to end the day the way he did, but he now chose to be thankful.

In a moment of time things change so quickly, Lord, but You're never surprised. Whatever You have for tomorrow, help me to be ready and thankful for Your care.

Suddenly realizing he wasn't the least bit tired, Cash relit the lantern and opened his Bible. He read for almost an hour, and when he did fall asleep, it was with the sweet knowledge that God was still very much in control.

🌹 🌹 🌹

"I wasn't sure how you liked your eggs" were the first words that greeted Cash the next morning; he had barely taken two steps into the kitchen. "I scrambled them. Will that be all right?"

"Yes," Cash said, not used to having his opinion asked. Katy knew his likes and dislikes very well. Neither was he accustomed to having such a young, attractive woman flushed and working over the stove in his kitchen, but clearly she had found her feet. As efficiently as if she did it every day, she laid the table service where he always sat, set his plate in front of him, and filled his coffee cup while he watched.

"I found a small pitcher of cream and assume you take it in your coffee."

"Yes, I do. Thank you," Cash said, getting over his surprise enough to sit down.

Reagan put both sugar and cream in close reach, her movements relaxed but very capable.

"Now she might eat something for me," Reagan muttered good-naturedly, turning away to replace the coffeepot and lift a waiting tray that held a second breakfast.

"Katy's awake?"

"Yes, but she wouldn't eat a thing until you'd been served."

Cash's mouth tightened. "Well, this is the last day for that. Here, give me that tray."

Upon seeing his expression and hearing his tone, Reagan knew better than to argue. She stayed where she was, and realizing she needed to eat as well, fixed herself a small plate.

Cash, on the other hand, did not give his own stomach or cooling food a second thought. Tray held firmly in his large, work-roughened hands, he headed in to straighten a few things out with a certain stubborn old woman.

"Cash," Katy said in soft surprise. "Did you finish your breakfast already?"

"No, I have not," he said, his voice sounding more angry than she had ever heard him. Cash set the tray on her bedside table, pulled the chair close, sat down, and looked at her. "We will have one thing straight right now, Kathleen Sims. I am not the one in need of tender care."

"Well!" Katy said with a small spark of her old indignation. "What did she fix you that you're so put out?"

"I mean it, Katy," he said in a no-nonsense way. "You can lie in this bed and tell Reagan how you want things done until you're blue in the face, but you'll not tell her to feed me and take care of my needs first."

"What will you do?" Katy challenged. The pain was riding her hard, but she could not let this pup have his way.

Cash sat back and crossed his arms.

"That's easy. I'll forbid her to see to a single one of my needs. No food cooked, no clothes washed, nothing."

"I'll just tell her otherwise."

Cash stood, moved the tray so she could reach everything and then put his hand on the headboard to lean over her once again.

"This is still my home," he said with deadly calm. "It was a surprise to see Reagan at the door last night, but after a few hours of thinking it through, I see her as a blessing. But her main purpose here is to take care of *you*. If she doesn't understand that, I'll get someone who does." Cash straightened, his voice returning to normal. "Start your breakfast, Katy, and I'll ask Reagan to check on you as soon as I've explained the situation to her."

Cash left the sickroom without a word. He found Reagan in almost the same position as he'd left her. As he sat back down at his now-empty place, movement caught his eye. He looked to see Reagan using the corner of her apron, and taking his meal from the oven. She set the hot plate before him.

"Please sit down, Reagan. I need to tell you a few things."

Reagan obeyed, her face sober, but rebellion growing in her heart. She was not leaving here, no matter what he said!

"You're not here to take care of me," Cash stated. "I can understand Katy's distraction with that since she's done nothing but see to my needs and the needs of others for many years, but if she's ever going to get out of that bed and walk again, she needs to take care of herself."

Reagan's heart turned with pain at the thought that Katy might not make a full recovery.

"If it makes her feel better to have you changing beds and doing other household chores, that's fine. But you're never, and I repeat, never, no matter what Katy says, to set her needs aside for mine. You won't hear this from her, but it's what I expect."

"What do I do if she tells me otherwise, like this morning?"

Cash looked her in the eye and admitted, "After getting over my surprise, I'm glad you're here, Reagan, but I know how I want this done. Katy sometimes forgets who's in charge. If you can't do as I expect, I'll find someone who can."

Reagan had no argument for that. Indeed Katy's very commanding presence had caused Reagan to forget whose home she was in. All remaining fight drained out of her. It was more than reasonable that Cash get his way in this matter, especially in light of the fact that he only wanted his housekeeper to be well.

"Do you have any questions?"

"No. I should tell you, though, that she was awake in the night and has some pretty aggressive plans."

"Like what?"

"She says she hasn't done the windows in a while, the rugs need beating—things like that. She also said your bedroom and office need turning out, and she was going to get to it next week."

Cash shook his head a little. "I think you should run everything through me for a while. You can take notes or whatever you need to keep track of what she wants done, but before you start any large projects, see me."

"All right."

"I need to tell you, Reagan," Cash added, "I'm very thankful that you've come to help her."

"It's all my fault, Cash. No matter what you say, I'll believe that." She shrugged and added, "There was nothing else I could do."

The rancher knew there was no point in arguing with her.

"Nevertheless, I thank you for your willingness to come and help." He paused suddenly, as he fully realized what a huge job they would both have. "Reagan," he went on, "the doctor said that Katy must keep still if her hip is going to heal properly so she can walk again. I don't want you to lie to her, but between the two of us, we need to keep her as calm and happy as we can manage. I'm not sure she'll make it easy, and I'm not going to let her run you ragged, but—"

Cash cut off when Reagan put her hand up.

"I know what you want, and I'm willing to do that."

Cash stared at her. He genuinely liked her, he realized, and at the moment he was more grateful to her than he could say. That it had been her bicycle that caused the accident was of little importance to him. She was willing to help, and he was very glad to have her.

"I did tell Katy that you would check on her after I talked to you."

Reagan pushed out of the kitchen chair.

"I'll go right now."

Cash ate his again-cool breakfast, his mind covering the things he had to do. Reagan could not keep sleeping on the floor of Katy's room, and his family needed to know what had happened. He ate without giving much thought to the taste, his mind on the full day ahead.

🥀 🥀 🥀

"What is that noise?" Katy demanded not long after Reagan started giving her a bath. She'd eaten a small breakfast and had been fairly subdued. Reagan had been the one to suggest washing up when she noticed the hair around Katy's temples and forehead was matted with sweat.

"I don't know."

"Well, go check!"

"As soon as we're done and you're settled."

"Oh, for pity's sake!" the old woman exclaimed in very real frustration. "I tell you, Cash does not know what he's talking about! I'm fine. Go see what that is!"

Reagan stood to full height, a glint in her eye and, surprisingly, a smile on her face.

"As me Irish father would say," she said, dropping into a remarkable Irish brogue, "'Dinna fash yourself, woman.'"

"What?" Katy was so taken aback, she forgot about the noises.

"'Dinna fash yourself.' In other words, don't fret yourself, don't worry."

"Easy for you to say," the older woman sniffed, turning her head with as much dignity as she could muster.

Reagan ignored her and went back to the bath. She made swift work of it, and by the time someone knocked on the door, Katy was bathed and in a fresh gown.

"Come in," Reagan called.

Cash's head came around the corner.

"I need to show you something, Reagan. Do you have a minute?"

"Coming right up."

"What were those noises?" Katy demanded.

"I'll tell you as soon as I get finished talking with Reagan," Cash said, waiting for Reagan to come to the door so he could take her out into the hall.

"If you're stirring up a bunch of dust, Cash Rawlings..." they both heard Katy begin, but neither one turned back to hear the rest.

"There's a small storeroom around here next to the pantry," Cash said, as they headed down the hall. "It was never meant for a bedroom, but if the closet door in Katy's room is open, you can hear everything in that room."

Reagan suddenly smiled at him.

"You sound as though you speak from experience."

Cash smiled at being caught out and laughed when he volunteered, "My mother's great uncle visited one time. With the way he snored, you could hear it all over the house, but my brothers and I did hide in this room one night just to get the full effect."

Reagan had a good laugh over this as they finished the journey to the room. She passed odds and ends of furniture and even some sacks of food that had been stacked against one wall of the narrow hallway. When she got to the room, she could see that someone had been busy.

The room was very small, but already there was a bed with a small table near the head. Suddenly, from behind Cash and Reagan, one of the ranch hands showed up with a small dresser.

"Right in the corner there, Luke," Cash directed. "Now, Reagan, we've got rugs to spare and just about anything you want to make this liveable. I don't want you sleeping on the floor for the next six weeks. It's simply not practical, and I don't think you'll be able to move around comfortably if I put another bed in Katy's room."

"But I can't be too far away and still hear her if she calls in the night," Reagan finished for him.

"Exactly. Now right here, on the other side of the wall, is the closet. We're going to try a few experiments and see..." Cash stopped talking, his voice trailing off for a moment.

Reagan watched him, as did Luke, both waiting for further instructions.

"Do you sleep soundly?" he finally asked.

Reagan shrugged. "I don't know. I've never given it much thought."

"Did you wake easily when Katy called you in the night?"

"I think so."

"But you were sleeping on the floor," Cash said as he did some thinking out loud, "and that couldn't have been very restful."

"Reagan?" Katy's voice suddenly came through the wall.

"Is that closet door open?" Cash asked as he turned to Reagan.

"I don't think so."

Cash worried the edge of his lip for a moment.

"I'd better see what Katy wants."

"Right!" Cash was brought back to reality. "Before you go, though, do you think you could be comfortable in here, Reagan?"

Reagan couldn't stop her smile, her eyes sparkling and white teeth flashing at him.

"You haven't seen my house, have you, Cash?"

With that she turned and went on her way. Not until then did Cash notice that Luke had not taken his eyes from Reagan. Remembering that night with Ty in front of the hotel, the ranch owner had all he could do not to pat Luke on the back and warn him that the lady would not be interested.

❧ ❧ ❧

"I spilled my water!" Katy all but snapped at Reagan when she crossed the threshold. "Cash should just come in here and put me out of my misery. I can't even get myself a drink!"

Reagan did not comment. The thought of Katy dying horrified her, and for a moment she could not speak. She came close to the bed, lifting a towel from the basin on her way past. She mopped the water without overdo fuss, but inside she was shaken.

I've caused all of this. Katy's misery and all the inconvenience are my fault.

"Okay," Cash stated with enthusiasm, coming through the open door unannounced. "Here's the plan, Kate. Reagan and I are going to clear the stuff from this closet and then shut the door. You're going to hear a lot of cutting and pounding because I'm going to put a doorway through on the other side."

"Whatever for?" Katy asked, mouth open.

"Reagan's going to sleep in the little storeroom by the pantry, and the new door will give her access in here. I don't want another bed in this room, but she needs to be able to hear you."

The older woman looked so upset that Cash went to her. Reagan felt they needed time alone, but for some reason she couldn't move.

"Katy." The big cowboy said her name quietly, taking the chair and leaning close. "I want you better, and to do that you can't get out of this bed. Reagan has to be close to help you, but she can't sleep on the floor."

"But it's little more than a closet. Never has a guest in this house been treated that way."

"I know, and if things were different, it wouldn't have to be this way now, but Reagan understands."

"Maybe we should move to my house. I wanted Reagan here to take care of you, but maybe we should get out of your hair."

Cash picked up her hand.

"This is where you're staying until you can walk out on your own. When you're on your own two feet—bossy as the day is long—you can go home. Until then we're going to live together and probably drive each other crazy at times, but that won't change the facts. The three of us are going to do everything we have to do to get you out of that bed."

Listening to him from where she felt frozen in place, Reagan saw for the first time how much Cash loved this old woman. This kind of love was foreign to her. She didn't know what to do with it; indeed, it frightened her, but at the same time she was strangely touched by what she was witnessing.

"Okay." Cash stood, clearly ready to get to work. "We'll make it as fast as possible, but it will be noisy."

"Who's helping you?" Katy demanded.

"Luke."

"Well, that's at least something."

Cash went on his way, and Katy decided to take her mind off what she thought of as an intolerable situation.

"Have you met Luke?"

"I don't think so," Reagan said. She wasn't ready to talk, but keeping Katy's spirits in mind, she answered.

"I think he's about your age."

"Now, what would you be knowing about my age?" The brogue was back, and Reagan was smiling.

Katy snorted. "You can't be more than 20."

Reagan had a good laugh over this, and without even knowing it, Katy was drawn away from her pain as curiosity got the best of her.

"You don't mean to say you're older!"

"Indeed, I do," Reagan said as she straightened the room and even dusted the dresser.

"Twenty-one?"

Again Reagan laughed.

"No!" Katy exclaimed. "I refuse to believe it."

"I'll have you know," Reagan informed her, brogue still in place as she came to the end of the bed, "that I will be 24 later this year."

Katy's mouth opened and with good reason. Reagan did have a youthful appearance about her. And with her gutsy, sometimes zany, approach to life, Katy naturally thought her younger.

"What year were you born?" Katy prodded, certain Reagan could not be telling the truth.

"Eighteen fifty-nine. How about yourself?"

The number on the tip of her tongue, Katy opened her mouth but caught herself just in time.

Reagan smiled, and Katy shook her head a little in mock despair. But all of this fun came to an end just moments later when pounding and lots of movement started on the other side of the wall. Reagan went over and swiftly began to empty the closet so she could shut the door, but there had been no missing the pained look on the bedridden woman's face.

❧ ❧ ❧

Reagan had never been so glad to sit down. Prior to speaking with Cash, she had been determined to clean the entire house *and* see to Katy's needs, but right now she saw that in no uncertain terms Cash had rescued her.

Katy was finally asleep. There was now a new passageway between Katy's room and her small bedroom. Katy had eaten and told Reagan she wanted to sleep, and Reagan had figured out that if she left the doors open, she could sit on the porch in a rocking chair and still hear if Katy called.

Her feet throbbing, even though she'd put them up on a small wooden bench, Reagan let her head fall against the high-backed rocking chair, her eyelids lowered just enough to find the horizon going to dusk. In that position, she was ready to think about the day.

Katy had received a surprising number of visitors, almost all food-bearing: the Bennetts; Max; Brenda and her daughters; two other cowhands; Pastor Ellis and Noelle; Lavinia from the general store; and Dr. Bruce again. Reagan had been introduced to the ones she did not know, but she did not visit with any of them or even stay close by. Katy still had things she needed from her little house, and finding them had taken some searching. Reagan also had her own room to clean and put together, wanting it done before nightfall. All had been accomplished, but by the time Reagan had started dinner, she'd been nearly cross-eyed with exhaustion, and the day wasn't done. Cash had turned out to be a marvelous help in the kitchen, but he'd gone to be with Katy while Reagan worked on the dishes. Never had Reagan been so glad to hear anyone say she wanted to sleep than when Katy made this announcement not long after the dishes were completed.

Reagan now shifted a little in her chair, thinking she should just head to bed, but before she could do that, her thoughts went back to the way Cash had dealt with the patient all day. Panic almost gripped the new caregiver. Cash's tenderness was still too much for Reagan to take in.

For the first time in a very long time, Reagan found herself asking her own heart why she could not let people love her. As a child she'd been starved for love and affection, but when she'd grown into womanhood and men were actually willing to marry her, her young heart had felt frozen in her chest.

And then today, having to watch the love between a pair who were like mother and son had been just as painful. *When*, Reagan asked herself, *had all love become a threat? When did I go from needing it so badly to being terrified by it? And where, if anywhere, does God fit into the whole picture?*

Not having answers to these questions was so confusing and painful to Reagan that she didn't even want to think about them, but one question would not go away, and that one was directed at God.

Do You really love people in a way they can survive?

The question repeated itself over and over again in Reagan's mind until she thought her head might burst. When she knew she couldn't think on it anymore, she rose wearily to her feet and made her way inside. A swift check on Katy told her that for the moment she was still off duty.

Trying not to long for the little house behind the Bennetts', Reagan took herself off to bed.

Twelve

DEAR SLATE, THE LETTER STARTED, the third one of the evening. *Katy has fallen and broken her hip. The doctor predicted that she will be laid up for about six weeks, but if she remains still during the healing process, she should be able to walk again with very little trouble.*

I won't try to go into details on how it happened, but there is a young woman from town who has moved in to help her. At first I didn't want her, but Katy was so glad to see her that I didn't feel I could send her away. I will keep you informed of Katy's progress, but if any business should bring you into the area, I know she would appreciate the visit.

Greet Duffy and the family and give my love to Libby. You're to take good care of her right now. God bless you all.

Love, Cash

Cash had deliberately kept all the letters short, but it had still been a lot of writing for one day. He would ride into town first thing in the morning and get them posted. Thoughts of town caused him to remember that, between him and Reagan, they would have to keep tabs on the pantry and other house supplies and needs. Max might be a help in that area, and he had offered to do all he could.

Cash sat up straight and thought about what a long day it had been. From his office he'd heard Reagan go onto the porch and now rose to check on her.

The porch was empty.

147

Lantern in hand, he made a swift check on Katy, found her sleeping, and knew it was time to close up for the night. He had no more gotten to her doorway, however, when she called Reagan's name.

"No, it's Cash," he whispered, going over to shut the closet door so Reagan would not be disturbed. "Do you need something?" he asked, approaching the bed.

"No. What time is it?"

Cash told her as he sat down.

"Why aren't you in bed?" she wished to know, but her voice was calm.

"I was just headed up."

"Good. You need your rest."

"I just finished letters to the family, letting them know you'd been hurt."

"You didn't have to do that."

"How do you figure?"

Katy had no reply. She knew very well that if she said anything, he would only remind her of what she would have done if the situation had been reversed.

"Cash?" she asked quietly.

"Yeah."

"Do you pray for me?"

"Yes, I do. What made you ask that?"

"Do you think God let this happen because I've sinned?"

"Not specifically, I don't, but at some point we all have to face the fact that we sin. If the fall you took helps you to do that, then I would say that was good."

"So you don't think I'm being punished?"

"No, but you know how I feel about God getting your attention, Katy. I think you've needed Him for a long time."

"What if it's too late?"

"I don't believe that, and God's Word doesn't support that idea either."

Again Katy had no reply. Cash wasn't sure what he should add or say, so he opted just to pray this time so that she could hear.

"Father in heaven," he began quietly, "thank You for Katy. She means so much to me. I ask You to help her heal well so she can be on her feet again, but even more than her body, Lord, I know her heart needs to be healed of sin, like mine did before I found You. Bless Katy this night and in the days to come. Thank You that Reagan could be here to help. Help us all to sleep so we can work hard tomorrow. In Your name I pray. Amen."

Cash stood, bent over the bedridden woman, and kissed her brow.

"Good night, Kate."

"Good night, Cash."

Cash opened the closet door again and then made his way from the room and up the stairway, thinking that his own bed was never going to feel so good. And he was right. Much as he was thankful for an opportunity to pray with Katy, knowing she was thinking about God, he could not stay awake to give it much contemplation.

❧ ❧ ❧

"Did I see Reagan at the church party?" Brenda asked of her husband the morning after he arrived home. He had surprised her by coming in very late on Thursday night when she hadn't expected him until Friday.

"I don't know," Brad said. "Did you?"

"I thought I did. Did you happen to notice her?"

Brad smiled, his eyes flirting with hers.

"You're the only woman I notice."

Brenda shook her head. "When I start believing that, Bradley Johns, it'll be a cold day in August."

Brad only laughed.

"Why did you want to know?"

"Because I'll go over and give Reagan a break with Katy if she wants to attend church."

"It's only been a few days, Bren," he said out of genuine concern for his wife's current condition. "I mean, it's a nice thought, but you're tired yourself these days."

"Nevertheless..." she said pointedly, hands going to her waist. Brad raised his own hands in surrender.

"You do whatever you think is best. I'll be talking to Cash about what he wants done on the ranch, but if you want to help out on Sunday, I'll watch the girls."

Smiling with pleasure, Brenda slipped her arms around his neck and kissed him. Brad found himself rather glad he'd agreed.

❧ ❧ ❧

"How does Doc say she's doing?" Brad asked of Cash later that same morning.

"He says she'll be all right if she keeps still."

Brad's brows rose.

"I know," Cash said, having read the foreman's mind. "We're doing all we can."

"What can I do?"

"Take care of the ranch."

Brad nodded, not surprised, and more than willing and capable. The foreman was about to ask some detailed questions when Reagan came through the kitchen door, set the tray down very hard on the table, and turned to both men, eyes blazing.

"There is *nothing* wrong with this food."

"Did Katy say there was?"

Reagan's voice grew tight with sarcasm.

"This isn't the way she bakes her bread. She likes a firmer loaf."

With a hand to his employer's arm, Brad went on his way. Cash waved him off and then went to the tray.

"Is this the same bread that I had for breakfast?"

"Yes, it is."

"I thought it tasted fine, very good even."

"But my patient doesn't."

Cash nodded, looking down into her flushed face. She was awfully easy on the eyes, especially when the color was high in her cheeks.

"I'll tell you what, Reagan," he said quickly to get his mind back on the business at hand. "When she gets hungry enough, she'll eat. Just give her a little time."

Reagan sighed. "The last thing you need me to do is get upset at her." She glanced up at him. "If I'm not careful, you'll have two unreasonable females on your hands."

Cash's smile seemed to say *I'm not too worried about it.*

"You don't upset easily, do you, Cash?" Reagan couldn't help but ask.

"Not as a rule."

"How have the two of you worked together all these years?"

Cash smiled again but didn't answer.

"Well, I'll try again." Reagan picked up the tray and went back to work. Cash told her he'd be in the office and left her on her own.

Reagan heard him go and thought that if she wasn't careful she could become very depressed. She was a people person. She liked to take care of things, and under all her bravado was pleased when folks were happy. Katy's dislike of the bread she made every day was a little hard to take.

But she still has to eat, and you've got to feed her.

This little pep talk over, Reagan started on another meal.

❧ ❧ ❧

"Cash," Brenda called when she spotted him outside. Both of her girls were healthy again and back in school.

Brenda had appreciated her husband's concern for her, but she was feeling fine and very much wanted to help Katy, who had helped them out so many times in the past.

"How are you, Brenda?" Cash asked as the two covered the distance and met between the two houses.

"I'm doing well. How's Katy this morning?"

"I think she's already tired of that bed. She wasn't too happy with what was on her breakfast tray, so Reagan was going to try again."

"I'm glad I caught you then, because I wanted to tell you that if you and Reagan want to go to church on Sunday morning, I'll stay with Katy."

"That would be great, Brenda. Thank you," Cash said with genuine relief. He had been thinking on that very problem as he wondered whether he should offer a wagon to Reagan so she could attend or simply go without her. This solution allowed him to go no matter what she wanted. "I'll let her know of the offer, and one of us will get back to you."

"All right. Or if Reagan just needs some time off, please come and tell me, Cash. Brad is rather fussy about me right now, but I'm sure I could give Reagan a half day's break with no problem, especially if the girls are home from school. They can always cheer Katy up."

"Thank you, Brenda. How are the girls, by the way?"

"Doing well. Robin's cold was nothing serious. I think she might have been a little worked up about her father's trip."

Cash smiled in compassion, albeit a bit distractedly, and Brenda said goodbye, sensing his need to get back to work.

"Thanks again, Brenda."

"You're welcome."

Cash moved to go on his way but ended up just walking back to the house. He couldn't remember the last time he'd had so much on his mind. He'd been headed somewhere when Brenda stopped him, and right now he couldn't recall what his destination had been. It didn't help to walk in the front door and hear Katy yelling. Cash figured that Reagan was tied up somewhere, so he rushed to her aid.

To his surprise and dismay, Reagan was standing at the foot of the bed, taking Katy's ill humor with a placid face.

"What in the world, Katy?" Cash began.

"She won't do it!" Katy nearly shouted. She was puce in color, her eyes bulging with rage. She looked as if her heart could fail at any moment. "I'm telling her she has to start in the office, and she won't go!"

"Please calm down," Cash began, trying not to think about how many weeks they had to go.

"But she won't listen. Did you hire her to take care of things or not?"

Cash knew right then that all those years of ignoring Katy's moods had been a mistake. He had let Katy have run of the house—much as his mother had—and now it was coming around to haunt him. He had never wanted to be too hard on her when she bossed him and everyone else. Indeed, it was something of a joke around the ranch, even with the woman herself, but now he could see that he'd not done any of them favors by letting it continue.

If he hadn't been afraid she might try to get out of that bed and hurt herself worse in the process, Cash might have called Reagan from the room and left Katy to stew in her own juices. Right now he didn't want to take the chance.

"Please explain to me exactly what you want Reagan to do."

"Your office!"

Cash paused and nearly shook his head. Katy had been on the verge of hysterics over his office not getting cleaned? Knowing that he had to get more sleep this night, Cash worked to question her calmly.

"What about my office?"

"It's got to be cleaned! She has to go over every shelf and book."

Cash turned to Reagan, whose eyes gave nothing away but whose face was pale.

"And is there a reason you don't want to do that?"

"You said that Katy's needs came first, and she still hasn't eaten a thing today." Reagan gestured rather helplessly with her hands. "That and the fact you've been trying to work in there."

With sudden clarity of thought, Cash turned stern eyes to Katy and knew that he was long overdue in explaining some things to his housekeeper.

"What gives you the right to put us all through this?"

Katy blinked in surprise. Cash's voice was utterly normal, but his words were astounding.

"Reagan comes out with her bicycle to give you a good time, you get hurt, and now you somehow think you have the right to make all of us fit into your agenda. I couldn't be more sorry that you got hurt, Katy. I wish it had been me. But it hasn't even been 48 hours, and you're doing everything in your power to make us all miserable."

Katy was still silent with shock.

"If you don't want anything to eat, that's fine, but Reagan isn't here to listen to you rant and rave. From now on, whatever you tell her to do, she'll do, even if you lie there and starve, but not once will you raise your voice to her or be disrespectful in any way. Do I make myself clear?"

The housekeeper was too shocked to answer, and Cash's mouth tightened in anger.

"I said, do I make myself clear?"

Katy could only nod.

Cash turned to Reagan now, not caring that it was right in front of Katy.

"You're here, Reagan, because you feel guilty. You're here because you think this is all your fault, and I understand and appreciate that, but no one should have to put up with what Katy is handing out. I'll understand if you want to move back to town. I'll even take you. Just say the word, and I'll find someone else."

"No, it's all right," Reagan responded, swiftly shaking her head. It had been a terrible scene to witness, and she just wanted to get away and be alone with her thoughts, but she made herself stay and listen. After all, this was her fault. "I'll be all right. As soon as you're done in your office, I'll start in there."

"Fine. I'm headed to the barn, so you go right ahead."

Cash left without another word.

Reagan was left alone with the bedridden woman.

"I'll just be across the way in the office, Katy. Call if you need me."

Still feeling very awkward about the entire scene, Reagan had not actually looked Katy in the eye as she said this, so she didn't notice whether the other woman nodded or acknowledged her in the least. Either way she was glad to escape. She was so tense she thought she might burst.

Dusting cloths and broom in hand, Reagan entered Cash's office a few minutes later and, at a first glance, could not find a speck of dust. Nevertheless, she got to work, thinking that when she was done, the room would never have been so clean.

❧ ❧ ❧

Cash finally remembered what he'd needed to do in the barn, but when he got there, he didn't start to work. Familiar sights and smells surrounding him, Cash stood and prayed.

Do I go back and apologize for speaking to her as I never have before or for letting her have her way for so long? Or do I let it go and hope I haven't ruined the relationship for all time? I don't know what to do, Father. I said what needed to be said. Katy needed to hear it, but she's not used to that from me. I'm not going to let her lie there and pout, and I can't let her slowly tear Reagan apart.

Cash tried to think. He couldn't be certain, but it seemed to him that Reagan was looking very tired. And why wouldn't she? Her hours at the hotel had been from morning into the early afternoon. Here she was on duty almost 24 hours a day.

After a few more minutes in prayer, Cash opted not to say anything else to Katy about the incident. When he finished in the barn, he would return to the house and carry on business as usual. He wasn't certain what to expect from Katy, and he was willing to allow her to deal with this in her own way, but only as long as the rest of them could still stand to live with her.

❧ ❧ ❧

Reagan's back hurt a little—there had been a lot of books to move—but the office looked great. She had polished, dusted, and swept, even going so far as to wash the inside panes on the windows. Now on her way out the door, Reagan took a moment to study a portrait on the wall.

A man and woman looked back at her. The woman had Cash Rawlings' eyes, and Reagan didn't have a hard time figuring out who they were. Neither one smiled, but Reagan thought that to have had a son as caring as Cash, they must be very kind.

"Reagan," Cash said as he came through the door, "I'm glad I caught you..." He started again but stopped talking without warning.

Reagan watched him walk around the room, not touching anything but smiling with pleasure at the job she'd done. He turned to face her when he was finally behind his desk.

"The office looks great. Thank you."

"You're welcome," she said with a smile, glad she could please someone.

"Those are my parents, by the way."

Reagan's eyes went back to the frame.

"I figured as much. You have your mother's eyes."

"So I've been told," Cash said as he moved to join her by the picture.

"What are their names?"

"Charles Sr. and Virginia Rawlings."

"Who's Junior?"

"I am."

Reagan frowned up at him.

"'Cash' was all the better my brothers could manage, and the name just stuck."

"How many siblings do you have?"

"Two brothers, both younger. In fact, if you look at my father, you'll just about see an older version of Dakota."

"Dakota? That's an unusual name."

"It is, but it fits him."

Reagan looked back at the portrait, and Cash studied her. Again he found himself feeling rather drawn to her.

"Reagan's not all that common either."

"No," she said with a smile, "but I think it fits me too."

"It does," Cash had to agree. "What's your middle name, by the way?"

"Reagan."

Cash laughed. "Okay, what's your first name?"

"Eileen."

"Eileen Reagan Sullivan?"

"That's it. A fine Irish girl must have a fine Irish name," she told him, brogue in place.

Cash was delighted and wished she'd do it again.

"Who were you quoting? Your father?"

"That's the one. Mother got away with Reagan as a middle name only because it was her maiden name."

"How did you get away with not going by Eileen?"

"I didn't—not around my father at least."

"Why didn't you like Eileen? It's a beautiful name."

"It is, but I wanted the connection to my mother."

Cash saw the sadness in her face and was certain he knew why.

"Did she die, Reagan?"

"No, she left my father and me not long after my ninth birthday." Reagan looked up at him, her look almost daring him to pity her. "My father finished drinking himself to death three years later."

"I'm sorry."

"I'm not," she stated flatly. "After that, there was no one to stop me from being Reagan."

Cash thought it was the kind of comment she would exit on, but she stayed right where she was, her face still set.

"Before I forget," Cash said, changing the subject as tactfully as he could manage and walking back to the desk to pick up an envelope, "I have your pay ready. You can expect it every Friday."

"Pay?" Reagan asked as she moved to the desk and took the packet from his outstretched hand. She looked inside, not believing him until she saw the bills. She set the envelope back down.

"You're not paying me."

"Says who?"

"Says me."

Cash laughed. "Let's get something straight right now, Reagan Sullivan. I didn't hire you in the same way I did my other employees, but you've got yourself a job."

She began to shake her head, and Cash's brows rose.

"Don't even think about saying no to this, Reagan." He handed the money packet to her again. "You won't win."

Now Reagan's brows elevated.

"We'll just see about that, Mr. Rawlings."

Cash smiled at her tone.

"I'm not trying to play power games with you, Miss Sullivan. It's just that I'm a businessman with a ranch to run, and you are one of my employees. It's no more complicated than that. You're doing your job, and I'm paying you for it."

"But you wouldn't even need me if I hadn't—" Reagan began, but Cash wasn't listening. She could see that by his face.

"Take the money, Reagan," Cash stated for the last time, not really caring if he sounded high-handed. "I won't hear of anything else."

Cash went to his desk chair then, and Reagan knew the conversation was over. She did leave with the money as she exited the office, but even as she cleaned up so she could check on Katy, she was thinking of ways to get around her new boss's having to pay her.

Thirteen

"I COMPLETELY FORGOT TO TELL YOU something yesterday, Reagan." Cash started Saturday morning with these words.

"What's that?"

"Brenda says she'll stay with Katy while we go to church."

There was no mistaking the relief on her face.

"Did she really?"

"Yes. I usually leave around 9:20 if that will work for you."

"That would be fine," she said, but then hesitated. "Should I ask Katy?"

Cash shook his head no. "Has she spoken to you yet?"

"No. She had a good meal last night and again this morning—better than she has eaten—but other than thanking me, she hasn't said two words."

Cash's unconscious sigh told of the pain he was feeling. Katy hadn't spoken to him either.

"Just leave her be," he finally said. "You can't read her mind, so unless she asks for something, let her alone."

"I'll work on the house some more and check on her often."

"Good."

And they both discovered that it *was* good. Cash ate his breakfast, and Reagan went to work on Katy's regular chores. That it was Saturday and she should have gone to town for supplies was lost on her. She dusted, swept, and started the meat for dinner, all the while checking on Katy at regular intervals.

Cash went about his day as well. As usual on a Saturday night, the boys would be done a little early so they could head into town with their pay, and his own schedule was one he liked to keep monitored so that he was fresh for Sunday morning.

He worked in his office for a time and then went to check the livestock in the barn. It didn't take long, and as he made his way back to the house, the Bennetts' wagon came up the drive. He stopped, a big smile on his face, as it drew abreast of him.

"Well, hello," he greeted Holly and all three of the kids, even as he lifted Elly so he could swing her down from the wagon bed. Jonah scrambled behind his sister.

"Hello, Cash. I hope you don't mind the intrusion, but I have two little people who need to see Reagan."

"I don't mind at all, and she's going to be very pleased. Here, let me get Alisa."

The baby smiled at him as soon as she was in his arms, and Cash kissed her soft, pudgy cheek.

"How is Katy doing?" Holly asked after Cash had given her a hand down.

"She's having a pretty hard time with it all, I would say. How are things in town?"

"There she is!" Elly suddenly cried before Holly could answer, and both adults turned to see Reagan come out the front door. From across the yard they could hear Reagan laugh as Elly and Jonah ran to hug her. The three sat down on the front porch steps together, heads close as they snuggled and talked.

Cash looked back at his guest just as Alisa reached for her mother.

"And you, Cash Rawlings," Holly said as she settled Alisa on her hip, her voice low to give them privacy. "How are you doing?"

Cash smiled, knowing she could read him well after all these years.

"I think I'm still surprised that it happened at all. I keep expecting to see Kate in the kitchen and bustling through the house, but it's Reagan."

"How is Reagan doing? Is it dreadfully uncomfortable?"

"Actually, it's not. She's very competent, and she works quietly and effectively. Compared to Katy's bossing me around, the place is silent."

"So you're not sorry she came?"

"I was at first. I didn't think I could manage it, but she did so well with Katy that I didn't feel I had a choice." Cash laughed a little. "Katy's not even speaking to us right now, but Reagan just keeps on."

Holly's face told him she sympathized.

"We're praying for you, Cash."

"I can tell. I'm getting very little sleep, and it's probably the only way I'm holding up. But tell me, why did you visit when we'll see you tomorrow?"

"We weren't sure if Reagan would come."

"She's planning on it," Cash was glad to tell her. "Brenda Johns is going to fill in for her. You should have seen Reagan's face when I gave her the option."

"Relieved?"

"Definitely. I'm not certain if she's coming because she wants to be in church or get away from Katy, but either way, she's coming."

"I'm glad."

Up on the porch, Reagan was glad too. She had missed the children so much, and she thought if she had to go another hour with Katy's silent treatment she just might scream. She had just about decided to take a spin on her bike when she looked out the window and saw the children.

"How is school?" she asked them.

"It's good. We still like it."

"But we miss you, Reagan," Jonah told her. "And not just for rides on the bicycle."

Reagan laughed and hugged him a little closer. She thought about taking them in to see Katy, but if that woman was still pouting, the children would be hurt by her actions and wouldn't understand the reason.

"You know what?" Reagan said as she stood, taking the kids' hands in hers. "I need to see that baby."

Holly and Reagan hugged when the groups joined, and as everyone had come to expect, Alisa had a smile for whoever was holding her.

"I've missed you, Alisa," Reagan told her softly, and not for the first time Holly was struck by the fact that this woman did not want a husband and family. It didn't make sense to her.

The baby only smiled at Reagan and reached for her face.

"Is Katy up to company?" Holly asked.

Cash's and Reagan's eyes met. Reagan shrugged, and Cash nodded in decision.

"Why don't I just go in and check with her?"

Cash didn't wait for anyone to acknowledge his idea but headed to see his housekeeper, a few things on his mind. Without preamble he stepped into her room and began. "Holly Bennett and the children are here to see you. Do you want visitors?"

Katy's eyes swung to Cash and then away. The cowboy stood where he was for a full minute, but the prone woman did not look back at him.

"I'm not going to put up with this much longer, Kate."

"What are you going to do about it?" she shot right back, her eyes turning to him and showing her frustration.

Cash shook his head. "Is that what this is about, Katy? Not speaking to the people who are bending over backward to help you is your way of having a say?" He shook his head again in very real regret. "You ought to be ashamed."

Not giving her any time to reply, he turned for the door.

"Cash!" she called to him.

That man stopped and looked back, his brows raised in question.

"Please tell them to come in."

"I'll get them right now," he said, all rebuke gone.

Standing in her little room down the back hall where she'd dashed to get a small music box to show the children, Reagan stood very still, having heard a good bit of the exchange. Fresh waves of something foreign and frightening came over her, and she was again filled with wonder over this man's care of his injured housekeeper.

"Hello, Katy," Reagan heard Holly saying. She realized she'd been missing for some minutes. She made her way around through the kitchen, going slowly to give herself time to settle down.

❧ ❧ ❧

"And then what did you do?" Katy was saying just as Reagan entered the room.

"We ran a race around the schoolhouse, and Elly almost won!" Jonah filled her in.

"How did you do?"

"I was first after all the big kids."

A fond light entered Katy's eyes, and unbeknownst to her, both Cash and Reagan knew comfort at the sight of it.

"Reagan," Katy suddenly said, "there's a tin of salty peanuts in that cupboard over the large counter. Go and get some of those for the children, will you?"

"Coming right up."

What followed was a wonderful half hour. Katy spoke with some of her usual brusqueness, but all the remarks were kind with very few orders given, and more than one sentence was directed to Cash or Reagan. By the time Holly and the children headed back to town, things seemed to have righted themselves.

"I've got a roast in the oven, Katy," Reagan popped in to say after having seen the guests off and claiming four more hugs. "I'll check on it and then be back."

"That little Jonah is a corker and a half."

"Yes, he is. He can't wait to have legs long enough to ride—" Reagan cut off, but it was too late. Katy knew just what she was going to say.

"Now that's enough of that, Reagan Sullivan. We'll have no bad feelings on this. What's done is done!"

Reagan only nodded and slipped from the room, but she was distracted as she checked the meat and put some vegetables into a pot. She was getting ready to make gravy when Cash came on the scene.

"How was she after they left?"

"Back to herself, only nicer."

"Good."

Reagan turned fully to him.

"How did you convince her to see them?"

"I reminded her of all that's being done for her, and it seems to have softened her."

Reagan nodded. "When does the doctor come again?"

"I'm not sure. Do you think he's needed?"

"By Katy, yes. She needs to have hope that her hip is coming along and this whole thing will come to an end."

"Maybe I'll pop in tomorrow after church and let him know that she could use a visit."

Cash went back to work then, this time in his office, and Reagan went back to the meal. As she had come to expect, fatigue hit her at this time every day, but she kept on. At least her patient was speaking to her. Reagan found that made all the difference in the world.

❧ ❧ ❧

Katy listened for the wagon wheels to pull away on Sunday morning but could hear nothing. Brenda had brought the girls with her, and they were both eager to visit. Utter sadness filled Katy over the loss of her mobility. Many were the times these girls had come to the back door and she had had cookies for them. Now she lay in bed, more helpless than a baby. Never had she been so frustrated. Her good sense had told her to take a quick ride on that bike and be done, but she had wanted to show off for Cash.

For a moment Katy's eyes closed on his memory. Prior to her accident, he had never spoken harshly to her, but he was right, she needed to be shamed. Giving Reagan a hard time when she had quit her job to come and help and then repaying her with orders and anger was simply not to be tolerated. Katy didn't know what had come over her.

"All right, girls," Brenda said, entering with a fresh pitcher of water. "You've talked enough. Go see how your father is doing and if he's still in bed, tell him it's late."

"'Bye, girls," Katy called to them as they hurried away.

"I forgot how much they talk. I hope they didn't wear you out."

Katy only smiled, but it did the trick. Brenda assumed she was tired and left her on her own, but in truth, the older woman just needed time to think. For a woman who only darkened the door of the church out of guilt, she was certainly having a strange reaction to not being able to attend this morning. It wasn't guilt that filled her right now but longing. She could hear Brenda moving around not far outside the door, sounding as though she might be headed back her way, but still Katy wanted to pray.

I've spent so much time trying not to think about You that I don't know how to do this. Cash says You're there for everyone, even sinners, and I can see now that I am. She paused, her breathing coming hard as she tried to find the words to say what was in her heart, feeling more fear than she had been prepared for. *I think I might need to know more about this before I can do anything, but if You'll help me to get out of this bed, I'll try to learn about You and not run away anymore.*

Almost on that exact note, Brenda reentered the room. Had Cash been home, Katy would have asked for him, but he had only just left. She made herself lie still, even as Brenda moved quietly around the room, hoping she could fall asleep and not have to think about it when there was no one there to help her.

⚜ ⚜ ⚜

"Is God always in control?" Pastor Ellis asked on Sunday morning. "I mean, constantly, 100 percent of the time? Or is He a God who decided one day to wind up the universe, stand back, arms crossed over His chest, and watch to see what happened?"

Reagan's mouth opened a little. That was exactly the way her father had believed. When she was a child, he had said time and again that God might have created things, but He was not a part of the everyday dealings of humans.

He just wound up the universe and let it run. And who could blame Him? That's what I would do if I were God. I wouldn't want to be bothered with humans any longer than I had to.

"Do you think God really cares about the people He's created?" Pastor Ellis now queried. "The answer to that question might tell you about your view of God. Is He a sovereign ruler who enjoys seeing His creatures suffer, or is He a sovereign ruler who's there to love and aid His people in hard times? Maybe He's a God who isn't completely in control. Maybe He loves His creation, but He can't actually help it."

Reagan watched Pastor Ellis smile.

"I'd like to read to you from the book of Jeremiah. Don't turn there. Just let yourself listen for a moment. This is Jeremiah 32:17-19, and then verse 27. Just listen now to some of my favorite verses in all of Scripture.

"'Ah, Lord God! Behold, thou hast made the heaven and the earth by thy great power and stretched out arm, and there is nothing too hard for thee. Thou showest lovingkindness unto thousands, and recompensest the iniquity of the fathers into the bosom of their children after them; the Great, the Mighty God, the Lord of hosts, is his name, great in counsel, and mighty in work. For thine eyes are open upon all the ways of the sons of men, to give every one according to his ways, and according to the fruit of his doings.'

"Now to verse 27: 'Behold, I am the Lord, the God of all flesh. Is there anything too hard for me?'

"If you'll open your Bibles to the last chapter of the book of Job, I'd like to read to you again, but this time I want you to follow along. Job had been through so much, but the Word says he trusted God through it all. If you still doubt God's ability to be in control, follow along as I read from the first few verses of Job 42."

Not until that moment did Reagan realize she'd left the Bible Holly had loaned her in the little house. She searched around, hoping someone had left a Bible nearby, but saw that Cash already had his open and was holding it between them.

Reagan smiled at him; she had not even remembered he was there but now leaned a little to read along, even as the pastor began.

"'Then Job answered the Lord, and said, I know that thou canst do everything, and that no thought can be withheld from thee.' Now skip down to verse 12. 'So the Lord blessed the latter end of Job more than his beginning, for he had fourteen thousand sheep, and six thousand camels, and a thousand yoke of oxen, and a thousand she-asses. He had also seven sons and three daughters.' Now to verse 15: 'And in all the land were no women found so fair as the daughters of Job, and their father gave them inheritance among their brethren. After this lived Job an hundred and forty years, and saw his sons, and his sons' sons, even four generations. So Job died, being old and full of days.'"

Again the pastor smiled at the congregation. "You might be tempted to say that was the least God could do. After all, He allowed Satan to touch Job's life. But don't miss the point I'm trying to make: God is powerful, loving, and able. He did not sit back once He created us, happy to just watch us struggling to survive. Even today He's active and very much a part of any life that will allow Him room.

"But maybe you don't know what I'm talking about. Maybe you've never experienced what a personal God we have. Don't wait another day to find out. Don't be uncertain about tomorrow ever again. Don't be frightened of death for one more moment.

"I want you to bow your heads right now—no one looking around so all have privacy. This is not something I do very often, but all week I've felt a great burden to share this with you. Some of you don't know me very well, so you might not come to me or anyone else in this church, but you might be desperate to settle this issue between yourself and God. If you are, then I would urge you to pray this prayer with me. Just say the words in your heart after I say them. If you mean them, God will save you. You'll be a new believer in Jesus Christ.

"Just pray like this," Pastor Ellis continued, and then proceeded very slowly. "Father in heaven, I know I am a sinner. I know I am lost without You, but You sent Your Son to die for my sins, and I want to believe on You right now. I know You are willing and able to save me, and at this time I wish for Your salvation, so I can live my life for You.

"Dear friend," the pastor started, but needed to add, "let's keep our eyes closed for just a moment more. Dear friend, if you prayed that prayer with me, you are a new creature in Christ, a new believer. You don't need to tell me about it, but I would urge you to tell someone, and if you do tell me, I have a list of verses from God's Word that will help you understand what you've done and help you grow.

"We're just going to have a moment of silent prayer right now. I won't keep you too much longer, but let us just be quiet a moment to give all of our hearts some time to think."

Another minute passed, this time in silence, and finally Pastor Ellis closed the prayer with a few words. He then invited the congregation to stand and join him in a closing song.

"Is it really that simple?" Reagan turned to Cash and whispered. Her eyes were huge. She had not even made a pretense of reaching for the hymnbook or attempting to stand. All she could think about was the prayer she had just prayed. She had not planned to, but suddenly she'd wanted to so much that she ached. To her amazement, the ache was gone.

"Yes, Reagan, it is," Cash confirmed, keeping his seat as well, glad they were in one of the last pews.

"But there's so much I don't know," she told him, feeling slightly overwhelmed.

"That comes in time. When a person truly believes, he's new in Christ. The desire to learn fills him because God's Spirit now indwells him and can teach him all about the Word."

"You mean the Bible."

"Yes. A desire to know more about the Lord and live for Him is one of the ways we know that true salvation happened. It doesn't mean we never sin again, but our attitude is changed about sin, and we don't want to live in it anymore."

Reagan bit her lip just before she admitted, "I prayed the prayer."

Cash's smile was as warm as a spring day. "Did you, Reagan?"

She nodded rather helplessly.

"I hadn't planned to—not really—but suddenly my heart wanted to so badly. He said I would never have to fear again, and he said I could get this settled between God and me right now, and I wanted that."

"That sounds like great news, Reagan," Cash said sincerely. The congregation was milling around, but neither one noticed. "Our God is a saving God, and the benefits of knowing Him are without measure."

"That's the way Holly has talked."

"And she's right. Tell me something, Reagan; what happened to your fear of someone else being in control?"

"What do you mean?"

Cash looked her in the eye. "Listen to me, Reagan. I do not want to put a damper on your prayer in any way, but there is something we all have to understand. We need to understand who we are accepting when we are saved. God is huge, and He is a righteously jealous God. He does not want to share us. This needs to be a whole-heart experience for you, or me, or anyone who desires that relationship. Does that make sense?"

Reagan nodded.

"Your life will be taking a new direction. You won't be living for self, but for God. It's a wonderful life—there is none better—but I want to be sure you understand. I wouldn't want you to be confused about that."

Reagan stared at him for a moment and then began without warning: "There was a girl I knew in New York. She worked with me at the factory, and I was there on her first day. I remember her hands were bleeding by the time we broke for lunch. She'd obviously never worked a day in her life. Some of the girls asked her about it, but she didn't say very much."

Cash was hanging on every word, his face intent.

"Over time Veronica and I talked. I found out that she was from one of the wealthiest families in the city. She didn't want all the girls to know since they would never have understood. They would never have grasped why she would walk away from all that money to work like a dog in the factory, but she summed it up for me in a few words. She said she couldn't take the responsibility anymore."

Knowing that Reagan understood him so clearly caused Cash's heart to thunder in his chest.

"That's it, isn't it, Cash? My father, God, is the wealthiest man in the city, and I've got to act as though I belong to Him."

"Yes, Reagan, but our God doesn't leave us alone to do that. Just as Pastor said, He doesn't wind us up and let us go. He helps us every step of the way. He makes the changes in us. His love makes it worth living for Him—as you put it, 'acting like we belong to Him.'"

Reagan's heart and mind were so full she didn't know what to do or think. She sat quietly, trying to pray, but all she could do was express her gratitude.

"Do you thank God for saving you, Cash?" Reagan suddenly asked.

"Not as often as I should," he admitted. "I think that might be something I should thank Him for all day."

"He really does save, doesn't He?"

"Yes, He does," Cash agreed, that warm smile back in place. "When I first came to Christ, I had times when I didn't think it was real, but there was no denying the changes going on inside of me. God has a way of affirming us when we most need it."

"You weren't saved as a child?"

"No. I've only been saved for about five years."

"So you know what I'm feeling?"

Cash could only laugh at her look of wonder.

"Am I interrupting?" a voice cut in, and both turned to see Holly Bennett had come to stand just behind the pew where they sat.

Reagan rose to her feet, her face alight with wonder as she faced her friend.

"Oh, Holly," the younger woman whispered. "I'm so glad you came over. I have something wonderful to tell you."

Fourteen

"I DON'T HAVE TO GET MARRIED NOW, do I, Holly?" Reagan asked suddenly. She had talked with Russell and then Pastor Ellis, and now Holly was walking her to the wagon.

"What has you so worried on that issue, Reagan?"

The young woman sighed. "I don't know exactly, but the whole idea repels me. I can see how Russell loves you, but it's just not something I want."

"What if a man loved *you*?"

Reagan shook her head no.

"What if you loved a man?"

Reagan looked surprised.

"I've never been in love," she admitted, "but I've seen it happen and don't think it's for me."

Holly knew she should not debate this with her. As far as she knew, there was no command in Scripture that all women and men must find spouses. And Holly couldn't help but think that a person's preference was valid. At the same time, there was a correct way to view marriage, an institution God Himself created.

"You're worrying about this, Reagan, and there's no need. If God has marriage for you, He'll prepare your heart. Don't get in the habit of telling Him what He can and cannot do, and also don't fall into the sin pattern of worrying over what He *might* do."

This said, Holly smiled at her, and Reagan relaxed. She hugged the older woman and thanked her.

"I certainly have a lot to learn."

"You're not alone in that."

"Thank you, Holly. Thank you for everything."

"You're welcome. And don't give the little house another thought. I keep a close eye on it, and it's waiting for you whenever Katy's back on her feet."

The women hugged again before the men showed up and they parted. Once in the wagon, Russell told the children what had transpired, and they were very pleased. Elly, however, had a question.

"Will one of the men marry Reagan now?"

This wasn't an unusual question for a child in this situation who had watched it happen in the church family several times before.

"Reagan doesn't wish to be married," Holly told her gently. "So we'd probably better not watch for that."

But as soon as they arrived home and Russell had a moment alone with Holly, he returned to the subject.

"Maybe she won't feel that way after today."

"Yes, she will," Holly informed him. "She brought it up to me the moment we were alone."

"Did she really?" Russell asked, clearly surprised.

"Yes. I told her not to panic. But if the men in the congregation are smart, they'll keep their distance, because the lady is not in the market for a mate."

When Russell and Holly took so long, Jonah came looking for them, so they dropped the subject again. But for some reason, it lingered in the minds of both adults.

¾ ¾ ¾

By the time Reagan had talked with Holly, Russell, Pastor Ellis, and Holly again, and then she and Cash had asked the doctor to visit, they did not return to the ranch

until quite late. Brenda met them at the door, something
that caused momentary alarm, but all fear melted in the
light of her smile.

"How did it go?" Cash asked.

"Just fine. She was a little tired, I think, but we got along
just great."

"Thank you, Brenda," Reagan told her sincerely.

"Anytime, Reagan. Just let me know."

"Next Sunday?" Reagan said, a lilt in her voice.

"I'll plan on it."

Cash saw Brenda on her way and then went to check on
Katy. Reagan was already in the room.

"Cash," Katy said as soon as she saw him, her voice
urgent. "I need to speak with you."

"All right."

As he brought the chair close, Reagan bowed out with a
few words.

"I'll be in the kitchen working on Sunday dinner."

"Thank you, Reagan," acknowledged Cash before he
turned back to Katy, who surprised him by reaching for his
hand.

"I did something," she said, her eyes anxious as they
searched his.

"Okay."

"I made a deal with God."

Cash was surprised and didn't bother to hide it. "What
kind of deal?"

"I told Him if He'll let me get out of this bed, I won't run
from Him anymore."

Tenderness filled the rancher's heart. With his free hand,
he reached over and carefully smoothed the iron-colored
hair from Katy's brow.

"And tell me what you'll do with God if you never get
out of this bed?"

Her hand tightened on his. "Do you think He would do
that to me?"

"Not *to* you, Katy, but maybe *for* you."

Her brow deeply furrowed with confusion, she asked, "How could that be?"

"I can't say that I know God's mind on this matter, Kate, but maybe you've been running so long that this was His way to slow you down and get your attention. Maybe by staying in this bed, you can grow to be more help than you ever dreamed of."

All she could do was ask again, "How can that be?"

"Ask me what I want, Katy." Cash bent closer to her face to command in tender urgency. "Ask me whether I want clean clothes and a hot meal or to have you with me in eternity?"

For only the second time in his life—the incidents within a week of each other—Cash watched Katy cry. He didn't know when he'd felt so helpless, but he moved gently and put his arms around her. This act was not a first, but it had been years since he'd felt welcome to help her.

"I don't know what to do!" she finally wailed. "I thought this was God punishing me, but if I'm going to be punished, why did He send His Son to die?"

Cash smiled amid Katy's pain.

"You've been listening in church after all, Katy."

She sniffed and tried to calm herself, but it was a struggle.

"I'm going to get Reagan," Cash told her.

"Why?"

"Because something happened to her this morning, and she needs to tell you about it. Will you let me get her?"

Katy nodded, and Cash pressed his handkerchief into her hands before he left. Seconds later he was in the kitchen.

"Reagan, would you mind coming in and telling Katy about your decision this morning?"

"No, not at all," Reagan said right away but then hesitated. "She looked so glad to see you when you came in. I could tell something was bothering her."

"Yes, it is, and I think it would help to hear about this morning."

Reagan put aside the food she was working on, wiped her hands clean, and preceded Cash as he politely waited to follow.

"Take the chair, Reagan," Cash directed as soon as they were in the housekeeper's room.

"What happened this morning, Reagan?" Katy asked the moment she sat down.

Reagan could see that she'd been weeping and hoped she could explain this thing that was almost too huge to take in.

"I prayed to receive salvation from God. The pastor prayed, and I prayed with him."

"Why, Reagan?" Katy asked almost desperately. "Why now? Why today?"

Reagan shook her head a little. "I hadn't really planned on hearing what I did this morning, Katy, but Pastor Ellis said something my father used to claim. It was about God not being involved in people's lives. But Pastor showed us how involved He really was and is, and I knew a spark of hope for the first time. I've been asking myself if it could be true. I've been wondering if God could really want a relationship with me, and today it was so clear that He did."

Reagan sighed and went on quietly. "I'm a hard worker, Katy. I can do anything you ask of me, but sometimes when the lantern is dark and I can't get right to sleep, I ask myself who I really am. You have Cash. You have a place. You belong to someone. I've been on my own since I was a child. Most of the time it didn't matter. It couldn't matter, or I wouldn't have been able to keep on. I would ask myself why I needed God at all, and it took awhile, but eventually I figured out that it's not really whether or not I need God. The biggest worry was whether or not He would reject me. After I admitted that was the problem, and then someone showed me He *does* want me—" Reagan gave a little shrug. "There was nothing else I could do."

Katy's eyes filled with sadness.

"Look at me, Reagan. I'm old and worn out. Why would God want me?"

Reagan smiled at her. "I want you," she admitted. "I wanted your friendship so badly that I rode my bicycle out here so you could ride it." Again Reagan gave that little shrug. "Unlike God, I'm just a person with all kinds of faults. His reasons for wanting you wouldn't be selfish. Mine probably were."

It was Katy's undoing. No one had ever told her she was wanted as a friend. She cried, her hip hurting with how tensely she held her body, but her heart hurting more. It was some time before she could calm down enough to ask for help, but in the next half an hour, Cash questioned Katy and answered her questions in return before praying with her as she made the same choice Reagan had made earlier.

For a time the three sat in silence. Cash didn't know when he'd been so drained, but there was no denying the peace that filled his heart. He remembered the wonder he felt when his grandmother had come to Christ, and then Slater and Dakota. He knew his family was going to be stunned and delighted when they learned of Katy's salvation. It also gave him great hope for his parents.

And Reagan! Cash was still in a state of shock over that. Her heart had been so open, and she had been completely unguarded for the first time since he'd met her.

"Did Brenda give you lunch, Katy?" Reagan asked with wonderful practicality.

"No, I wasn't hungry."

"I'll bring something in."

"You go ahead and eat, Reagan," Katy said quietly. "I'm not that hungry, so go ahead."

"Okay."

"Do you want me to set up a table in here for the three of us?" Cash offered, not having thought of it before.

Katy smiled at him, an unusual sight. "I'm tired, Cash. Maybe later."

"All right."

The redhead bent low and kissed her cheek. Reagan did the same thing. The two exited on a quiet note, each feeling his own level of weariness. Reagan put Sunday dinner on the table and they ate together, but there was not a lot of conversation.

After the meal, Reagan checked on Katy and found her sleeping. She then felt free to spend some time on her own. Cash did the same, both understanding that the last few hours had given them a lot to take in.

☙ ☙ ☙

Katy was settled in for the night, and Reagan was headed to her room. Earlier, Cash had come to the younger woman with a Bible and told her she could use it for as long as she liked. Reagan didn't bother to tell him that Holly had done the same thing for her, but now that the house was completely quiet for the day and Katy's closet door was shut against the lantern light, Reagan sat in her room, the lantern turned high, and started on the verses Pastor Ellis had given her.

The first was in Romans 10, and when Reagan read it she saw that that was just what she'd done: confessed Christ and believed on Him. But the next verses were of a different sort.

Romans 8:38,39 said, *For I am persuaded, that neither death, nor life, nor angels, nor principalities, nor powers, nor things present, nor things to come, nor height, nor depth, nor any other creature, shall be able to separate us from the love of God, which is in Christ Jesus our Lord.*

Reagan read this in quiet amazement. She didn't know when she'd read such a comprehensive list. And if the list missed anything, it was covered in the last part about "any other creature." Reagan was so pleased and surprised about this that she sat on the edge of her bed and smiled.

Truly it had never occurred to her that God might rescind His love, but if the thought ever tormented her, she now knew where to turn.

Reagan found the next verses on the list just as amazing. She read John 10:27-30. *My sheep hear my voice, and I know them, and they follow me. And I give unto them eternal life, and they shall never perish, and neither shall any man pluck them out of my hand. My Father, which gave them me, is greater than all; and no man is able to pluck them out of my Father's hand. I and my Father are one.*

Reagan had not been positive who it was that was speaking until the last verse. *This has to be Jesus Christ,* she thought, *or He would not be claiming to be one with God.*

Without warning Reagan knew she shouldn't read anymore. She had been growing tired, a good tired that meant she would sleep well, but now questions were coming to mind that were going to keep her awake.

Setting the Bible aside, she readied for bed, her heart amazingly full of what she was learning, but her brain trying to maintain control so she would sleep. Eventually her mind won over. Reagan fell asleep in the darkness, her heart never once wondering who she was.

🌹 🌹 🌹

"Well, now, Katy, have you been lying still like a good girl?" the doctor asked Monday morning a few hours after breakfast.

"I've been out dancing," she told him, a small twinkle in her eye.

"How's the pain?"

It was on the tip of Katy's tongue to brush it off and say she'd had worse, but that wasn't true.

"More intense in the morning."

"That's the usual complaint. Another three weeks and we'll have you up in a wheelchair."

"Not walking?" she asked, wondering how she'd missed this.

"No. You'll have to stay off your feet for another three weeks after that. You don't want to risk falling again. And even when you start to walk, it's going to have to be slow."

Katy was stunned. She had thought that Reagan could go home as soon as she could get out of the bed, but the housekeeper knew she would never be able to help herself in and out of a wheelchair.

"We don't have a wheelchair," she reminded the doc, wondering why Cash remained quiet through this whole exchange.

"I've got one you can use," he said calmly. "And by the way, you're coming along fine. This is all very normal."

Katy felt herself relax. The news of the wheelchair wasn't a surprise she enjoyed, but there was no doubt that she found comfort in the doctor's other words.

☙ ☙ ☙

Reagan was doing laundry. She'd meant to attack the kitchen that morning but realized the laundry was piling up. The washing and dusting would still be waiting for her, but at least their clothes would be clean.

I didn't think a task as mundane as the laundry could be done with such peace, Reagan thought to herself, even as she washed. The same strength was needed for the hard wringing-out after rinsing and the lugging of wet, heavy clothes, but knowing God loved her somehow made the burden lighter. Nothing had changed around her, Reagan understood, but things were certainly different on the inside.

Even while pegging out the wash in the swiftly warming air on the clothesline at the back of the house, Reagan's thoughts lingered on what she knew about God. Sheets went up amid thoughts of God's Son. As towels and tablecloths were hung, she wondered about heaven. Jeans, shirts, dresses, blouses, skirts, and underclothing were pegged out in tidy order, but the work was done rather unconsciously. In fact Reagan didn't even hear her employer approaching.

"Move along," the rancher ordered mildly.

"Move where?" Reagan stopped and asked, having misunderstood.

"I wasn't talking to you."

Reagan frowned at him.

Cash nodded his head, and Reagan looked behind her. Four ranch hands were walking away, two of whom still turned to look behind them.

"You don't want them outside?" Reagan innocently guessed.

"They can be outside all they want, but I didn't think you needed an audience."

Reagan's brows rose, and she asked before thinking, "Why were they watching me?"

Cash laughed. "They have great hopes," he explained.

Having been confused by men's reaction to her for a long time, Reagan asked with candid curiosity, "Of what exactly?"

"Of catching your eye."

Reagan nodded and Cash went on.

"You might smile or speak to them. If you do that, you open the door so one of them could ask you out on Saturday night."

Reagan shook her head a little, and Cash misunderstood.

"Come now, Reagan. Were there no men who wanted to court you in New York?"

Reagan looked to where the men had been, her eyes thoughtful. "Do you really think one of your ranch hands wants to court me?"

"He might. His intentions might not be honorable, but this can be lonely country. Some cowboys don't figure they could ever support a wife and don't even try, but some work a ranch like this, dreaming of a time when they could own their own. When a man does that, he wants a woman by his side."

Reagan almost asked if Cash wanted that very thing but decided she might not like the answer. She wasn't blind. She could see that men stared at her, but she also figured that they knew, just by looking at her, that she was not the love-and-cherish type.

"Doc just left," Cash said, appearing not to notice Reagan's hesitation.

"What did he have to say?"

"That she's doing well, and all is as it should be. Right after the fall she didn't hear him when he talked about her time in the wheelchair, so that was a surprise to her."

"Where will you get a wheelchair?" Reagan suddenly thought to ask.

"The doc has one, but what I want to know from you is, did you hear that she'll not be completely back on her feet for about six weeks?"

"No, but it doesn't matter."

"You're sure? I didn't know what arrangements you made with Sally or Russ and Holly."

"I'm still paying my rent, and Sally wants me back no matter when I can come."

"She's a good employer, isn't she?"

"Yes, she is," Reagan said. Then her eyes grew huge. "I've got to tell her. I've got to tell her about Christ!"

Cash blinked at her sudden vehemence.

"Just this morning I read a verse in Matthew about letting people see your light. I've got to tell her!"

"Do you think she wants to hear?" Cash asked with maddening calm.

"Does that matter?" Reagan's face and question were so comical that Cash laughed all over again.

He knew they would have to discuss her evangelism tactics, but Reagan was already calming. Her mind had gone back to the Christians in New York and the first time she realized Russell Bennett was a Christian.

"I could turn her away from me, couldn't I?" she asked quietly. "If I don't tell Sally the right way, she won't want anything to do with me."

"It's entirely possible, and I don't think you want to take that risk."

Reagan's head tipped to one side.

"How did you tell people?"

"I told a few without invitation, but my family started asking why I'd changed. Then the door was open. The same thing has happened with some of the other ranchers in the area."

Reagan was asking herself if that might happen between her and Sally when she spotted something that made her gasp.

"What is that?" she asked in horror, moving a little closer to Cash and trying to get behind him.

"Go on now." Cash raised his voice and waved his hand.

The armadillo that had wandered into the yard stopped his clumsy progress and stared over at them, so Cash waved him on again. Reagan's eyes nearly swallowed her face as she looked at the strange armor-plated creature as he waddled back the way he'd come.

"What is it?" she gasped out loud.

"An armadillo. Have you not seen one yet?"

"You mean, they live around here?"

"Sure."

Her hands to her waist, she turned fully to face Cash Rawlings, her eyes filled with astonishment. In a brogue as thick as though she'd just arrived from Ireland, Reagan demanded, "What kind of employer are you not to let a girl know about such creatures? My heart could have been scared into stopping on the spot."

Cash could only smile, wishing she would do it again.

"Were you born in Ireland?"

"We were discussing armordillos!"

"Armadillos," he corrected softly, his eyes alight with amusement.

"That is entirely beside the point! I want to know that one of those creatures is not going to visit me in my room some night."

"No, they don't like the house. It's too active."

"They?" The brogue was back. "How many might there be?"

To which Cash could only laugh. "I've got to get back to work, Reagan," he responded, turning with a wave. "I'll talk to you later."

Reagan was not at all sure she wanted to end this conversation, but she was given little choice. She also knew her employer was right. Katy hadn't been checked on since the doctor left, and some of the laundry was still in the basket. The day was moving on, and if she wasn't careful, it would move without her.

Fifteen

"I'VE GOT TO GO TO TOWN tomorrow," Reagan told Katy later that day. "We're low on supplies. Do you go to Mrs. Unger's?"

"Always. And for everything except the molasses candy that Cash likes."

"Is that what's in the bowl in the living room?"

"That's it."

"I've got paper here." Reagan sat down and began to read what she had on her list.

"We're low on brown sugar? Have you checked the tall cupboard by the door?"

"No. I'll do that," Reagan said, head bent, making notes.

"Are you sure you're saved, Reagan?" Katy suddenly asked quietly.

The younger woman looked up at her. Their eyes held for a moment, and then Reagan nodded affirmatively.

"Are you having doubts, Katy?"

"A few. I just don't feel saved. I want to get out of this bed. I want to do so many things, and I can't! Would I be feeling this restless if I was really saved?"

Reagan had no idea what to tell her. "Why don't you ask Cash? You know he'll help you."

Katy sighed with relief.

"Maybe I will. I know from church that Satan is a powerful enemy. He lies all the time. Maybe he's lying to me, and

I'm lying to myself, and God knows that I'm just fine with Him."

"Except..." Reagan began but halted.

"Except what?"

"Isn't worry a sin?"

Katy's eyes got big.

"I think it is."

"Talk to Cash, Katy. Don't lie there without answers."

The older woman nodded, and Reagan smiled at her. As Reagan bent back over her list, Katy found herself thanking God for the younger woman and almost instantly realized she'd never done such a thing before.

"Okay," Reagan said. "How about beans? We're very low. Is there another bag I'm not seeing?"

The conversation went back to the matter at hand, namely, Reagan's trip to town. They covered the entire list before Katy told her that Lavinia would expect the order to be charged and that if Cash needed his candy from Reynold's, the money jar was in the big cupboard.

Reagan finally left the sickroom, a dozen thoughts filling her head, the first one being that she would have to tell Katy how much she was needed. She ran the house with ease, seeing to every need. Did anyone ever tell her how vital she was to the ranch? It seemed like something Cash would do often, but whether or not he did, Reagan decided that at some time she needed to add her own voice of admiration.

❧ ❧ ❧

"I appreciate this, Brenda," Reagan told the other woman the next morning.

"It's my pleasure, Reagan. Do you need anything special done?"

"No. She's had her bath, which made her a little cold, so now she's under an extra blanket and reading a book."

"All right. I'll check on her and see if she wants anything from her house."

"Good. I've been over a few times, but I'm always in a rush."

This established, Reagan took her list and small coin purse with money from the jar and walked outside to the barn. The day felt as if it was going to be hot. Little by little, as the weeks passed, it had been warming up, and Reagan knew that very soon she would have to look into some lighter-weight clothing. Today however, she had supplies to purchase. She wasn't comfortable spending someone else's money, but if this was what it took to get Katy back on her feet, she would do it.

Reagan worked all of this out in her mind before she got to the barn. Never very comfortable around horses, she forced herself not to think about what must be done. If she could have figured a way to get supplies back to the ranch on her bicycle, she would have done it.

The barn was scarier than she thought it would be, and not until she was inside did she remember that the horses were kept in the paddock outside. The thought of having to catch one gave her no comfort, but as she walked down the length of the barn, a horse's head came out over the door of its stall. At first Reagan was startled but realized suddenly that she'd been rescued.

"Hey, fella," she began coaxingly, not missing the gray muzzle and sunken eyes. "You look about my speed."

The horse stretched his neck out in a friendly fashion, but Reagan was still uneasy. She glanced around and spotted a buggy, one that looked light and manageable. She went into that stall and, taking the shaves, manhandled the buggy out into the lane between the two long rows of stalls.

"Okay," she panted, still speaking to the horse, which looked half asleep, "we'll just get you out of there, and you can take me to town."

Reagan flipped the latch, and as soon as the horse heard it, his ears perked up and he moved to come out. A moment later, the door swung fully open and the horse came straight at Reagan, his nose smelling her clothing for sugar or a handful of oats.

"Oh, no!" Reagan cried as she backed up. "Stay back now; stay back."

But the old horse just nuzzled the front of her dress and then stood still. When Reagan saw that she was not going to be trampled, she relaxed a little and began to give orders.

"All right now. You just back yourself up to the buggy."

The horse's ears twitched, but already his eyes had half-closed again.

"Come on, now. I've got things to do. Just get hitched to this buggy, and we'll go."

Reagan reached out and pushed a little on the horse's side, but the animal didn't appear to notice.

Reagan cast about for some other plan, and that was when she spotted him. Watching her intently, Cash Rawlings stood about 20 feet away, shoulder propped against a column.

"Oh, Cash," Reagan began, "I didn't see you."

"Reagan, what are you doing?"

"I'm trying to get this horse hitched to the buggy. I have to go to town."

Cash could only laugh.

"And what were you doing just standing there, Cash Rawlings?" Reagan wanted to know. "I could have been trampled."

"Not by Misty. I think she's older than I am."

"Oh, it's a girl?" She looked with new interest at the animal's face. "How can you tell?"

Cash's laughter echoed off the barn's interior, even as Reagan turned red and refused to look at him.

Pushing away from the column, the rancher finally took pity on her and came forward.

"Didn't Katy tell you I always assign one of the men to take her to town?"

"No. We never got to that." Reagan glanced at him. "How did you know I was out here?"

"I saw Brenda in the kitchen, and Katy told me where you were headed. I was actually getting ready to saddle my horse and head after you, sure you'd taken off on your bike."

"I would have if I could have figured out a way to do it!" she told him indignantly, a slight brogue entering in.

"I'll take you," Cash told her, moving to put Misty back inside with soothing words and a handful of oats.

"But you're busy, Cash, and the whole point of my being here is to help."

"I need some things in town too, Reagan. If I didn't have time, I would send someone else."

Reagan looked suspicious but let it go. He was a big boy. If he didn't want to go to town, he didn't have to.

"By the way," Cash began again, "were you really hoping Misty would just back her way into the harness?"

Reagan's chin went into the air. "As old as she is, I thought she must know how."

"But Misty's never been a cart horse. She's a cattle pony."

"Oh, there are different types?"

Her eyes were so big with interest that Cash couldn't find it in his heart to laugh again, but he wanted to. The things he'd taken for granted nearly all his life were so wondrous to her. In fact, it wasn't all that unusual to spot armadillos in the barn, but he didn't think he would mention it.

"So, are you ready to go?"

"Yes, I have my list and some money for your candy."

"Are we out of candy? I haven't been eating it much."

"Katy didn't want to run out."

"She spoils me."

I'm glad someone does was the first thought that sprang to Reagan's mind.

Because she had no idea where it had come from, it disturbed her all the way to town.

🌿 🌿 🌿

"Okay, Reagan," Lavinia said, having checked over the list again and been even more picky than Katy. "I think that's the lot. Anything more?"

"I don't think so."

"Here—" The proprietress grabbed a tin of lady's powder—it was scented with flowers—and pressed it into Reagan's hands. "Take this to Katy; no charge. Tell her to come back soon."

"I'll do that, Mrs. Unger. Thank you."

"Sally misses you," Lavinia said, acting as though she had all day even though there were other patrons in the store.

"I miss her too. If Cash doesn't get back before I'm done, I may go down to see her."

"I can always tell him where you went."

"I'll do that, then. Thank you again."

Lavinia waved Reagan away, but in truth she was just barely holding her tongue. Had she seen something in Cash Rawlings' eyes when he'd dropped Reagan off?

"He's tall and she's not, and I always think that makes for a cute couple."

"I don't need a couple," Mrs. Guthrie said in Lavinia's ear. The woman's hearing was not what it used to be, and she also had a habit of starting conversations in her head. "Don't try to sell me more than I need, Lavinia Unger."

Lavinia only shook her head, moved to assist her customer, and held her peace yet again.

🌿 🌿 🌿

"You look tired," Sally told Reagan, hugging her again. "How much time do you have?"

"Not much, but I wanted to see how you were doing."

"I'm tired too, but then we both knew I would be. How is Katy, by the way?"

"She's coming along. It's hard to be in that bed all day, but she's coping."

"I thought she'd be verbally tearing the house down."

"She started out that way, but there's been a change in her."

"Good. Do they give you any time off?"

Reagan smiled. "I have as many days off as you gave me."

Sally had a good laugh over this, and both women saw Cash come in the front.

"I just wanted to tell you I'd be at the livery," he told her as he started to turn away.

Reagan stopped him.

"Cash. I don't want to leave Brenda alone too long."

Cash waved in understanding and went on his way.

Reagan would have enjoyed going to see Holly, but she still had to get the candy her boss liked.

"I'd better go."

"Are you and Cash starting to get along?" Sally asked suddenly.

Reagan frowned at her. "We've always gotten along."

Sally only nodded, her face impassive. She thought the relationship was changing, but maybe she was wrong. Then again, she figured she might be right and Reagan didn't see it.

"Take care," Sally said, not bothering to answer the question that was still in Reagan's face.

"All right. You do the same."

Reagan went on her way but wondered what might have come over Sally. She dismissed it before she reached Reynold's, however, where she made her purchase and was the first one back to the wagon. Cash was just behind her, and in good time they were on their way.

"Was I hard to get along with before?" Reagan asked Cash out of the blue; they hadn't even cleared downtown.

"Before?"

"Before I came to Christ."

"Not really hard to get along with, Reagan, but a little closed off to certain topics."

"So you didn't find me rude?"

"No."

Reagan sat staring straight ahead, and after a moment Cash glanced at her profile.

"Did I say something that made you think that?" he asked after a time.

"No, but Sally said something about our getting along, and I thought we always had."

"Ahh."

Now it was Reagan's turn to look at Cash.

"What did 'ahh' mean?"

At first Cash didn't answer, but Reagan continued to look at him.

"I'm afraid, Reagan, that people are going to talk. They're going to see us together and make wrong assumptions."

Reagan took no time to catch on. She thought Sally would have known better, but clearly she'd misjudged her. And because Reagan wasn't a woman who went in for coyness and flirtations, she came right out with her feelings on the matter.

"You don't make wrong assumptions about us, do you, Cash?"

"No, ma'am, I don't," he told her, his voice as it always was.

Reagan sighed with relief, not caring if she was heard or not. The last thing she needed was her boss mooning over her. If he started that—Katy or not—Reagan would be on her way.

Reagan's mind was still on the matter—that is, men in general and their relationship to women—when she and Cash pulled down the long driveway, and for that reason she knew without having to be told why their wagon was met by three cowhands.

"Hello, boys," Cash greeted them as he pulled up.

All three men had removed their hats, but the tallest of the three stepped forward to speak.

"When we realized that you hadn't assigned anyone to go to town with Miss Sullivan, we thought you might want help with the unloading."

"Well, boys, that's right kind of you. Miss Sullivan can tell you where things go."

The pointed look Reagan gave Cash was rewarded only with a smile.

"I'll just go in and check on Katy and tell Brenda she can go."

"Thank you," Reagan told him, her eyes saying otherwise.

As soon as Cash left, two of the hands came forward to help her down, but Reagan told them she could manage. When she caught sight of one trying to get a glimpse of her ankles, she became all businesslike. In a matter of minutes the job was done, and the men were thanked and sent on their way.

"Did you give them cookies?" Katy asked when Reagan told her of the episode.

"They weren't looking for cookies," Reagan stated in no uncertain terms, and Katy chuckled.

"You can laugh all you want, Katy, but I could have done without them."

Cash, who had just entered the room, exchanged a look with Katy, both sets of eyes holding laughter.

"So how was Lavinia?"

"She misses you and sent you some powder."

"Now wasn't that nice! What scent?"

"Wildflower, I think."

"Mmmm..." Katy showed her appreciation after Reagan had handed her the tin and she had opened it enough to get a whiff. "Who else did you see in town?"

"Before Reagan fills you in," Cash inserted, "I saw Pastor at the livery, and he wanted to know if the three of us are planning to have a Bible study together. I told him we hadn't gotten that far."

"I want to," Reagan said without hesitation. While reading her Bible that morning, she'd had several questions.

"I do too," Katy added.

"All right. We'll start this week. How's Thursday night—in here after dinner?"

"What will we study?" Katy wished to know.

"I'm not sure just yet. Do you have an interest?"

Katy looked thoughtful. "I missed some of the work Pastor Ellis did on God's promises. Can we go over that?"

"Sure. Is that going to work for you, Reagan?"

"Anything," she told him. "I feel completely lost in the Bible."

"Okay. Thursday night it is."

Cash went on his way, and Reagan turned to Katy.

"Did you talk to him about your doubts?"

"No, because I remembered what he would say."

"What would he say?"

"That all feelings have to follow the truth of Scripture. If I don't feel saved, but I know in my heart that I took care of things between God the Father and me, then I'm saved forever."

"You know so much, Katy," Reagan said in amazement. "How do you know so much?"

Katy did not look pleased. "I sat in that church just trying to be good enough to get God's notice without admitting that His way was the only way He would accept. I did my level best not to listen, but a few things got in!"

Reagan bit her lip in an effort not to laugh, but it didn't work. A giggle slipped out and then another.

Just realizing what she'd said, Katy began to laugh as well. Before many moments passed, the two of them were having a loud session of laughter and giggles.

Across the way, Cash sat in his office and listened. He was in the midst of trying to catch up on his correspondence, but for a time he couldn't lift the pen. This miracle that had happened in his own household was just too big to take in.

⅜ ⅜ ⅜

One week and six days after Katy was hurt, Dakota and Slater Rawlings rode up the drive to the ranch. They hadn't planned on arriving together but had met up on the road and come in at the same time. It had been a good time to catch up as Dakota had taken a new job, but both men were preoccupied with the news about Katy. She was not a young woman anymore, as they knew all too well.

Dakota and Slater quickened their pace when the ranch house came into view, but a scene in front of the house—Cash and a young woman arguing—caused them to finish the ride very slowly. When they got close enough, they saw that a contraption stood between the warring couple—one they'd both seen in St. Louis but never in Texas.

"Why have you brought me out here?" Reagan asked loudly enough for the visiting Rawlingses to hear. "And why do you have my bike out?"

"I want you to go for a ride."

"To town?"

"No. Just for pleasure."

"Why?"

"You need a break."

Reagan's hands came up.

"I have work to do, Cash."

"It can wait. Get on the bike."

"What if Katy needs me?"

"I'll keep an eye on her. Get on the bike."

"This is ridiculous."

"No, it's not. What's ridiculous is that you haven't had a moment to yourself since Katy fell, and I know you love to ride. Now get on the bike."

"Stop saying that."

"As soon as you get on the bike, I will."

With eyes that told him she thought him demented, Reagan took the bicycle handles and, with the ease of breathing, hopped on and began to ride. Planning to keep it short, she started around the house, fully intending to stay in the barnyard.

"Make it a long one," Cash called after her, "or I'll send you out again."

Not until that was settled and Reagan was riding out of sight did Cash look up to see his brothers. They were both smiling hugely, and Cash shook his head, not looking forward to explaining the situation to the two men with the Cheshire cat smiles.

"Well, now," Dakota began. "Who was that?"

"You can get that gleam out of your eye, Dak. It's not what you think."

"What do we think?" Slater asked, smile still in place as he dismounted, went forward, and hugged his oldest brother.

Dakota was next, and the middle brother's mouth was opening to say more when he spotted Reagan again on the bike. His gaze drew the others, and for a moment all three watched as she made a wide circle by the barn and headed once again toward the back of the house, looking for all the world as though she was having the time of her life. Dakota finally spoke when she disappeared.

"Is that the woman from town? The one in the letter?"

"Yes. Her name is Reagan Sullivan."

"A woman who owns her own bicycle, Cash," Dakota said, eyes hopeful. "Just the kind of girl you need. Any chance she's a believer?"

Cash had all he could do not to shake his head. Since their marriages, his brothers had one thing on their minds: to see him married as well.

"Well?" Slater put in now. "Is she?"

"As of about nine days ago, yes."

"She's not taken, is she?"

"You two take the cake, you know that? I strongly suspect you're here for Katy, but all you want to know is whether or not I've found someone to marry."

The younger brothers' faces became very sober, and Cash saw in an instant that he should not have teased them.

"Come on in," he said. "Katy will be surprised speechless."

"How is she, Cash?" Slater said seriously. "I mean, really?"

Cash smiled, absolutely delighted to be able to say, "I'll let her tell you herself."

Sixteen

"THAT WAS JUST WHAT I NEEDED!" Reagan announced as she spotted Cash in Katy's room, rushing in before seeing that they had guests. "At first I thought you needed your head checked, but then I just—" Reagan came to an abrupt and awkward halt. Two men were in the room, both cowboys, and Reagan had interrupted.

"I'm sorry," she said as she began backing toward the door. "I'm sorry," she said even more softly before anyone could speak.

"Come in, Reagan." Katy's voice stopped her; she had never heard her so excited. "These are my other two boys!"

Reagan looked to Cash.

"My brothers," he supplied. "Dakota and Slater, I'd like to introduce you to Reagan Sullivan."

"Hello," Reagan greeted them, still embarrassed. The men were perfect gentlemen, however, and came forward to shake her hand, neither one seeming the least bit put out.

"It's a pleasure," Dakota said, his smile genuine.

"Cash and Katy have been telling us about all you do. We can't thank you enough."

This had come from Slater, and Reagan blinked in surprise. She had known that Cash was a gentleman, but three in the same family was almost too hard to believe. And they were all so different in appearance!

"You're not from Texas, are you?" Dakota now asked, his voice a deep drawl.

Reagan smiled. "How could you tell?"

"No one else here rides a bicycle."

Reagan couldn't help but laugh at that; she knew it was probably true. But as much as the men genuinely seemed to enjoy her company, Reagan wanted to leave them on their own. If the light in Katy's eyes was any indication, she was near to bursting with pleasure over having them there.

"I've got some things to do in the kitchen," she said, backing toward the door. "I'll see you at dinner."

"Thank you, Reagan," Cash said, even as he hoped she wasn't leaving for another reason. He had caught a glimpse of vulnerability in her face, something he was not accustomed to seeing in Reagan. It left him uncertain about how to respond.

Reagan was feeling very much the way Cash had guessed. She knew that she was still needed, but interfering with this family reunion was the last thing she wanted. Katy needed to see "her boys" on her own. And too, she just hadn't spent much time with families. She thought that Russell and Holly's family was unusually close, but now she was seeing it again in Cash and his brothers.

To get her mind off the feelings she didn't understand and didn't know how to handle, Reagan threw herself into a wonderful meal, one that would celebrate the return of the brothers. Glad she'd baked a cake earlier that day, she frosted it and then worked hard on the potatoes and vegetables to go with the meat.

"We're going to eat in Katy's room tonight," Cash announced about 15 minutes after Reagan got down to work, Slater right behind him.

"That's a wonderful idea. Katy will love that."

While Reagan remained over the stove and oven, the men took a small table and four chairs to Katy's room. Reagan did not understand the complete plan, however, until after they came and took all the bowls of food as well. Reagan was getting ready to serve herself from the pot when she heard a voice.

"I'll get her," Slater called over his shoulder as he came back to the kitchen. "Come on, Reagan. We're waiting for you."

Reagan shook her head.

"I'll be fine in the kitchen, Dakota. I see Katy all the time."

"I'm Slater, and Katy wants you to come."

Reagan looked suspicious. "Did she say that?"

He nodded like a schoolboy, and Reagan had to laugh. Nevertheless he was very persuasive, and before long Reagan found herself in Katy's room. A prayer was said and dishes were passed. The men bantered constantly, teasing Katy almost nonstop and still managing to compliment Reagan on the food.

"I made cake," she said at one point, and the men were appreciative to the point of making Reagan think they had never had it.

"We have molasses candy too, don't we, Reagan?" Katy put in.

"Yes, ma'am. I just filled the jar."

"I may never go home," Dakota said outrageously.

"I'll go home," Slater added, "but I might have to take that candy dish with me."

Cash snorted in disbelief. "If I know you, Slate, there won't be any candy left in the jar when you leave tomorrow night."

Slater looked innocent at this remark, and even Katy laughed.

"Do you have to leave so soon?" Reagan asked. These three had a way of making everyone feel right at home.

"Yes. My wife is having a baby soon, and I don't want to miss anything."

"You shouldn't have come," Katy worried from the bed.

"It's all right, Kate. You're too important to me not to be here, and Duffy says that Libby probably has another week at least, maybe two."

"Libby is Slater's wife, and Duffy is her stepfather and doctor," Cash supplied for Reagan.

"Do you hope for a boy or a girl?" Reagan asked the blond brother.

Slater smiled. "My wife has three younger siblings, a brother and two sisters. They are the sweetest kids in the world, which makes it impossible for me to choose among them. For some reason I feel the same way about the baby. I know if it's a little Laura or Jeanette, I'll love her, and if the baby's a little Zach, that would be just as great."

"You should have brought them with you," Dakota said. "I could go for a conversation with Laura or Zach at just about any time."

"Then you're going to love the latest, Dak," Slater filled them in. "Just before Libby and I moved into our own place, Laura would come into our room in the mornings and look around. At first she wouldn't tell Libby why, but then Libby got her to admit that she was looking for a nest."

"A nest?" Cash asked. "What was that about?"

"We think it was about Duffy teasing Liberty and her mother one night, saying that he always knew when Katie was going to give birth because she'd start nesting up a storm."

All the occupants of the room had a good laugh over this. Slater went on to tell of some other conversations with Laura and Zach and how fast Jeanette was growing, and Reagan could only sit in quiet amazement. It was with nothing short of relief to be able to serve the cake, have a small piece herself, and then escape to the cleanup needed in the kitchen.

She was almost halfway done when Cash joined her. He picked up the dish towel—something he did for her often—and began to dry the heavy pots she'd used.

Tonight, however, instead of talking to her about general topics or answering her questions on Scripture, he came right to what was on his mind.

"What happened in there, Reagan?"

"What do you mean?" she asked, head still bent and hoping it wasn't what she feared.

"You looked about ready to cry when Slater was talking about his wife's siblings."

"I never cry," she told him, as though that were the end of the subject.

"Why is that, do you think?"

"It doesn't do any good."

"I don't know about that."

Reagan looked at him but then went right back to washing.

"So answer my other question. Why was it upsetting to you when Slater was talking?"

More than anything in the world, Reagan wanted to lie and say she wasn't upset at all, but she couldn't do it. She knew it was wrong, and this was Cash. She would never lie to him.

"I don't want to talk about it," she opted, her voice tight.

"All right," Cash said easily, his voice as calm as ever.

"Are you always so nice?" Reagan demanded, turning to him, her face red with emotion. "Aren't you ever grouchy or mean?"

Cash looked at her for a moment and then spoke, his voice filled with wonder.

"What possible reason would I have for being mean to you, Reagan? You're my sister in Christ. You're a part of my household. You take care of Katy and me as though you've been doing it all your life. You give of your time and energy all day long. What possible reason could I have to reward all your kindness and hard work with meanness?"

Feeling very shamed, Reagan went back to the dishes. She thought Cash would walk away and leave her to finish on her own, but even though she'd acted like a shrew, he stayed. They were almost done when Reagan began to quietly admit what was on her mind.

"I've never had a family like yours, Cash. I've always wanted one, but just the thought of it scares me to no end."

"Why does it, Reagan?"

"Because families take something from you."

"What do you mean?"

Reagan turned to face him.

"Your brothers and Katy are here now, but they're not going to live forever. What will you do when they're gone?"

"I'll be very sad. I'll grieve for a long time, but I still won't hold back on my feelings for them today. I'll still pour my heart into them so that today can be all God intended and so when they do ride away from here—even if it turns out to be the last time I see them on this earth—I'll have no regrets.

"You're right, Reagan, families do cost something, but they're worth every cent."

Reagan was so shaken that she almost dropped her washcloth. Her complexion went very pale, and she looked helplessly at Cash.

"Reagan." Cash's voice was the kindest she'd ever heard. "I'm sorry to upset you. I promise it was the last thing I wanted to do. You didn't want to talk about it. I should have let it go."

"You did let it go," she reminded him. "I brought it back up." She turned to the dishpan and admitted softly, "I don't know why I'm the way I am."

"It's not hard to guess, the way your mother left and your father turned to drink."

Reagan nodded. "But there's no excuse for worry or fear, is there, Cash? You told us how huge our God is and how powerful and able to look after our every need He is. You told Katy and me that last Thursday night, and Pastor Ellis said something about it on Sunday too."

"That's true, Reagan, and it's great you remembered, but don't be harder on yourself than God is. When you fall into the sin of worry or fear, confess it to God as you would any other sin, and ask Him to change you."

They heard laughter coming from Katy's room, and Reagan listened to it in silence. Cash was right. Those men with her had no guarantee that Katy would be alive the next time they visited, but they'd traveled—one leaving an expectant wife—to see her because she was loved, because she was family. Even if she died an hour after they left, they would not be the least bit sorry they had come. In fact, Reagan thought with a sudden certainty, it would probably be quite the opposite.

Without warning the young woman relaxed. She had not been thinking logically. Her fear had clouded her judgment. If she knew that she had a last chance to see Sally or Holly, she would not stay away. She would go to her side and be with her no matter how hard it was to say goodbye at a later time.

For a moment Reagan was transported back to the day she realized her mother was not returning. For a long time she had blamed herself. She convinced herself that her mother would have stayed if she'd only been a better little girl. Then her life became consumed with her father's drinking, and some of her mother's memory faded into the background. She had started to wonder if she'd caused her father to drink, but by then a wall had grown around her heart, and she didn't care if she had or not.

Today she was able to see that she had not been responsible. Just by thinking about her own life, she knew that she couldn't blame someone else for the choices she made, no matter how tempting that might be.

With a heartfelt sigh, Reagan turned to thank Cash for the help his words had been but found herself alone.

And isn't that just like him, Reagan thought with pleasure. *He's so thoughtful and caring. It's too bad he doesn't have children,* she said to the Lord. *Their upbringing would be far removed from my own.*

❦ ❦ ❦

"We have to talk."

Cash had been dead asleep. He was emotionally drained these days, and most nights when his head hit the pillow, he was gone.

"Dakota?"

"Yeah. Slater too."

Cash heard the strike of a match just as light came into his eyes. Both his brothers were standing fully dressed at the side of his bed. For a moment he wondered what time it was and then realized they must have stayed up talking after he'd gone to bed.

"Is something wrong?"

"No, but with Slater leaving tomorrow night, who knows when we'll get to talk again?"

Cash was finally awake enough to look into their eyes. He caught steely determination.

"Talk or browbeat me into agreeing with you?"

"He knows us too well," Dakota said without repentance and proceeded to sit on the edge of the bed. Slater took the floor.

"I know she's a new Christian and that these things take time," Dakota began. "But Slate and I want to know if you've noticed Reagan."

"She lives in my house," Cash stated calmly.

"That doesn't mean you've noticed her," Slater said. "Dak told me that if you hadn't pointed out to him that he was falling for Darvi, he might never have given it a thought."

"And you think I've fallen for Reagan?"

"No. We think she's fallen for you."

Cash had no trouble shaking his head.

"Now there you're wrong. If ever there was a woman who did not want a family, it's Reagan Sullivan."

This stopped both men. Their brother's voice told them he was completely serious.

"Listen," Cash went on, "I appreciate your caring—you know I do—and as I've told you, I want to fall in love and get married. But it doesn't seem to consume my thoughts like it does yours. I'm happy and at peace with who I am right now. If God has someone for me, you'll be the first to know, but for now, I can't push this, especially not with Reagan. Her heart can't take it."

"We're sorry we woke you," Dakota said sincerely. "Thanks for telling us, Cash. We'll keep praying."

"Thank you. I'll see you in the morning," he murmured, sounding as tired as he felt.

"All right. Good night."

Slater said his goodnight as well, but the moment the two men were out in the hallway, Dakota signaled his brother into his room. They shut the door so they could finish the conversation.

"He's in love with her," Slater stated.

"I think so too, but he doesn't know it, and right now it looks like that's for the best."

"Do you think he does know but has held his feelings in check? I mean, she did *just* come to Christ, and Cash would not even entertain the notion of marrying an unbeliever."

"He might have, but I don't think so. I think his heart is as tender as it's always been, and Reagan is just another one of the many recipients."

The younger Rawlings brothers were tired as well and didn't have much more to say. With few other words, each man sought his own bed, but before they could rest, each was convicted of his thoughts and actions.

A major miracle had happened with both Katy and Reagan coming to Christ, and all they could do was play matchmaker. In the morning, both men planned to seek Cash out and apologize.

❧ ❧ ❧

"You want to ride?" Reagan asked in surprise, staring up at Slater.

"Sure. I've seen them in St. Louis but never been close to one. Or don't you think I'll fit?"

"Oh, no, you'll fit. I'm just surprised."

"Why?"

Reagan looked uncertain and then knew she had to come out with it.

"I'm the reason Katy broke her hip. I brought the bike out and talked her into riding."

"That's not what Katy said," Slater told her with a smile. Reagan blinked.

"What did Katy say?"

"She said that she knew she should have stopped and didn't. She was getting tired but wanted to show off for Cash, so when she put her leg out, it couldn't support her."

Reagan's mouth opened and Slater grinned. Her hands came to her waist, and the accent slipped into place.

"So you've been chattin' behind Reagan's back, have you now? Well, I'll tell you a thing or two, Mr. Rawlings," Reagan began, stopping when she saw that Dakota had come on the scene and was staring at her.

"Do it again," he ordered, but Reagan only laughed.

"I thought you were here to visit Katy," she accused them, her voice returning to normal.

"She's asleep. I think we wore her out last night and then again this morning."

"I still want to ride this thing," Slater put in, and Reagan acquiesced and gave him a quick demonstration.

"She just hops right on! Did you see that?"

"Yes, I did. I think I'll have a try."

"Wait your turn, Dakota."

Before long Cash joined the threesome, and in little time they had Reagan in near hysterics with their antics on the bike. To the amazement of all, Cash was the most proficient.

"Have you been practicing in the barn when I wasn't looking?" Reagan challenged him.

"Every night," he teased. "I sneak down after dark and ride among the horses."

"Wouldn't Darvi love to see this," Slater called as Dakota took a turn.

"I was thinking of some of the Rangers I used to work with. I'm glad they're not around now."

"Rangers?" Reagan questioned Cash.

"Dakota and Slater were both with the Texas Rangers."

Reagan's mouth dropped open as she did nothing to disguise her amazement.

"Real Texas Rangers?"

Cash smiled.

"Who's a real Texas Ranger?" Dakota asked as he rode up and stopped.

Reagan could only stare at both of the younger Rawlingses.

"What's so amazing, Reagan?" Cash asked her.

"I don't know. I just never thought I'd meet any. I've been hearing about the Texas Rangers since I was a little girl."

Once again Cash was given a glimpse of life through Reagan's eyes. The very things he thought nothing of were special and amazing to her.

"Is it too personal to ask why you're not with the Rangers anymore?"

"Not at all." Dakota filled her in, explaining the way Rangers had to be on the move and how hard it was to meet that expectation and also be with his family.

Reagan was still looking stunned over who they had been when she realized she hadn't checked on Katy for a time.

"I'd better get inside."

"Thanks for the lesson," they called to her, but Reagan only waved them away. Once inside she found Katy still asleep and thought it might be a good time to dust and sweep upstairs. She tried to make quick work of it but found it was quite warm and was reminded that she still hadn't gotten a chance to shop for cooler clothing. Having arrived in this hot country in January, she had not made summer clothing a priority, but suddenly Reagan felt awful.

Not caring whether or not she was needed, Reagan moved down to Katy's bedroom and sat quietly in the chair. The window was open, and for a time she let what little breeze there was blow in on her as she prayed for Katy's hip to heal.

"Are you all right, Reagan?"

Reagan turned from the window to find Katy looking at her.

"I'm just a little warm."

"Have you nothing cooler to wear?" the older woman asked, taking in the long sleeves and dark material of Reagan's dress.

"No. I haven't had a chance to shop."

"Well, go today."

"No. I'll just take some time the next time we need supplies."

"Oh, stuff and nonsense! It's only April, Reagan. You're going to need cooler clothing. Go now while I have the boys to look after me."

"It's not the same," Reagan informed her, knowing Katy would understand her meaning.

"I don't have any needs like that right now. I'm fine. Now go. No, wait. Get Cash in here. I'll ask him to take you. Do you have money?"

"Yes, thank you, I do have money, and I'll just ride my bike."

"How will you get your dress home?"

"Mrs. Unger will wrap it, I'm sure." Reagan smiled before adding, "Dinna fash yourself, woman."

Before it was over, Cash ended up hearing about Reagan's plans and did offer to take her into town, but she would have none of it. Before lunch, so the sun was not quite as fierce, Reagan—with instructions to take all day if she needed—took herself off in the direction of town, her mind already going over what she should buy. She also had a letter in her pocket from Katy. It was to be delivered to Lavinia. Reagan assumed it was a thank-you note for the powder.

And she was partially correct.

Had Reagan but known it, Katy was plotting against her. All her life Katy Sims had had tender thoughts for the ones she loved, but never before had she felt she could express them or do anything about them. It had been her lot, or so she felt, to cook and clean as a way to say the words she could not utter.

Now she knew better. And the letter to Lavinia was only the start.

Seventeen

"I'M HAVING A SALE FOR SPECIAL customers," Lavinia whispered to Reagan not many minutes after she was handed the letter. "Buy two dresses, get one free."

Reagan's eyes rounded.

"When is the sale?"

"Today only."

Katy had not asked the mercantile proprietress to lie to Reagan; nevertheless, in handling it her own way, she was going to accomplish Katy's goal.

That Lavinia had received a note from Katy thanking her for the powder and telling her to talk Reagan into buying an extra dress and putting it on her bill was enough to surprise her into sitting down, but she fought the urge. Staying on her feet and helping Reagan, Lavinia was able to see that in just under an hour's time, the younger woman left the store with three new dresses, all very lightweight and comfortable, and some new underthings and stockings too.

Never in her life had Reagan been able to afford more than two dresses. Her shoes were not going to last another year, but for the moment, Reagan felt as though she was set for life. She was so excited about her purchases that she wanted to tell someone. At the same time, she wanted to ignore Katy's orders to take her time. Telling herself she would just take a few minutes, she rode her bicycle toward Holly's house.

As Reagan knew she would be, Holly was very surprised but also pleased to see her.

"You came in on your own? Cash didn't have one of the men bring you?"

"No, I rode my bike."

"I'm surprised Cash didn't do the job himself."

"He wanted to, but his brothers are visiting, one of them just until tonight, and I didn't want any of them to have to come to town with me."

"Will you be able to get things back on your bike?"

"Yes. It's just a small bundle of clothing."

"For you?"

Reagan nodded.

"Show me!"

For a time the women enjoyed looking at the purchases, but before long Reagan put her hand on Holly's arm and spoke intently about what had been lingering in her heart on her ride into town.

"I understand now, Holly, why you wanted this for me. I was reading my Bible on Monday morning and realized that your prayers were answered with a yes. You knew how much God's Son would do in my life, and you wanted that for me."

"Oh, Reagan," Holly said quietly, "you have no idea what you do for my heart."

"I don't know how," Reagan said with a laugh. "There's so little I know."

"But you want to know, and that's such a blessing, Reagan."

Reagan frowned a little.

"Think of how delighted you were when the children loved your bike and Elly wanted to ride it. You were thrilled to have them share in something you love."

Reagan nodded with new understanding.

"It's coming up on noon. Do you have time to walk with Alisa and me to give Russell his lunch?"

Reagan hesitated, but she wanted to see the large blacksmith who was missing from her life on the ranch.

"All right, but I'd better take my bike and go right from the livery."

Holly pushed the bike so Reagan could hold Alisa. They walked swiftly to the livery, talking all the way, and when Russell saw Reagan he gave her a hug.

"We miss you. How is it going at the ranch?"

"It's going well. Cash's brothers are visiting. Slater leaves tonight, and I'm not sure when Dakota leaves. Katy was so glad to see them."

"I'm sure she was. How is she coming?"

"She's doing very well. I think she'll be in that wheelchair right on time, and once she gets out of that bed, there will be no stopping her."

Russell and Holly were both very glad to hear it, and with Alisa going from one adult to the next and even spending some time falling in the dirt on her own, the three of them had a quick session of catching up.

The time flew swiftly, however, and all too soon Reagan said she had to go. Getting hugs from both Holly and Russell and a grimy one from Alisa, she hopped on her bike and started out of town.

It didn't take long to see that the sun was going to be very hot for her ride back, but it was good to know that she could wash the dress she was wearing and put it away for a time. Come next winter, she would be glad to have its extra weight.

Without really planning to, Reagan stopped riding. There was some shade ahead, and she walked the bike and stood for a moment in it. The thought of winter caused something like sadness to come upon her. She didn't know why, but the future—even knowing that God loved her and would take care of her—was somehow daunting. She couldn't put her finger on the exact reason, but she feared that the sameness of her life, the day in and day out working at the hotel and dealing with the customers, would eventually grow old and tiresome.

Reagan was still thinking on it when a rider came into view. She stood still and watched as Dakota Rawlings came abreast of her.

"Hello," she greeted him with a smile.

"Hello, yourself."

"Where are you off to?"

"To find you."

Reagan looked concerned. "Is something wrong with Katy?"

"No, but she wanted me to look for you."

"You didn't have to do that."

"She was growing anxious," Dakota explained. "She was doing her best not to show it, but she just kept asking after you."

"I knew I should have stayed and seen to her needs."

"I don't think that's it. She felt that she pushed you into going and said that you looked overheated even before you left. She also said she told you to take your time but didn't believe you actually would. I think your being gone this long convinced her that you must have collapsed on the side of the road."

"I'd better get right back."

"I'll go along with you. In fact, we can just walk. She started to relax as soon as I volunteered to go."

"Oh, all right."

Dakota swung down from the saddle, took Reagan's parcel and hung the string on his saddle horn, and then took the handlebars of her bike. That he did nothing to restrain his horse or prompt him to follow was not lost on her.

"Will he just come?"

"The puppy? Yes."

Reagan laughed at the term, but in a moment saw what he meant. Dakota's horse did not want him far from view.

"So how did your shopping go?"

Reagan looked pleased when she said, "Very well. It's fun to get new things, isn't it?"

"Yes, it is. Too bad my wife wasn't here to go with you. She loves to shop."

"How long have you been married?"

"Since January."

"Well, congratulations."

"Thank you."

At any other time Dakota might have been tempted to tease her a little about a marriage of her own, but Cash's words were still strong in his mind. For some reason, this woman's heart was vulnerable where marriage or men were concerned. Maybe she'd been married before and deserted. Dakota didn't know, but after he'd apologized to Cash that morning, he realized his first concern needed to be for Reagan's spiritual growth, not whether or not she wanted to marry his brother.

"Do you miss New York?" he asked.

"Just some of the people. I like Texas."

"What brought you here?"

"I applied for a job as a nanny, but then it was taken when I got here."

"I think Cash told us you work at the hotel."

"I did until Katy got hurt."

"What will you do when she gets back on her feet?"

"Go back to the hotel."

Dakota glanced her way and wondered if he caught a note of sadness.

"How do you like having Russ and Holly as landlords?"

"They're wonderful. I love the children too."

"I haven't seen much of the baby, but that Jonah is a keeper."

"Yes, he is. He can't wait for the day when his legs are long enough to ride the bike like his sister does."

"Isn't that just like a little boy?"

"What's that?"

"To wish his childhood away."

"You sound as though you speak from experience."

"I do."

"What was your wish?"

"To be a Texas Ranger."

"But then you gave it up."

Dakota smiled. "You haven't met Darvi. If you met her, you'd understand."

A wave of such longing swept over Reagan that she almost gasped. The thought of having someone speak like that of her, his voice sounding so caring and intimate, was almost more than she could take in. It was nothing short of relief to see the gate to the ranch come into view.

"My feet are starting to hurt," Reagan said honestly. "I hope you don't mind if I ride the rest of the way, Dakota."

"Not at all. Just leave your package with me."

"Thank you. And thank you for walking me."

"My pleasure."

Reagan was off just a heartbeat later, her mind gearing up to get back to work. Dakota didn't waste any time, but he did follow more slowly. He didn't want to tarry too long since Slater was leaving later in the day, but suddenly he had much on his mind.

❧ ❧ ❧

"You'll take care of yourself and get out of this bed as soon as possible, right?" Slater asked quietly as he leaned close to the woman who had helped raise him, knowing he needed to leave very soon.

"I will if you'll take care of Libby and that baby."

"I'll do it."

"Send word as soon as he's born."

Slater smiled. "What if it's a she?"

"I never had one of those to chase," she said, her voice almost wistful. "I'm not sure I'd know what to do."

"Well, we'll bring him or her as soon as we can so you can find out."

Slater gave her a warm hug, his heart squeezing with love.

He made his way from the room, his thoughts in a quandary. His wife needed him, and he very much wanted to be with her, but Katy's joy at seeing him had been impossible to miss.

His horse was saddled and waiting for him out front, but the only people he could see standing in the yard were his brothers. A swift check in the kitchen told him Reagan was elsewhere, so he tried upstairs. When he still didn't find her, he checked the kitchen again and found her coming from the pantry.

"Thank you for everything," he began.

"Oh, you're welcome. Did you get the food I wrapped for you?"

"Yes, ma'am. I appreciate it very much."

Reagan smiled. "Have a good trip."

"Thank you, Reagan, and I do mean thank you for everything."

Not wanting to be made over, Reagan only nodded and gave a little wave when he turned and went on his way.

Outside his brothers waited, and Slater found it hard to leave them as well. He made his goodbye a brief one, but the older brothers stood in the yard for a time.

"I sure hope that baby doesn't come before he gets back."

"It doesn't sound like that will happen."

"But he looked a little anxious."

"I thought he did too."

The two looked at each other.

"When are you pulling out?" Cash asked.

"I'll go Friday. Darvi isn't looking for me too soon."

"I'm glad you're staying. It'll do Katy's heart good."

"From what I can see, you and Reagan are about all she needs."

Cash shook his head. "When I think of how panicked I was when she showed up at the door..." Another shake accompanied this. "I could not have done this without her."

"Any word from the folks?"

"No. I'm not certain they're home. I know Mother would have been in touch if she'd gotten my letter."

"Yes. She would have."

The conversation dwindled to a comfortable silence as they both watched Slater and his horse ride out of sight. Neither man needing any further words, they both turned for the house.

⁂ ⁂ ⁂

Reagan was working hard in the kitchen when Cash came down the next morning. She had scrambled eggs, a large pot of coffee brewing, and also hot biscuits and sausage staying warm in the oven.

"It smells good in here," Cash commented.

"Are you hungry?" Reagan asked with a smile, turning as Cash approached.

She didn't see his hesitation as she spun his way. Since she was a good deal shorter, all she noticed was the blood on his chin.

"Are you cut?" she said moving closer, her face showing concern. "Your chin is bleeding."

"Oh, is it still bleeding?" His hand came up. "I nicked myself while shaving."

His voice conveying it was nothing, Cash walked toward the mirror that hung over the washbasin to inspect his chin.

Reagan stayed where she was, but it was happening again. Her heart had an odd feeling around it, as though someone were squeezing it hard. It hurt her to breathe deeply, and she had the funny feeling she might need to cry. Since she never cried, this was very foreign to her, but she thought if she didn't stop thinking about him being hurt, she would weep on the spot.

"Do you want anything?" Reagan asked in a voice she didn't recognize. She cleared her throat in an effort to hide the squeak.

Cash turned to her.

"No, it's fine. Thank you. I already washed it off."

When Reagan didn't answer, Cash watched her for a moment, his brow showing that he was somewhat puzzled. Reagan quickly schooled her features and went back to work on the meal. Cash spoke again, but she did not turn.

"If my lazybones brother ever gets out of bed, tell him I'm headed out for a quick check on the stock."

Reagan only nodded, and Cash felt he needed to add, "I'll grab a plate when I get back in."

"I'll leave it for you in the oven."

"Thank you."

Reagan didn't see that her hands were shaking until after she heard the door close on his exit.

What is the matter with me? I'm going to drop something or burn myself if I keep this up! He said he was fine. Men cut themselves shaving every day.

But Reagan was not convinced. She was still feeling upset about the whole episode even as she put a full plate of food in the oven for her employer and took a tray to Katy. She did so hoping the older woman was in a chatty mood. She would welcome anything that would get her mind off the way her heart was acting.

❧ ❧ ❧

She had to buy new dresses, Cash thought as he heeled his mount a little harder. *As if she didn't look good enough the way she was, she's now decked out in flowers and gingham. And that yellow dress next to her hair. I could barely take my eyes off her face.*

Cash refused to let his mind go any further. He rode his horse across the flats of his land, praying and trying hard to clear his thinking. He had known that Reagan was headed to buy clothing, but he didn't think she would find anything quite so attractive.

"Katy shops in that same store, and she never looks like that," Cash muttered, his mind missing the obvious.

The rancher had come out to check on some fence line and the stock and now forced his mind to those tasks. As he was riding out, he had passed his foreman, who said he would join him soon. In the distance Cash could see him on the way.

Brad's horse covered the distance in an easy gait, and Cash waited in the saddle for him to arrive. The two addressed ideas to repair some fences, and Brad filled him in as to his plans for the next few weeks.

Cash rode back to the ranch house, confident that his foreman had things under control. As to his own control, that was yet to be seen. Reagan had made her view of marriage very clear. He knew she wasn't against men in general, but she certainly wouldn't welcome the warm thoughts he'd had about her earlier. If he continued to feel the way he did, his intentions would be more than honorable, but no more welcome.

Giving his horse a break even as his stomach rumbled with hunger, Cash made his way slowly back to the house, asking God to help his confused heart.

ᘓ ᘓ ᘓ

"Good morning," Dakota greeted Katy as he came into her room and found both women inside.

"Have you eaten?" Katy asked, some of her mothering ways coming to the surface.

Dakota looked to Reagan.

"Have you ever known such a woman for wanting to feed a man? Does she constantly try to put food into you all day?"

Reagan laughed but also added, "There is food in the kitchen. Did you find it?"

"I found a plate in the oven."

Reagan's mouth opened a little, but she wasn't sure what to say. That had been Cash's food. Neither Dakota nor Katy seemed to notice her thoughtful face, and just as soon as she had an opportunity, she made her way from Katy's room to the kitchen, but it was too late. Cash was scooping the remains of the pan onto a plate.

"I'm sorry," Reagan began.

"For what?"

"Dakota ate your food. I just found out."

Cash smiled. "If Dak ate it, then why are you apologizing?"

"Because I should have put two plates in the oven. Are those eggs even warm?"

"They're fine."

"So you've tried them?" Reagan pressed him.

"Not yet."

"So how do you know?"

"I know I'm hungry enough to eat anything."

Reagan closed her mouth while he took his plate to the table, but she wasted no time in bringing him a cup of coffee. She was going to set it next to his plate and start on the dishes when he invited her to sit down.

Reagan did so, always a little wary when this happened, but Cash looked completely at ease.

"How are you?" he asked, his eyes on hers.

"Fine."

"Are you sure? You don't get a lot of time off, and I don't want you wearing down."

Reagan made herself think about it. She was often too fast in answering questions about herself as it was a subject she never wished to discuss.

"I'm fine."

"Not too tired?"

"At times I am," she admitted, working to be honest. "But not right now."

"Okay. For a time a couple of women from town were coming out to help Katy with some of the housework, but for one reason or another, they both had to quit. I'm thinking about getting someone else in, just to lighten the load, and if I do that soon, it will relieve you a little."

"How will Katy be with that?"

"I think she'll be fine," Cash said, even as his heart was asking how Reagan would deal with it. "Doc should be out today," he added. "I know Kate is hoping for a good report."

"She says the pain lessens all the time. I think she'll be out of that bed next week."

"That would be right on schedule. I'm going to do a little rearranging of furniture so she'll be able to get around in that chair."

"All right. There was a woman in New York who lived in a wheelchair. She wouldn't allow anyone to help her. She moved the wheels and propelled herself anywhere she wanted to go."

"Sounds independent."

"She was."

"That must be common to New Yorkers," Cash said with a small smile, his eyes watchful.

Reagan looked at him.

"Was that a compliment or an insult?"

"Depends."

"On what?"

Cash didn't answer. He only smiled and stood, getting ready to take his plate to the counter.

"You're pretty confident, you know that?" Reagan said to his retreating back.

"How's that?"

"You think you can tease me and still get a hot meal tonight."

Cash smiled, much as he had at the table, his eyes warm as he looked at Reagan for a moment and then went on his way.

The housekeeper didn't move for a time. She had work to do certainly, but for the moment she wanted to figure out her enigmatic employer. Her eyes half-closed in thought, she sat and looked at the place where he'd been sitting.

It didn't help, and after just a few minutes, she pushed to her feet. Time was wasting, and she still didn't know what to think of the man.

Eighteen

"OKAY, KATY," CASH DIRECTED AFTER dinner that night. "You read the verses in John 14, and Reagan, you put your finger in 1 Corinthians 10:13 so you can read that in a minute."

Katy took a moment to find the passage and began. "'In my Father's house are many mansions; if it were not so, I would have told you. I go to prepare a place for you. And if I go and prepare a place for you, I will come again, and receive you unto myself, that where I am, there ye may be also.'"

"Did you see all the promises in there?" Cash asked the women. Dakota's own head was bent as he studied the verses with them.

"But the word 'promise' isn't in there," Reagan said quietly.

"That's true, but God can't lie, so anything He tells us in His Word can be taken as a promise."

"That's the part!" Katy exclaimed. "When Pastor Ellis said that in church, I didn't understand it. And both times he and Mrs. Ellis have visited, I haven't known how to word the question."

"But it's clear to you now?"

"Yes."

That settled, Cash had Reagan read her verse.

"'There hath no temptation taken you but such as is common to man; but God is faithful, who will not suffer you to be tempted above that ye are able, but will with the temptation also make a way to escape, that ye may be able to bear it.'"

"Do you understand what that means?" Cash asked and watched Dakota nod.

Reagan and Katy were still studying their Bibles, so he waited.

"I think it means that I have no excuse to sin," Reagan said.

"That's true, Reagan, but there's more to it than that. God always provides a way out. We never have to be slaves to sin again, because He always gives us some way to escape every time we're tempted."

From there, Cash took them into Psalms. For the next hour they studied verse after verse on the promises of God. Only when Katy began to flag did Cash bring things to a close.

"Thank you, Cash," Katy told him as the men kissed her and left the room. Reagan stayed to ready her for the night.

"Did you learn as much as I did?" Katy wanted to know.

Reagan smiled as she filled the water glass and put everything within reach.

"I might have learned more. You keep forgetting, I haven't heard any of this."

Katy patted the chair, and Reagan sat close to her. The older woman took her hand and held it.

"Tell me about Wednesday."

"Wednesday?"

"Yes. Isn't that the day you went shopping?"

"Yes, but I don't think there's anything to tell."

"How did you end up with three dresses?"

Reagan smiled. "Lavinia was having a one-day sale." Reagan paused and looked deflated. "I should have shopped for you too."

Katy grinned in delight and confessed to Reagan what was in the note she'd sent. The younger woman looked shocked but also very pleased.

"Go on now," Katy finally shooed her away. "You've had a long day. Go sit and put your feet up."

Reagan kissed her goodnight and then walked out to find the men talking in the living room. She had rarely let herself sit on one of those beautiful sofas—she never felt she had time—but did so now, hoping she was not intruding.

"I'm glad you joined us," Cash said. "Put your feet up."

He smiled at her when she settled in and then turned to his brother.

"What will Darvi be doing tonight?"

"She'll probably have dinner with some of the friends we've made. The church family there is small, but it's very close. The townsfolk are kind too."

"What do you do for a living now?" Reagan felt free to ask.

"I'm filling in for a sheriff who's been hurt, so I'm still in law enforcement."

"And what will you do when the sheriff comes back?"

"I just heard that that's not going to happen for a while, but when he does return, I have two options: I could get another job in law enforcement, or Darvi and I could come back to the ranch, build our own place, and work with Cash."

Reagan turned immediately to her employer.

"Will you be expanding if that happens?"

Cash blinked. "As a matter of fact, I will, but how did you know that?"

"Well, you have things completely under control right now. If you're going to add another full-time man, I assume you'll be letting your foreman go or expanding your herd."

"And what would you be knowing about herd expansion?" Dakota asked, his mouth open a little.

"Well, sometimes I look at the books Cash has on the office shelves, the ones that talk about ranching," she answered, clearly embarrassed, and then looked to Cash. "I hope that's all right."

"Of course it's all right. Do you have any questions?"

"Actually I do." She leaned forward a little, her eyes alight with interest. "Do you brand just in the spring or more than once a year? And why do you brand when you have fences? I thought branding was going out of style with fences becoming so popular."

Cash had all he could do not to gawk at her as he answered.

"Brands are still important when we go to market. Also, fences don't always hold, and with more ranchers moving into the area, I want to be certain I can claim my own herd. We're also not immune to rustling."

"I wondered about that. How often do you come across head that have lost some of their brand?"

"Off and on."

"Do you redo it?"

"Yes, ma'am."

"You sound rather interested in ranching, Reagan," Dakota put in.

"Oh, I am," she told him honestly. "I think it would be wonderful to own my own ranch. Even a small place would be exciting."

"And how would you work things?"

"Like Cash does. He does a great job. Although I would probably put the barn and paddock further from the house to cut down on the dust."

The men smiled.

"Our mother felt the same way, but by the time she realized it, it was too late."

A few moments later, Reagan stifled a yawn and asked to be excused. Out of courtesy, the men stood when she rose and left, but sat back down to talk some more.

"How long has she lived here?" Dakota asked.

"Since January."

"And she's from New York?"

"Yes."

Dakota stared at his brother. "She reminds me of Father. He was so city bred, but he sure took to Texas."

"I hadn't thought of it, but you're right. Other than the heat before she got lighter clothing, she hasn't batted an eyelash over much of anything."

Cash had no more said this when he remembered the armadillo. He laughed as he explained to Dakota.

Dakota had all he could do not to mention how well suited she seemed for his brother, but he restrained himself and remembered once again to pray only for God's will and not his own concerning his oldest sibling and the two women living in his house.

❧ ❧ ❧

On their way to church, Cash was thinking about the good time he'd had with his brothers, and how nice it would have been if Dakota could have stayed to see the church family. He did this in an effort to ignore how Reagan looked in another one of her new dresses, this one a medium blue that made her skin look like fresh cream.

He was praying for both his brothers, their wives, and the new baby—whether he or she had arrived or not—when he realized that Reagan was staying very close even after they'd arrived at church and walked into the building. Brenda had filled in with Katy as she had before, and Cash and Reagan had come at a good time to visit. Reagan, however, seemed unwilling to move from his side.

"Everything all right, Reagan?"

"Um hmm."

Cash looked down at her profile; she was worrying her lip a bit, her eyes watchful.

"Why do I have a hard time believing that?"

"I don't know," she said with a complete nonchalance that Cash wasn't buying.

"All right," he said, his voice dropping as he stepped in front of her. "What's going on?"

"Can't I stand with you?"

"You know you can."

"It's just until Holly comes."

"What happens then?"

"I'll have someone to stand with."

"Why must you stand with someone?"

With that, Reagan's mouth shut. She looked up at him and then away, but said nothing more.

"You may stand with me all morning if you want to."

"Thank you."

There was no missing her relief, and Cash was glad he didn't press her, but he wasn't done. Almost as soon as they left the church, he asked her again.

"Has someone at the church seemed threatening to you?"

Reagan's eyes grew.

"No."

"Has someone made improper advances?"

"No."

"Has someone done anything that I need to know about?"

"I don't think so."

"You didn't sound as sure that time."

Reagan fiddled with the fabric in her lap and fingered the Bible she'd brought.

Cash waited in silence for her to speak.

"It's hard to explain."

"What is?"

"Why I stayed close to you."

"I'd really like you to try, Reagan."

Not for the first time she noticed that his voice was always kind. Even when he was giving orders, he managed to use a tone that never frightened her.

"I think some of the men have heard about my decision for Christ. And so I think some of them want to catch my eye, like you said about the ranch hands."

"And that doesn't happen if you stay with someone?"

"Well, it might happen if I'm talking to Holly, but I know it won't happen if I'm with you." Reagan suddenly heard what she'd just said, and her head turned swiftly to look at him. "I'm sorry."

"For what?"

"I think I just admitted that I used you this morning," Reagan said with some exasperation, thinking he should know.

"No, you didn't. If I ever feel used, I'll tell you."

"So you don't mind?"

"That you stand with me? Of course not. I can't honestly think of a single man at church who would mean you harm, but if you don't wish to encourage any of them, that's fine."

Without warning, Reagan's head filled with one question: *What if I wish to encourage you?* She was horrified by this thought and put a hand to her face just thinking about it.

"Are you all right?" Cash asked as he watched her go quite pale.

"Yes. Well, sort of."

Cash continued to study her.

"I will be," she said at last, feeling her face flush. She never remembered blushing in New York, but it happened here quite often. What was the matter with her?

"I think I need more sleep," she said out loud, not really intending to voice that thought.

"Well, you'll be glad to know that I spoke with Meg Patton today, and she would be happy to come and relieve you one day a week. When I spoke to Katy about the idea this morning, I could tell she wanted only you but also that she understood."

"I was going to talk to you about that, Cash. I think I'll be fine to keep on as I'm doing. It's only a few more weeks, and I know just how Katy wants things done."

Cash didn't reply.

She looked a little more worn each day, and Cash was growing concerned about her health.

"I worked every day for Sally," Reagan reminded him.

"Not all day, you didn't. And unless I've missed something, you were never called in at night."

Reagan chewed her lip some more, the ranch gate coming into view.

"Let me tell you what I have in mind," Cash began gently. "I thought if Meg came on Saturdays and gave you the entire day off, and Brenda still took over for you on Sunday mornings, you would get a nice long rest each week."

"I've been meaning to talk to you about that, Cash."

"About what?"

"About Brenda's filling in for me. I feel badly that she and Brad can't go to church."

"Brenda and Brad have no interest in church, Reagan. He's been my foreman for several years now, and we've had many conversations on spiritual matters. He feels his life is fine. He believes in God and even says he prays to Him, but Brad doesn't believe he needs more than that."

Reagan nodded. She thought that might be the case but hoped she was wrong. She enjoyed Sunday mornings off, but not at someone else's expense.

"Would I go back to my house on Saturdays?" Reagan asked.

"I hope not, but you could if you wanted to."

It was on Reagan's mind to ask why he wanted her to stay when she wasn't working, but for some reason she thought the answer might be unsettling.

"Well," Reagan said at last, feeling as though she needed to be rescued. All spunk was gone from her these days.

Maybe she was more tired than she realized. "You tell me what you want me to do, and I'll do it."

"All right," Cash agreed without hesitation as he pulled up to drop her in front of the house. "You'll work Monday through Friday, as you have been, but come Saturday, Meg will arrive and give you the entire day off. You'll stay here on those days, but you won't work. Someone can take you to town; you can go for a ride on your bicycle; you can sleep late; lie around and read, visit with Katy, or any number of things; but you can't clean, wash clothes, or even cook for yourself. On Sundays Brenda will come, and you'll go back on duty after church until the next Saturday. And we'll do things that way until Katy is completely back on her feet."

Had Cash not been a strong man, he'd have kissed Reagan on the spot. Her mouth was hanging open in a way he found adorable.

"Is that clear?" he finally asked when she only stared at him.

"I think so. You may have to go over it again."

"Anytime," he said easily and climbed down to help her out of the wagon.

She looked at him, still feeling slightly amazed, but he only smiled.

Reagan made her way into the house, telling herself not to try and take it all in at that moment.

❧ ❧ ❧

"How are you doing?" Russell asked Cash at the elders' meeting that Sunday afternoon.

Cash looked at him, knowing if he could tell anyone what was going on, he could tell Russell.

"I'm all right, I think."

"How is it going having Reagan living under your roof?"

Cash stared at him. He should have known this friend would be perceptive.

"It has its moments."

"I'm sure it does."

Cash stood still, his mind on the woman who was wreaking havoc in his heart.

"Have you fallen for her?"

"I'm not sure, but something is happening."

"In both of you or just you?"

"That's a good question. Sometimes I see a softening in Reagan when she's with me, or maybe 'interest' would be a better word, but I can't be sure."

"Are you even sure of your own feelings?"

"Not to describe them. I do feel very protective of her, but at the same time I'm afraid of her."

"Why would you be afraid of her?"

"Not of her, I guess, but for her. Because she doesn't want a relationship. I've asked myself if she feels that way because of where she's been and how she's been treated, and maybe I would be different for her, but if that doesn't happen—if she doesn't see it that way—I would be in love alone."

It was not the clearest sentence, but Russell got the full meaning.

"I'm praying for you, Cash. Holly and I both are."

"Thank you. If Holly has any insight into Reagan that she thinks would help, I'd be glad to hear it."

The meeting was going to be starting soon, so the men joined the others. The first thing the elders did was take prayer requests and pray together. Cash asked the other men to remember his unusual situation and felt a peace over having them pray for him without having to go into specific details that might have embarrassed Reagan. And then Cash was the first to pray. He started by thanking God for allowing him to work with the caring elders of the church.

❧ ❧ ❧

The rocking chair moved swiftly under Reagan's body as she tried not to think about all she could be doing in the house. Before Cash had left for his meeting, he told her he just wanted her to see to Katy's needs on Sundays and to keep the cooking light. And that was all.

"But I was going to get a jump on the washing," she'd argued.

Cash had shaken his head.

"That might be why you're getting so tired. You need to take a day off. I don't work on Sundays any more than I have to, and that's how I stay strong the rest of the week."

Reagan could hardly argue with that, but at the moment she wasn't tired. Katy had dozed off, and normally Reagan would have been flying around to get a head start on the week.

"And why did Cash wait until this week to tell me?" Reagan muttered, wishing he was there so she could have it out with him.

But her feelings didn't last long. The longer she rocked, the more slowly she moved. She thought she should check on Katy before she got too comfortable but couldn't manage it. She nodded off while thinking about the work she would have waiting in the morning.

❧ ❧ ❧

Reagan opened her eyes to find she wasn't alone. Cash was in the other rocking chair, his feet up on the stool.

"I'm sure glad you got a jump on that wash today," he teased her.

Reagan blinked owlishly at him.

"How long have I been asleep?"

"I don't know."

Reagan leapt to her feet. "Katy!"

"I just checked on her. She just woke up too."

Reagan sank back into the chair with relief.

"I must have really conked out," she said, her hands wiping her face as she worked to remove the last vestiges of sleep.

Cash only stared at her.

"How was your meeting?"

"It was fine."

"What do you do?"

"Well, the elders are responsible for the church family. We need to make certain that folks are taken care of, both spiritually and physically, but we can't do that unless we're taking care of ourselves, so we meet once a month for prayer and Bible study, and then we discuss the needs of the rest of the church family."

"And that's right in Scripture?"

"Yes. The Bible asks the question, If a man can't order his own life, how can he lead the church? I can give you the passage if you want."

"Thank you."

A short silence fell, but Reagan was still thinking.

"Will I ever know what you know?"

"Certainly," he was able to answer honestly. "You study very hard, Reagan, and there's nothing slow about you."

Reagan was pleased to hear this, and she wanted to thank him, but at the moment the thoughts in her head made her embarrassed to even look at him.

"I'd better check on Katy."

"Reagan." Cash stopped her when she was right in front of him.

She reluctantly looked at him.

"This is how I want you to spend every Sunday, taking it as easy as possible."

"But now you're giving me Saturdays off, Cash. Before it's over, I'll be working on Wednesday from noon to three and that will be my whole week!"

Cash could only laugh.

"I wasn't making a joke," Reagan told him, her hands coming to her waist.

"But you're still funny."

This got him frowned at, so he added, "Why don't you ride your bike or go back to sleep for a while?"

"I have to check on Katy."

"I told you I just did. She's reading and making a list for town next time you go."

This put Reagan completely out of her element. She cast around for something to say and ended up storming off the porch. She stopped at the bottom of the steps and glared back at her employer.

"I'm going for a walk, Cash Rawlings, but not a pleasure walk. I'll be thinking about all the work I have to do this week and planning how to get it done in less time!"

This said, she stomped off. Much as he wanted to, Cash didn't follow or comment. He had all he could do not to laugh again.

Nineteen

REAGAN'S FIRST SATURDAY OFF WAS a fiasco. Meg came and worked hard, but Reagan could not keep still. Katy had been in her wheelchair for two days, and Reagan felt she had to be on hand at all times. Cash watched his plan fall apart and put a new one into action for the very next week. When Reagan got up he told her to change into an older dress and meet him in the yard.

Reagan did as she was told and arrived expecting him to ask her to wash windows, but instead, she found two horses waiting, both saddled and ready.

"We're going for a ride?" she asked, her skepticism showing in every way.

"Yep. I'll show you some of the land."

Reagan did not look pleased.

"I've never ridden a horse before. I don't like horses."

"Why not?"

"Because."

"Because why?"

Reagan's face told him he should already know this, but she still explained.

"What if it decides to bite me or buck me off?"

"I didn't choose a horse that would do that to you. This animal is very gentle."

"You want me to break my neck, don't you?" she asked, but it was apparent to Cash that she wasn't really speaking to him. She was circling the animal and mumbling to herself.

"What if I don't want to?" she demanded as she came to stand in front of Cash.

"How are you going to run your own ranch someday if you can't ride?" the cowboy countered, and Reagan bit her lip.

"It might happen," she said quietly.

"Yes, it might."

"I mean, it would take a miracle, but God can do that, can't He?"

"Yes, He can."

Cash watched her reconsider. While she was doing that, he reached for the hat that he'd hooked on her saddle horn and plopped it on her head.

"You'll need this."

"Oh, my," Reagan said as she took off the cowboy hat and examined it. "It's a woman's, isn't it? Where did you find it?"

"It's my mother's. She leaves it here."

"And she won't mind?"

"Not at all."

Cash watched her set the hat in place and adjust the rim. She then smiled up at him, and he had to ask himself what he'd been thinking to believe this was the answer to getting Reagan to relax on her day off. If the day continued as it started, he would be so weary from fighting his emotions, he wouldn't be able to stand.

"You're sure I won't get hurt?" she asked, her little face looking up at him trustingly.

"I can't say for sure, Reagan, but as much as it's within my power, I won't let you be harmed."

"You promise?"

"I can't do that. I'm not God."

Reagan's eyes grew a bit.

"Are we not supposed to promise?"

"It's not a good idea. Our word needs to be trustworthy, but I can't promise because circumstances might enter in that are out of my control."

Reagan thought on this for a time.

"God promises. He promises all the time. But then He can do anything He needs to make the promise happen."

Cash was glad he'd stayed quiet so she could come to this on her own.

"All right," Reagan said after another moment of quiet. "I'll ride the horse."

Without ceremony Cash boosted her into the saddle and watched her immediately panic. She gripped the horn with white-knuckled fingers and said in a voice that was very high and soft, "It's too far up. I'm going to fall."

"I'm right here, Reagan," Cash comforted, but it took a moment to get through to her. She stared at him in horror until she realized his hands were still holding her waist.

"You're still holding me."

He smiled the smile that had become so familiar, and Reagan relaxed a bit. When Cash felt and saw it, he gave her some directions on what to do and stepped back. She looked ready to panic again but didn't say anything.

Cash climbed into the saddle of his own horse and maneuvered him close to hers. As he expected, Reagan's horse didn't even shift.

"Are you set?"

"I can't remember what to do first."

"Give her a little bump with your heels. That's it."

"We're moving!"

"You're doing fine."

Inside of an hour, Reagan was as relaxed as if she'd been riding for years. She joined Cash when he stepped up the pace a bit and in little time found the rhythm of the horse's gait. Her hat flew off to be caught by the tie at her neck, and her laughter could be heard from afar.

"I had no idea! The horse really does just what you tell it."

"She's a good mount. Her name's Bessy, by the way."

Reagan reached down and patted the side of the horse's neck. They rode on for some time before Cash wanted to show Reagan some sights from the top of the hills. They left the horses staked below and walked up a slope.

On the way up, however, Reagan lost her footing. With a small cry she began to fall. Cash steadied himself to catch her, but he was too late in responding. Almost before he knew it, he was tumbling backward. The slope wasn't extremely steep, and he'd have probably rolled down and laughed about it if not for the tree that got in his way. The back of his head slammed against the trunk and set his ears to ringing.

"Oh, Cash!" Reagan cried. Having righted herself, she began running as fast as she could to get to his side. He had already sat up by the time she got there, but he was shaking his head to clear it.

"Are you all right?"

"I think so, but that hurt."

Reagan knelt next to him, her hands clenched in fear. She wanted to touch his head and see if he had a bump, but she was afraid of hurting him more.

"Why don't you lie back," she suggested. "Maybe you'll feel better."

Cash was feeling poorly enough to take her suggestion. He scooted forward a little, not caring about his clothing, and lay back. There was a slight rise at the base of the tree that was comfortable for his neck, and he settled in and shut his eyes.

"How is it?"

"It still hurts, but it did help to lie down. Thank you."

"It's all my fault. I fell right into you."

"It's not your fault, Reagan. I couldn't get my footing."

Reagan didn't really feel any better, but it helped to have him sound normal to her. His eyes were closed, but he was still talking. Thinking it would help to change the subject, Reagan asked some questions about where they were.

Cash told her what he'd been taking her to see and said that if he rested for a time, they could still go.

"Is there anything you want me to do?" Reagan asked when Cash fell quiet.

Cash opened his eyes for a moment, put his head up, and looked back down the hill.

"Do you remember how far back it is to the horses?"

"Yes. It's not far at all."

"Would you mind getting the water I have on my saddle?"

"I'll go right now."

Reagan hurried, so it didn't take long, and after Cash drank, he closed his eyes again. By then Reagan had run out of words. She felt awful. She wouldn't have wanted it to happen to anyone, but especially not to Cash. Cash, who was always so strong and ready to take care of others.

Reagan looked into his face—it was rather pale—and felt her heart squeeze. She watched the even rise and fall of his chest and thought he must have gone to sleep. She didn't know if that was safe, but clearly his head hurt, and she didn't wish to disturb him.

Moving carefully, she picked up his hand and held it in her lap. It was a hand much larger and rougher than her own, and with gentle movements she touched his fingers and even laid her own palm against his. She prayed while doing this, asking God to heal him and not let him be permanently harmed. She was still holding his hand and praying when she looked over to find his eyes on her.

Reagan let go of his hand as though she'd been burned, color leaping into her face.

"You're in love with me, Reagan," Cash said softly, and for a moment she froze.

It didn't last long. In less than a minute her face crumpled, and try as she might, the tears would not be stemmed.

"I didn't mean for it to happen. I really didn't," she cried quietly, a few tears actually falling down her cheeks. "I just couldn't seem to help myself."

The quiet tears deserted her then, and she cried the real ones, the ones that hadn't been shed in more years than she could remember. She was near to choking when she realized that Cash was sitting up and trying to speak to her.

"It's all right, Reagan," he said. "Listen to me."

"But it's not all right," she told him, sniffling and shaking all over. "I have no right to love you."

"How do you figure?"

"I just don't. I don't have any right to think that I could have Cash Rawlings for my own."

"What right do I have to think I could have Reagan Sullivan?"

Reagan shook her head. "It's not the same."

Cash smiled that warm, wonderful smile. "If the men at church are any indication, it's very much the same."

Reagan looked into his eyes.

Cash looked right back. With slow movements, he reached forward and brushed the tears from her cheeks. "You've been very hurt by someone," he said quietly.

All Reagan could do was nod.

"I'm not that man, Reagan."

"No, you're not," she agreed without hesitation. "You're nothing like my father."

"Was he the one?"

"Yes. I see him differently now that I understand what a sinner I am, but the way fathers treat their children—good or bad—lasts a long time."

"Can you tell me about it, or is it too painful?"

Reagan gave a mirthless laugh. "Even in that you're different. My father would have demanded an answer, not given me a choice."

Cash waited, knowing he needn't say any more.

"All I can tell you," Reagan started, "is what I know. I don't know the details. I just know how it affected me. Not long after my ninth birthday, my parents had a terrible fight. There was yelling and screaming, and I was locked out of the apartment. When my father came storming out, I ran in to find my mother on the floor.

"To this day I don't know if he struck her or forced himself on her or what, but she was crying and her hair was a mess, and she sat up and said she couldn't take it anymore."

Reagan looked up and found Cash listening carefully.

"She was gone when I woke up the next morning, and I never saw her again. For a time I tried to be a very good little girl, certain that would bring her back, but no one even noticed. On top of that my father was addicted to the bottle, and that only grew worse after Mama left. He was angry all the time, and I became afraid of him when he came close to backhanding me. That only happened once, and he stopped short, but I remember it. I didn't answer him quickly enough about where I'd been, and he almost hit me.

"Day after day I would watch him drink until he couldn't move in the chair any longer, and I'd leave him alone until he roused again. I don't know how we ate or even stayed in the apartment, but one day he didn't rouse, and I went for the neighbors. He was dead, and I was alone. I wasn't going to let it get me down, so before I was even a teen, I found work. I worked hard and did my best to find adventure around every corner so I could forget the things that hurt me. That's why I took the nanny's job that didn't work out. That's why I was willing to come to Texas."

Reagan looked him in the eye.

"But there's one adventure that terrifies me. I never wanted to be married. I never wanted a man to have control over me or to love me and then leave me or hurt me."

Cash put his hand out, just holding it open and waiting. After a moment, Reagan placed her hand in his palm, but Cash did not enclose her hand. Still moving carefully, he put his thumb on the back of her hand, not too tightly, and not attempting to pull her toward him in any way.

"I must know your views on marriage better than anyone, Reagan. I've had to be very careful."

"What do you mean?"

With his thumb stroking gently over the back of her hand, Cash said, "You're not a woman a man can rush. Not that I tend to be reckless, but I knew I had to be extra careful with your heart."

"Oh, Cash," was all she could think to say. Her thoughts felt scrambled. He was so wonderful—her heart knew that—but her mind was still afraid. Even the way he held her hand was undemanding. She didn't think she had ever met anyone like him.

"You need to know, Reagan, how much I want to take you in my arms right now and kiss you." Cash shocked her with his words; the hold on her hand had given no indication. "But you may not want to be my wife. You may never accept my love, and as much as I want to kiss you, I'm not going to do that if you're not going to marry me."

"I've never been kissed."

"When I was 16, I had a girlfriend and we used to kiss. When I got a little older, I saw what a mistake that was, but I've not had anyone in my life since I came to Christ."

Reagan's face told Cash she was thinking again. Thankfully, she wasn't long in saying what it was.

"Kissing leads to other things."

Even though his head still hurt, Cash had to laugh. She was always such a surprise.

"Well, doesn't it?"

"Yes, it certainly can—it never has for me—but even talking about it can lead to temptation, so I think the two of us had better get back on the trail."

Cash came awkwardly to his feet, and Reagan touched his arm.

"How is your head?"

"It hurts, but my heart knows I'm not in love alone, and that's enough to make me ignore the pain."

Reagan smiled. She was not a woman who dreamed about a man falling for her and telling her how he felt, but if she were, this would not be what she imagined.

You've been fighting this for years, Reagan girl—it's the least you deserve.

The two made their way down the hill to the horses and then very slowly back to the ranch. Reagan kept a close eye on Cash, but he didn't look as if he was going to pass out as she feared. She offered to go for someone to help with the horses, knowing she was useless in the barn, and Cash accepted. One of the hands, looking very pleased to be following Reagan, came in a hurry and offered to help Cash to the house as well.

Cash said he could handle it but was glad to get to the living room.

"If this isn't the worst," he commented quietly as he dropped onto the sofa.

"What's that?" Reagan asked. She had remained close by, hoping for a bit more conversation.

"Finding out you love me and having a headache all at the same time."

Reagan smiled. She had never heard him sound so disgruntled.

"Should I go for the doctor?" Reagan asked, making herself be practical.

"I don't think so."

This was no more than said when they both heard the bunkhouse cook coming through the kitchen. Max had come to see Katy on occasion, but Reagan had never had much interaction with him.

"Cash," he called again. "Where are you?"

"In the living room."

Max's voice brought Meg from Katy's room, so she was standing nearby when he arrived.

"You hit your head?" the older man demanded.

"Just a bump."

"Let me see it," he grumbled, as though Cash were a pesky child. "You've got a good egg there. What were you doing?"

"I lost my footing and fell against a tree."

Max shook his head.

"You'll have to keep an eye on him tonight," he said to Reagan. "Don't let him sleep too long."

Cash tried to object, but Reagan was taking it all in. As though the ranch owner weren't even in the room, plans were made around him. Reagan was told to wake him twice during the night, three times if he went to bed early, and Max would check him again in the morning. Max then proceeded to Katy's room, where she had just gotten back into bed, to fill her in as well.

"I'm fine," Cash said for the umpteenth time and then gave up trying to convince anyone. Meg was busy putting lunch on as both Reagan and Cash had missed it, and Max headed out to tell Brad about the head injury.

Cash was sitting in the living room feeling as though the house were falling apart around him when he realized all was quiet and that he was not alone. He looked over to see Reagan sitting on a chair watching him.

"Do you feel like you've lost control of your own home?"

"That was perceptive of you."

"Not really."

Cash's brows rose in question.

"You're always the one in charge, always the one to take care of everyone else. Having anything happen to you makes the rest of us fall apart."

"You seem pretty calm right now."

"I'm not as calm as I look. I'm afraid you're not all right, but you won't admit it or don't realize it."

"May I be honest with you?"

Reagan nodded.

"My head hurts a little, but my real problem is my frustration in not being able to talk to you more."

"What would you say?"

"I would ask you if I can talk to Pastor or Russell about us. I know how I feel, and I know how you feel, but there are things to be worked out because of your fear."

Reagan nodded in understanding.

"Once in a while," she admitted, "I would have a vision of living here for always and being yours too, and sometimes it would feel scary to me and sometimes not."

"What does it feel like right now?"

Reagan had to shake her head and confess that she wasn't sure.

"I just wish," she whispered, her heart ripping a little around the edge, "that you could have someone who's not me. I think you deserve better."

Cash didn't say a word, but Reagan got the distinct impression that he was not happy with this idea. She suspected that he might even have addressed the issue, but Meg came through the living room just then to tell them she had lunch hot and ready on the table.

Cash and Reagan thanked her and moved to the kitchen, both knowing that the end of this conversation was going to have to wait.

Twenty

"ARE YOU SURE YOU WANT TO TRY this?" Cash asked Katy again.

"I'm sure. Are you sure?"

Cash smiled when her tone begged him not to say no.

Reagan had awakened him in the night, but even so he'd slept well. Now, after having assured the woman repeatedly that his head was fine, Cash had rigged up a ramp in order to push Katy's wheelchair into the back of the wagon. The plan was not without risks.

"What do you suppose the doc would say?" Katy asked conversationally as Cash tied her chair to the sideboards to steady it.

"You do know how to panic a man, don't you, Kate."

Katy gave a crack of laughter just as Reagan came from the house with all of their Bibles.

"Are we set?" she asked, her eyes alight with excitement. This scheme had been all her own, and even though Cash had originally been horrified by the idea, he was once again won over by Katy's pleasure.

"I think so. Are you still riding back here?"

"Yes. I have a quilt to sit on, and I'll just keep the chair steady."

Cash shook his head when she looked mischievous and then stepped forward to help her when she moved to climb aboard. She smiled down at him, and his eyes held hers for a moment.

"It's about time you two found each other," Katy stated, shocking them a little. She looked at the couple staring at her and snorted.

"My hip is broken," she reminded them. "Not my eyes."

"Katy," Cash began patiently, feeling very protective of Reagan, "it's not that simple. We're going to give this—"

"I know," she cut him off. "Reagan has to get over her fear of being married, but she will. And I'm not going to spread the news until the two of you do."

"How did you know, Katy?" Reagan asked from her place on the floor of the wagon bed.

The older woman's face was kind. "I live with the two of you, Reagan. Cash didn't even know it, but as soon as you came to Christ, his feelings toward you started to change. And you didn't want this, but no woman has ever been able to resist Cash Rawlings. He's never encouraged them, mind you, but when that man walks the streets of Kinkade, female heads turn from all directions."

It was an interesting start to the morning. They had to get going because the ride was going to be slower, but both Cash and Reagan were somewhat shocked by all of Katy's observations.

"I've been praying for you both," she added when the wagon was finally set into motion.

"And what exactly have you been praying?" Cash asked over his shoulder from his place behind the reins.

"That you would grow in the Lord, so that if He did bring you together you'd be ready. I prayed in God's will, but I must admit I've wanted to see it happen."

"Why did you never say anything?" Reagan asked.

"That wouldn't have been wise. If I had been mistaken, it would have just made you uncomfortable around each other."

"But why did you say something now?" Cash asked.

"Because something more went on yesterday than you bumping your head. I don't need to know what, but Reagan doesn't have to try not to look at you anymore, and you touched her arm twice last night, Cash. That's not something I've ever seen you do to any woman before."

Cash turned around and met Reagan's wide gaze before both started to laugh. Katy joined them, not knowing when she had felt so good. Her hip was mending, and she was headed to church—and not out of fear—but because God now lived inside of her. This thought, however, reminded her of something she needed to take care of with Cash.

"Cash," Katy called to him just as her chair shifted a little and her hip experienced some pain.

"Am I going too fast?"

"No. I've got something to apologize to you about."

"All right. Did you want to talk to me later?"

"No. Reagan can hear this. Remember how angry I was about your view of your parents' salvation?"

"I remember."

"Well, I can see what you were talking about now. I know your mother would have come if she'd received the letter you sent. She's that type of person. But I do see what you meant before. Being a good person is not what God has to say."

It had been said in Katy's way, but Cash understood her.

"Thank you, Kate. I appreciate that very much."

The three went on to church and had a wonderful morning. Less than a handful of folks missed the chance to greet Katy and wish her well, and she thought that if she died that day, she would do so the happiest person on earth.

"How many folks get a second chance at my age?" she asked Noelle Ellis.

"Not many take it like you have, Katy. Even at the eleventh hour God saves, but it seems that not many folks see their need in time."

Katy was so excited she could hardly speak. She was still sitting there smiling when Cash came to claim her.

"Are you about ready to head out?"

"Yes, I am. Is Reagan ready?"

"I believe so."

Several men were on hand to help Cash load Katy and her chair back into the wagon. It wasn't without discomfort to her, but if the truth be told, that lady barely even noticed.

≈ ≈ ≈

"Katy!" Cash called to her after he made a trip into town on Thursday morning.

"In the kitchen," she called back.

Cash just about ran to find her and saw Reagan in attendance as well.

"My parents are on their way!" he told them. "Davis at the telegraph office caught me just as I was leaving town. They had been out of the state, and while away my father had taken ill, but now they're on their way."

"We'll have to shop," Katy said decisively. "Do we have time?"

"I'm not sure," he spoke as he tried to scan the contents of the message again. "With this date, they could be coming in today."

Amid Katy's and his own excitement, it took a moment for Cash to notice that Reagan was missing. He called for her and began to check around the house, but not until he walked through the living room did he spot her out front, bicycle in hand, getting ready to hop on and ride. Without having to be told, he knew she was not headed out for exercise.

He was out the door in a flash, running faster than he had in years. He caught up with her just as she was giving the bike a push to jump on. He was thankful she heard his approach and stopped.

"Oh, Cash," she said quietly, her features strained and tense, "I have to go home for a little while. I should have told you, but you're here now, so now you know."

"Can I take you?" he offered, his chest still heaving some.

"No, no," she said, her eyes filling with panic. "I'll be back sometime."

"Reagan, honey," Cash said gently, "what's wrong?"

"I just need to go home. It's been a long time."

"Does this have anything to do with my parents' coming?"

"I have to go," she told him, not even looking at him. "I'll be back."

"Reagan," he tried again, but she just shook her head and started on her way.

Cash wasted no time. He moved swiftly back to the house, spoke with Katy, ran over to see Brenda, and then went out to the barn. He saddled his horse and was riding at a full gallop just ten minutes later.

He had waited a long time for that little black-haired woman to walk into his life. He wasn't going to let her escape him that easily.

❧ ❧ ❧

Reagan's heart was near to bursting by the time she reached the street on which she lived. For the first time since she could remember, she hoped Holly would not spot her and come to the porch to visit. She needed to talk to only one person at the moment, and she had run away from him. Outside of Cash Rawlings, she wanted to be alone.

For the last half block she had been off the bike, just pushing it along. Now she was almost to the yard and already wanting to cry. She thought if she could just get inside, she could let go. It would feel good to cry. It might give her a headache the way it had when she cried with Cash, but in the end she had been glad she allowed herself the release.

"Cash!" Reagan said his name when she spotted him, stopping short to see him leaning against her front door. After a moment she continued pushing her bike up to him.

"How can you possibly be here ahead of me?"

"I have a fast horse, and I know a shortcut."

Reagan looked into his eyes and then away.

"I shouldn't have run. I know that now, but I just panicked."

"Why did you?"

Reagan made herself admit the truth. "When your brothers came, I hadn't yet faced my feelings for you. Now it's different. What if I don't like your parents? What if they don't like me?"

Reagan gestured helplessly with one hand, wishing for some way to make herself clear.

"I've never had what you have, Cash," she tried. "Most people would be dying for it, but I'm afraid of it. You have brothers who love and care for you. They came from miles away to see Katy. Now your parents are on their way. I don't even have to see them to know that they won't be anything like my parents, but that doesn't mean we'll like each other."

"And what happens if they don't like you?"

Reagan's smile was sad. "It will no longer be an issue of me getting over my fears. The issue will be that you would never marry a woman your family didn't approve of."

"Here," Cash said. "Give me your bike."

He took it and leaned it up against the side of the house. He then directed Reagan to the bench in the yard. Once they'd sat down, he prayed and tried to gather his thoughts.

"It's funny, but I think many husbands and wives come from very diverse backgrounds. Have you ever noticed that?"

Reagan said she hadn't.

"I sometimes wonder if that isn't by design. I mean, you've been hurt by your family, but mine is very loving and supportive. I can see how you might find that threatening, but it could also serve to give you strength."

Cash turned his head to study her, and he could see that she was thinking.

"Do you remember last Saturday when I said I wished you could find someone better?"

"Yes."

"You didn't like that, did you?"

"No, I didn't because it's not true."

"But this is what I'm talking about. A woman should be glad to meet your family. I mean, a little bit of nerves is normal, but not panic and thoughts of escape."

"But I don't want just *any* woman. I want you. Even if you panic and run away. I want to give you as much time as you need to see that you have nothing to fear, but I don't want anyone else, Reagan."

The little Irish woman next to him said nothing, and Cash was suddenly glad that this had happened. There were some things she didn't know about him. It was time she did.

"Have you caught on yet that my parents are not believers?"

"Yes."

"It's interesting to me that all of their sons and even my father's mother have come to Christ, but they haven't. Now ask me Reagan—ask me why it's interesting."

"Okay. Why is it?"

"Because Charles Rawlings Sr. set out to raise three of the most independent children you could imagine. He hoped one of us boys would want the ranch, and I did, but he's always insisted that we step out and follow our dreams. He loves to travel and have adventures, and he's dragged my mother halfway around the world, but not in all of his ventures has he found Jesus Christ.

"He and my mother are starting to ask some questions, but it's taken a lot of years for that to happen."

"But God saved all three of you boys after you were grown and gone?"

"Yes, and that brings me back to us. You're right, I do value my parents' opinion. But you need to understand their expectations. Slater met Libby and fell in love before any of us met her. We all went to the wedding, but he was a man in love long before my parents knew.

"Dakota and Darvi had known each other for years but hadn't seen each other. He was escorting her back to St. Louis just last fall, and on the way they came here. I was the one to point out to Dakota that he was in love. He told me later that our mother came right out and asked him if he fell in love with Darvi because she shared his faith. They were married in January.

"You see, Reagan, my parents know exactly the type of woman my brothers and I are going to fall for. They know the women will share our belief in Christ because that's the life we've chosen for ourselves. They also know that the wives we choose will be people who are strong and independent because that's what they instilled in us from the time we were small.

"Hair color, where you grew up, how tall you are, what type of books you like—those are all just details. Everyone who meets you falls in love with you. My parents won't be any different. My love for you will cause them to love you, and when they see that you share my faith, they'll just see that as normal, even though they haven't embraced it themselves."

The couple's eyes met.

"All this to say, Reagan, that it's still about your fear of marriage. My parents are wonderful. You'll love them, and they'll love you in return. What is yet to be determined is whether or not you want to be my wife."

Reagan looked into his face and found what she always did: a wonderful man. His eyes were filled with caring, and she knew he was not a man to play games with a woman.

"I can't promise that the fear won't come back, Cash."

"So what does that mean? Do you want to wait until all fears are gone or what?"

She chewed her lip. "Can I think on it?"

"No," he teased. "I need to know right now."

Reagan smiled.

"Come on." Cash stood. "Let's get back to the ranch. I asked Brenda to fill in, but I don't want to be gone too long."

"I shouldn't have run like that. Will Katy be upset?"

"Furious."

They did stop to greet Holly but didn't find anyone home. They continued on to the edge of town where Reagan was going to ride her bike ahead of Cash's horse. The sound of the train heading out of town reminded Reagan of the Rawlingses' visit. She stopped and turned to Cash.

"Is that the last train today I hear?"

"No, I think there's one more."

"But your parents could have come in already."

"True."

"They could be at the ranch."

"Yes."

Reagan's mouth opened. "What are they going to say when they find you gone?"

"Nothing."

She began to shake her head.

"Reagan," he began patiently, "they really do want my brothers and me to live our own lives. They don't expect me to drop everything because they're coming."

Reagan was intrigued for the first time. Until now she'd been too wrapped up in herself to give them much thought, but now she realized she would be gaining a glimpse into Cash's life in a way that had not been possible before.

Wordlessly climbing back onto her bike, Reagan continued on her way to the ranch. Cash followed her with a smile, just glad she was still going in the right direction. It was hard to wait at times like this, but Cash asked God for patience.

It's my dream to have the ranch be her home, her permanent home, Lord, where she would feel safe and loved, but You know what You want here. Help me to trust, and help Reagan to see that I want only to treasure her.

🌹 🌹 🌹

"Reagan," Cash said with a huge smile, just moments after they arrived back, "these are my parents, Charles and Virginia Rawlings."

"Oh, Reagan!" Virginia shocked her by coming forward to hug her. "I can't think what Katy and Cash would have done without you. Katy's told us all about it. You dear, sweet thing."

Charles smiled into the wide, dark eyes that met his and was there to shake Reagan's hand as soon as Virginia released her.

"It's great to meet you, Reagan. Did I see you come up on a bicycle?"

"Yes."

"You're not from Texas, so where are you from?"

Reagan laughed a little. "New York."

"I love New York. Were you right in the city?"

"For most of my life, yes."

"Great place. What brought you to Texas?"

Reagan smiled. He was like an older version of Dakota. "Adventure."

"That's my kind of answer. Have you found some?"

"Yes. Sometimes more than I bargained for."

"Tell them what you think of armadillos," Katy directed, and both senior Rawlings enjoyed her face of horror and general description of what she called a "creature."

"You look a little thin," Cash said of his father when there was a break.

The older man shook his head and admitted, "I haven't had the flu like that in a long time. And it certainly wasn't fun not being at home."

The two fell into easy conversation, and before long Virginia was up wheeling Katy into the kitchen and signaling for Reagan to join them.

As elegantly as Mrs. Rawlings was dressed, Reagan was surprised to see her dig right into the kitchen work. She took over dinner preparations as though she had done so all her life, and Reagan was reminded that this had been her home.

Reagan listened to her talk to Katy, and even though they included her, it was clear that they were old and dear friends. Reagan found herself praying that Katy would have an opportunity to share the change in her life, but for the most part she just listened and laughed at some of Mrs. Rawlings' stories.

Everyone was on the tired side, so they had an early dinner. Again Reagan laughed at the easy banter and camaraderie. And it was just as Cash said it would be: They seemed to accept her wholeheartedly and without question.

Mrs. Rawlings insisted on cleaning up, coaxing her husband to help her, and as much as Katy was glad to see them, she was perfectly content to have Reagan settle her for an early night. She was enjoying the freedom of the chair, but her body still ached, and she grew fatigued in fairly short order.

Cash bid Katy good night and then waited for Reagan to appear. Without asking, he whisked her onto the front porch and spoke as soon as he had her alone.

"How are you? Do you wish you'd stayed in town?"

"No. I'm fine. They're both so kind, just like you said they would be. Why did I run away and act so foolishly?"

Cash bent and kissed her cheek.

"I don't want you to be too rough on yourself. It's a lot to take in, and I've told you I don't have a timetable that you have to meet."

"Maybe you should."

He shook his head, took a seat, and asked her to join him.

Reagan sighed, feeling as tired as everyone else. They talked for a short time, but Cash didn't try to dissuade her when she said she was ready to head to bed. He knew that emotional issues were the most wearying kind. He was tired as well.

"Thank you, Cash," she surprised him by saying just before she slipped inside.

"For what?"

"For coming after me."

"My pleasure," he said, able to mean it with all his heart.

❧ ❧ ❧

"You're in love with that girl," Virginia said to her son much later that night. They were the last ones awake in the house. Always the rancher, Charles had gone to the barn to check the stock, and the two were visiting in the upstairs hall.

"You think so, do you?"

Virginia laughed a little. "I may be tired, Cash, but I can still see straight."

The rancher laughed with her. "We're not moving very fast," he said.

"Is that your choice or hers?"

"It's ours."

Virginia smiled with pride. She loved knowing that she had raised three gentlemen. It meant the world to her.

"How long are you staying?" Cash finally remembered to ask.

"Probably just a few days before we head out to see your grandmother and brothers, but I think we'll be back on the way home."

"I'm glad. It's good to have you here, Mother. I know it means so much to Katy."

"She's changed," Virginia said, her voice thoughtful.

All Cash did was nod before Virginia said she was going to bed. Mother and son went to their rooms shortly after that, and until Cash fell asleep, he asked himself whether he should have told his mother why Katy was different or let the lady do it herself.

Twenty-One

"Now, didn't you tell me they had seemed open earlier this year?" Pastor Ellis asked Cash the next Sunday afternoon. The Ellis family had invited Cash, Reagan, Katy, and the Bennetts to lunch.

"Yes. When my brother was married in January, my parents were both very open, and I told them to write if I could be of help. I know they were planning to keep going to the church I visited while I was there, but they haven't brought the subject up, and I don't know how to go about it. They didn't even say what they thought of the service here last week."

"I didn't have a chance either," Katy put in. "I found out after they left that Mrs. Rawlings noticed a change in me, but I didn't have any opportunities to tell her the reason."

"It might still come," Pastor encouraged her. "Did you say they were still coming back this way?"

Cash nodded, and they all listened as Katy gave the schedule Virginia had shared with her.

"Maybe one of your brothers will have a chance to ask how they're doing, or even your grandmother." Russell added this hopeful note just before Noelle said she had cake for dessert.

"How are you?" Holly asked of Reagan as they finished with dessert a short time later. The two were sitting side by side, and there had been a lull in the conversation. The other people went back to talking, but the two women had a moment alone.

"I'm doing fine. How are you?"

"Doing great. Do I miss my guess, or are you and Cash getting rather close?"

Reagan smiled. "Cash has talked to Pastor, and I think he even spoke to Russell, but they must have taken him seriously when he said we were keeping it quiet right now."

Holly had all she could do not to squeal with excitement. Instead she asked with a false calm, "And what did Cash speak to Pastor and Russ about?"

"Just that we're starting to talk about a relationship."

The word was enough to jolt Holly back to earth.

"Reagan, are you all right with this? I mean, really?"

Reagan's face was wreathed with softness as she thought about this question.

"He's so patient, Holly. I didn't know anyone like him existed."

Holly Bennett knew she was going to burst into tears at any moment, and she had to get out of the room.

"I'm going to check on the children," she announced, raising her voice some to be heard by Russell.

He nodded and thanked her.

Reagan only let her get to her feet before saying she was going to join her. She followed Holly onto the front porch where the older woman stood with her hand over her mouth.

"Holly?"

"I'm sorry, Reagan." She was just barely holding tears. "I've just wanted this for you for so long. I've wanted you to know how loved you are, and if Cash can do that, I just—" She couldn't go on, but Reagan didn't really need her to.

"Thank you, Holly," she said when she hugged her.

"Hi, Reagan," Jonah called as he ran by, and that gave Holly the push she needed to dry her tears. She looked down at Reagan for a moment and then smiled and hugged her again.

"I just want you to know," Holly ended up saying, "that whatever you do, I'll love you like a sister forever."

Reagan had never had anyone say such a thing to her. For a moment she was speechless.

"Thank you, Holly. It's a wonderful thing to know."

Wanting to rejoin the group, Holly made a swift check on the children, but as soon as she was finished, she and Reagan went back inside.

❧ ❧ ❧

"What are you up to?" Cash asked Reagan after he'd taken her to the general store for supplies.

"Nothing," she said innocently, but Cash saw what she was trying to hide.

A thumb went up to push the brim of his hat back as he asked, "Wrinkle cream, Reagan?"

She frowned at him. "I'm not exactly a teen any longer, Cash."

The cowboy had all he could do not to shout with laughter.

"Let me see this stuff," he said as he took it from the hand she held behind her back.

Reagan looked innocently around as he read, but there was no escaping when he leaned close to her face.

"Now, show me these wrinkles you're trying to get rid of."

"You don't see any?" She looked up at him in that trusting way he was coming to know.

"No."

"What about those little lines next to my eyes?"

"Where?"

Reagan squinted, and this time Cash had to laugh.

"Shh..." she got after him, fighting laughter of her own.

"You don't need this," he said, plunking it decisively on the shelf.

"This dry heat is hard on the skin."

"I agree with you, but some regular lotion will do." Cash grabbed a jar from the shelf and handed it to her. It was a brand that he'd seen Katy use in the kitchen.

"This stuff?"

"I think Katy uses it."

Reagan read the description on the bottle before looking up to ask Cash if Katy needed any. The question was never voiced. Cash's eyes were on something further down the shelf, and as Reagan followed his gaze, she smiled. Never before had she noticed the full line of feminine apparel that covered half of those shelves. Clearly Cash had never noticed either. Reagan just stood and watched him.

"Reagan?" he asked before making eye contact with her.

"Yes?"

Cash turned to see that she'd been staring at him. His smile was full blown in an instant, and Reagan wanted to laugh.

"Do all women wear those pretty things?" he asked when they were finally back in the wagon and headed to the ranch.

"Well, maybe not as lacy and pretty as some of those, but something like them."

Cash nodded, still looking thoughtfully out over the horses' heads.

"Honestly, Cash, you do have a mother. Certainly you have seen some of those things before."

"Honestly, Reagan," he copied her, "a man doesn't give much thought to what his mother wears. The woman he's in love with is a different matter."

"I guess that makes sense, but don't you ever go down that aisle?"

"For what?"

"I don't know. Where do they keep the men's under-things?"

"In a different spot, and you can trust me when I tell you that they don't have the same effect. By the way," he asked, "do certain things come in certain colors?"

"No. That was all a mixture. There were blue bloomers, but also blue shifts and camisoles. All those things come in a variety of colors."

"What's a camisole? I've never heard of that."

Reagan cleared her throat, wondering how they had come to talk of this.

"You wear it under your blouse."

"Do you have a blue one?" Cash asked before he thought.

"Am I allowed to tell you that?"

Cash turned to look at her, his eyes straying a bit before he caught himself.

"Maybe you shouldn't," he said, fixing his gaze over the horses again.

In truth Reagan had a pink one, but she wisely kept this to herself.

"Don't decide to marry me too soon, Reagan," Cash said suddenly.

"Why is that?"

"Courting you is an education."

As she'd wanted to in the store, Reagan allowed herself a nice loud laugh.

☙ ☙ ☙

"Have I ever missed you," Sally said on the first morning Reagan went back to work at the hotel. Katy was back on her feet and going strong; Reagan had even stayed on for an extra week just to enjoy working with Katy in her element. It had been hard to leave the ranch, but everyone knew it was for the best.

Reagan smiled.

"Did your cousin ever show up?"

"No, and I've got bunions the size of eggs to prove it."

"Well, I'm here now."

"True, but I suspect it won't be for long."

"What do you mean?"

Sally looked innocent. "Rumor around town has it that you and Cash Rawlings are getting mighty friendly."

"Is that right?" Reagan asked, already tying on an apron and setting to work.

"Yes, that's right."

Reagan didn't respond.

"Well?"

"Well what?"

"Is it true?"

Reagan smiled. "I happen to think he's very special."

"And does he share that same opinion of you?"

Reagan looked at her. "He has said something along that line."

Sally grinned. "He's been a sought-after catch in this town for a long time, Reagan. A few hearts are going to break when word gets out on this."

"According to you, word is already out."

"I mean official word, the church bells ringing and all that."

Reagan only laughed and went to work in earnest. She was slightly out of practice after eight weeks off the job, but things were coming back fast. And indeed the morning flew. Long before she was ready, it was time to head to the dining room.

Reagan had to laugh. The men acted as if she'd been gone for ages, and their pleas for dinner or an evening out with her were more ardent than ever. Reagan was wondering how many more days of this she could take when she looked up to see Cash Rawlings come in the door.

He took a seat at an empty table, his eyes trained on Reagan, and when she was done with the order she was working on, she went to him.

"Well, now," she said softly, eyes on his face. "What brings you out this morning?"

"A man's got to eat," he said, his own eyes smiling right back.

"But you've got someone to cook for you," Reagan said, even being so bold as to sit down for a moment.

Cash leaned close, aware that every eye in the room was on them.

"I thought maybe these gentlemen needed a little notice that you're not up for grabs any longer."

"I never was."

"But they didn't know that."

Reagan smiled. "True. I think they believed if they just asked long enough, I would eventually succumb."

"That's what I'm hoping," he said as he reached up and brushed a finger down her cheek.

Reagan bit her lip to keep from laughing and stood, not bothering to take his order before exiting to the kitchen and returning with just the breakfast she knew he liked.

❦ ❦ ❦

About ten days later, Reagan and Cash walked along the pond, their hands linked. It was dreadfully hot, but dusk was beginning to fall, and they were happy just to be together. It was a Sunday, and Reagan had come after work for a late lunch that Katy had prepared and to spend the day at the ranch.

"I miss you," she said suddenly.

"The feeling is more than shared, Reagan."

"Mine's different."

"How's that?"

"It just is."

Cash's hand brought her gently to a halt. He looked down into her face, and in just a matter of seconds understood that she was there to stay. He studied her eyes, and with complete openness found her eyes staring right back.

"If I wanted to talk about the future, Reagan, would you run away?"

"Nope," she said, giving the word her best Texas drawl.

"How about children? Would you be afraid to discuss having a family?"

"Nope."

Cash's smile was tender beyond belief.

"And marriage, Reagan," he whispered. "How scary is marriage these days?"

"Not at all."

Moving ever so carefully, his hands coming up to cup her face, Cash leaned forward until their lips touched for the first time.

"Oh, my," Reagan breathed when he broke the contact.

"I was afraid of that," Cash said, his forehead laid against hers.

"What's that?"

"Of liking this no small amount."

Reagan laughed and went on tiptoe to kiss him again.

"I hope you know what this means," he warned her.

"What?"

"I'll be asking very soon, and I'll expect a yes answer."

Reagan stepped back, her hands going to her hips in that familiar way.

"You mean you're not going to ask this minute?"

Cash could only snatch her into his arms and hold on tight, his laughter coming in great waves that echoed over the pond. But they couldn't keep this event to themselves. In just a few moments, like children let outside to play, they ran for the house to see Katy.

"How did you know?" Katy asked after Cash shared their conversation. The three sat in the living room. "What changed for you, Reagan?" the older woman asked. "Why aren't you afraid any longer?"

"It's been coming for a long time, Katy," Reagan answered, her eyes on Cash. "I watched Cash deal with you and everyone in and around this ranch. Even people he didn't know very well were treated with such care and kindness, and then he said he loved me and wanted me to be his wife. If folks just passing through could be treated with kindness, what would he be like to a wife he loved? I realized I was a fool not to have seen it sooner."

Cash looked into her eyes, and for a moment the young couple forgot anyone else was in the room.

Katy sighed as if she herself had just fallen in love, and Reagan looked at her.

"Will you stand up with me, Katy?"

"Me?" her voice squeaked, giving Reagan the giggles.

"Yes. I want a big wedding. I'm planning on asking Holly and Sally too."

"You're going to have me bawling," she said.

"Do you want to know what else?" Reagan said, her eyes alight with mischief.

"What?"

"He hasn't even asked me yet."

Katy looked at her employer in shock and then came to her feet.

"Well, I'm getting out of here. You, Cash Rawlings, have work to do."

The couple had a good laugh as Katy took herself from the room. Reagan was about to say something to Cash, but he was coming to his feet as well. She watched as he slipped into his office and returned with a box in his hands.

"What's this?"

"A little gift for you."

Reagan loved gifts and swiftly opened it. Her mouth opening in surprise, she took out a small silver-colored bell.

"For my bike?"

"Yes, indeed."

"Where did you find it?"

"Lavinia had it."

Reagan gave the bell a little ring and then looked at him. "What would I do without you, Cash?"

"Marry me and you won't have to find out."

Reagan smiled, her eyes thoughtful.

"Reagan Rawlings. It sounds kind of funny, doesn't it?"

"Not to me."

"Oh, Cash, just name the day."

"I'll take that as a yes," he said, just before pulling her close and sealing her agreement with a kiss.

🌹 🌹 🌹

"It's a boy!" Virginia said as she burst in the front door of the ranch house and found the spacious living room empty. "Is anyone here?"

Katy came from the kitchen, not moving as spryly as she once did, but on her own two feet.

"What's that?"

"Libby had a boy! We were only going to stay a short time, but then she was so close, so we just waited. I held him, Katy," she said, her voice taking on a note of wonder. "I held my own little grandson, Reese Rawlings."

"A boy." Katy shook her head in surprise. She had been praying for Liberty just that morning. "How is Libby? How is Slater?"

"Everyone's doing great. Where's Cash?"

"In the barn, last I knew."

Virginia took off in the direction of the kitchen to use the back door, and only then did Katy look up to see that Charles had come in the front door behind his wife. He was standing just inside, a smile on his face.

"A boy," Katy said. "Now isn't that good news?"

"Yes, it is," Charles agreed, albeit a good deal calmer than his wife. He came forward, his eyes on the housekeeper.

"Sit down, Katy," he invited. "I want to talk to you."

Katy sat in complete comfort. They'd known each other too many years for anything else.

"You've changed, Katy."

"I have," Katy admitted without hesitation. She had been asking God for open doors with people and boldness when they came. "Do you want to hear about it?"

"Yes, I do."

"I believe the way Gretchen, Cash, Slater, and Dak do. I know I'm a sinner, but I'm saved from punishment."

Charles nodded, his face serene. He bent forward, his voice low as he admitted, "I am too, Katy."

Katy's mouth opened.

"But you've not said anything. Cash can't know. He'd have told me."

"No one knows."

"Why, Mr. Rawlings?"

"Virginia. She still doesn't know what to do with it all." He paused, his face so troubled. "Do you know all the places I've dragged her, Katy? She's been everywhere with me because I told her when we got married that I wasn't going to do things on my own. She agreed with me, and that's the way it's always been. But now I've done this without her, and I don't know how to tell her."

Katy's heart broke over this news. "When did it happen?"

"When I was ill. I honestly thought that was the end for me. I knew I was lost if it was, so I took care of things, and just like Dakota, God gave me another chance."

"He's good that way," Katy said. "I know all about second chances, Mr. Rawlings. I'll pray for you," she said suddenly. "I have been, but now I'll pray that you'll find a way to tell Mrs. Rawlings. Maybe just hearing from you will turn her heart."

"Thank you, Katy. I don't know if I've ever told you what you mean to us, and I don't think I could find the words now, but I do thank you."

Katy smiled at him, and Charles wanted to shake his head in amazement. The old Katy would have hushed him and left the room. The peace and serenity that surrounded this Katy was unmistakable. He had seen it even before they had left but had not had a chance to speak with her.

"Charles!" Virginia could be heard coming back through the house now.

"In the living room."

Mrs. Rawlings came rushing through, pulling Cash, who was laughing at her excitement, with her.

"Tell him, Cash!" she demanded, looking ready to burst all over again.

Cash smiled at his father.

"I've asked Reagan to marry me, and she's accepted."

Charles went to his son. The men embraced, and the older Rawlings found himself quite choked up. He knew he had to tell Virginia soon, so he could share his news with his son, this precious first child who loved the ranch as he did.

But the time didn't come. Anxious as she was to return home, Virginia wanted to spend only one night at the ranch, and then head to Dakota's before going back to St. Louis.

Cash, however, did find a letter on his desk after his parents left. He read it and then laid his head down on the desktop and cried with a mixture of joy and heartbreak. That God would save his father was the most amazing thing Cash had ever known. In years past, whenever he had pictured one of his parents coming to Christ, it was his mother, and here his father had been the first to believe.

A note on the bottom of the letter said that Katy knew also but to be careful of his mother's feelings in any future dealings with her. Cash went to Katy, glad she was close by, to see if she knew about the note.

"I didn't think he'd had a chance to talk with you, so I'm glad he wrote it," she said. "They were gone so fast."

"I just wish my mother knew."

Katy looked at him, her chin thrust forward a bit.

"You're not doubting, are you, Cash?"

"What exactly?"

"I know your father hasn't told your mother yet, but you don't doubt that she'll believe, do you?"

"I do at times, Katy. I want it very badly, but God does give us a choice."

"That He does," she said with conviction, "and I have to trust Him no matter what, but I think your mother will come around. I'm praying for that very thing."

"I am too, Katy. It's good to know I'm not alone."

Katy smiled even after he left the room. Neither one of them was alone. They would never be alone again.

Epilogue

Christmas 1883

DAKOTA AND DARVI HAD BEEN IN their new house at the ranch for almost a month, but they would still have Christmas in the main house. And the whole family would be gathered. Slater, Liberty, and Reese were already at the ranch, as was Grandma Rawlings. Charles and Virginia were due that day.

Married just four months, Reagan Rawlings had decorated to her heart's content, and her husband had even bought her a dark green dress that she was saving for Christmas day. She had been somewhat nervous about hosting this special day for the whole clan, but as usual, Katy was a lifesaver, and Cash took it all in stride.

Over at Dakota and Darvi's, Darvi held her little nephew, dreaming of when it would be her turn. Liberty and Darvi grew closer each time they saw each other, and the men always had catching up to do.

In the kitchen of the main house, Gretchen Rawlings and Katy were talking and working away, both elated to have the family gathered under one roof. They each knew the favorite dishes of the family and worked on what they termed their "secret" recipes.

Coming in on the train—due to arrive in just 45 minutes—were Charles and Virginia Rawlings. They were laden with packages, even though they'd sent many ahead of time, and Virginia worked at not worrying.

"Are you going to make it?" Charles asked, his eyes searching her face.

"I don't know. I almost wish I had written first. They're all going to cry, and that's not what we need to do at Christmas."

"When someone comes to Christ, especially when it's someone you love dearly, you can cry anytime."

Virginia leaned to kiss him.

"Why did it take me so long?"

He slipped an arm around her.

"I don't care how long it took. I just love knowing I never have to leave you behind. That's all that matters to me."

Virginia relaxed completely then, her husband's embrace telling her it was going to be all right.

In the main house at the ranch, Cash was looking for his wife.

"Reagan?" Cash called to her as he mounted the stairs toward their room. She didn't answer, but he found her sitting on the side of their bed.

"Hi," he said as he sat down next to her, scooped her into his arms, and settled her in his lap.

"Hello," she said, still giving him her profile.

Her voice told him she was thinking.

"What's up?"

"I was just thinking," she admitted, finally meeting his eyes.

"About what?"

"Your Christmas gift."

"What about it?"

"I couldn't stand for you not to like it, Cash, at least not in front of anyone else." She turned to look at him. "I want to give you your gift now."

"Now?"

"Now."

Cash started to laugh.

"Reagan, I know I'll like it."

He tried to reason with her for some minutes, but she had that stubborn tilt to her chin.

"I want to give it to you now."

"No."

"Yes."

This went on for a short time before Cash realized he didn't care. Looking like a conspiratorial child, Reagan took his hand and led him quietly down the stairs. At the bottom she peeked around the corner, and when it was clear, rushed him to the room that Katy had used to recuperate.

Cash was laughing so hard that he tried to hold his breath. Reagan was taking this all the way. She darted inside, shut the door, and leaned on it, breathing theatrically.

"What are we doing?"

"Shh," she told him. "They'll hear us."

Cash wanted to shake his head but found himself dragged along to the closet. It creaked a little when it opened, and even Reagan started to laugh.

"Come on," she urged him, having picked up a lantern. "Come through here."

"It's dark."

"Just hold onto me."

"Gladly," he agreed just before finding himself in pitch blackness.

"Okay, now close your eyes."

"It's dark, Reagan," he said indulgently.

"I know, but I'm going to light the lantern. Are they closed?"

"Yes."

He heard the strike of the match, and from behind his lids could tell that Reagan's little room had been illumined.

"Okay," she said, watching him carefully.

Cash opened his eyes and then blinked.

"You bought me a bike?"

"Yes. Do you like it?"

"You bought me my own bike?"

"Yes. It's taller than mine. It should fit you very well."

He walked toward it like a child on his tenth birthday. Reagan watched him, her hands clasped in front of her.

"You bought me a bike," he said with such pleasure that Reagan beamed.

"Look at me. I'm a city boy!"

Watching as he tried to straddle it in the tiny room, she suddenly realized what she'd done.

"Oh, no," she suddenly said.

"What's wrong?"

"You like it."

"That's bad?"

"No, but now I don't have anything to surprise you with for Christmas."

Cash set the bike aside and came to her. His arms were gentle around her as he gathered her to his chest.

"My entire family is coming for Christmas in the home I share with my new wife, and you think I need more gifts."

Reagan threw her arms around his neck, her lips seeking his own. She suddenly felt exactly the same. He was all the Christmas gift she would ever need again.

About
the Author

LORI WICK is one of the most
versatile Christian fiction
writers in the market today. Her
works include pioneer fiction,
a series set in Victorian England,
and contemporary novels. Lori's
books (over 2.5 million copies in
print) continue to delight readers
and top the Christian bestselling
fiction list. Lori and her husband, Bob, live in Wisconsin
with "the three coolest kids
in the world."

Books by Lori Wick

A Place Called Home Series
A Place Called Home
A Song for Silas
The Long Road Home
A Gathering of Memories

The Californians
Whatever Tomorrow Brings
As Time Goes By
Sean Donovan
Donovan's Daughter

Kensington Chronicles
The Hawk and the Jewel
Wings of the Morning
Who Brings Forth the Wind
The Knight and the Dove

Rocky Mountain Memories
Where the Wild Rose Blooms
Whispers of Moonlight
To Know Her by Name
Promise Me Tomorrow

The Yellow Rose Trilogy
Every Little Thing About You
A Texas Sky
City Girl

Contemporary Fiction
Sophie's Heart
Beyond the Picket Fence (Short Stories)
Pretense
The Princess

Gift Books
Reflections of a Thankful Heart
A Moment of Thanks Journal

Harvest House Publishers

For the Best in Inspirational Fiction

Linda Chaikin

TRADE WINDS

Captive Heart
Silver Dreams
Island Bride

A DAY TO REMEMBER

Monday's Child
Tuesday's Child
Wednesday's Child
Thursday's Child

Melody Carlson

A Place to Come Home To
Everything I Long For
Looking for You All My Life
Someone to Belong To

Debra White Smith

Second Chances
The Awakening
A Shelter in the Storm

Dear Reader,

We would appreciate hearing from you regarding this Harvest House fiction book. It will enable us to continue to give you the best in Christian publishing.

1. What most influenced you to purchase *City Girl?*
    ❑ Author   ❑ Recommendations
    ❑ Subject matter   ❑ Cover/Title
    ❑ Backcover copy   ❑ Other_____

2. Where did you purchase this book?
    ❑ Christian bookstore   ❑ Grocery store
    ❑ General bookstore   ❑ Other_____
    ❑ Department store

3. Your overall rating of this book?
    ❑ Excellent ❑ Very good ❑ Good ❑ Fair ❑ Poor

4. How likely would you be to purchase other books by this author?
    ❑ Very likely ❑ Not very likely ❑ Somewhat likely ❑ Not at all

5. What types of books most interest you? (Check all that apply.)
    ❑ Women's Books   ❑ Fiction
    ❑ Marriage Books   ❑ Biographies
    ❑ Current Issues   ❑ Children's Books
    ❑ Christian Living   ❑ Youth Books
    ❑ Bible Studies   ❑ Other_____

6. Please check the box next to your age group.
    ❑ Under 18 ❑ 18-24 ❑ 25-34 ❑ 35-44 ❑ 45-54 ❑ 55 and over

          Mail to: Editorial Director
                  Harvest House Publishers
                  1075 Arrowsmith
                  Eugene, OR 97402

Name _____

Address _____

State _____ Zip_____

Thank you for helping us to help you in future publications!